RECKLESS INDULGENCE

Sage of the Red Rose

RECKLESS INDULGENCE

Sage of the Red Rose

Author

Lorenzo

Editor

Dr. Sasha Eloi Evans

Najzma M. Williams

PUBLISHING

DEDICATION

Azrael Gyptian Brown, the reason behind it all, the little guy that keeps Dad focused.

And to the greatest Mom in the world, who no matter what never stopped believing in me.

To my brother Ralph, who's always game no matter how large and out of the world my plans may be. My Guy

PREFACE

This novel was an experiment of emotion, patience and understanding.   A journey of internal struggle and discovery through trail and error. Sometimes, in the darkest of times the hero is the most unlikely light.

Anyone can be that hero…

For in a world of color, the truth is often black and white…

Table of Contents

CHAPTER 1

Goyem

Confessions of a black soul,

The untarnished shine of black gold,

like fat folds on the belly of the greedy swine

on the rich and needy, I'll dine,

the blind, and the devoid of will

in blood-soaked orgies, the frantic night's noise is still,

by,

The Soul of the Kingu,

It was about 4:30 pm on a Friday. Enkill Jones had just walked out of the Parole building on W. 40th St. in midtown Manhattan, where like all freshly released parolees in New York State, he was mandated to report within twenty-four hours. The words of his new Parole officer, Ms. Brown - a dark skinned in her early twenties that he found slightly attractive with her waist-length braids and slender curves - played in his head.

"Mr. Jones, I am going to be perfectly honest with you. You have three violent felony convictions, that means Category One; intensive supervision!" The way she said those last two words were like a physical hand that pinned Enkill down to the metal folding chair he was seated in. To him, her small office became a cell, oppressive and suffocating.

"I'm not going to harass you, constantly reminding you about your business... business you're supposed to handle! I am not going to question you as to what your plans are; just make them legal. You follow me?"

Enkill nodded, "Yeah." His eyes on her cleavage.

P.O. Brown ignored his disinterest, " Hard work will take you a long way in this world. The outcome of your life is now in your hands. You've got three pieces of violence!" A passion flared in her gaze. "The next one is life. You might be lucky, and get out when you're damn near sixty, broke, black and broken. I've seen it. You don't want to.

"You have a chance. Don't fuck it up! Is there anything I've told, Mr. Jones, that you don't understand?" she asked, closing the thick manila envelope that detailed the more unfortunate events of Enkill's criminal career. She put it back down into the clutter with a sigh.

" I understand you perfectly," Enkill replied, staring across the desk into her hard, hazel eyes. There was a sympathetic softening around the edges that revealed how much she really did care. That was to someone who had the sight to see.

Enkill wasn't one of those people. In his hardened heart, he didn't believe in sympathy or mercy. Anxious to get out of her office, he said, "Six years and ten months is a lot of time to think and a lot of time to plan. I've made good use of my time... very good use."

Ms. Brown gave a half-laugh to the cocky man sitting in front of her, whose incarnation she'd seen before... many times before. "I hope you have Mr. Jones. I'll be seeing you in two weeks, and don't be getting high."

Enkill got up and headed for the door. In its open entrance, he turned, flashing his best suave smile, "It was nice meeting you, Ms. Brown. Until next time…."

Leaving the office, he stepped out onto the street, emerging under the towering weight of the city's countless skyscrapers. It was the peak of rush –hour as dusk gradually settled over the metropolis. The familiar scent of car exhaust and street vendor delicacies invaded his nose. The honking of car horns and the congested chattering of many conversations washed over him in waves. Finally, it hit him.

I am a free man! After all those years, he was finally free. I am finally free!

Enkill was a twenty-one-year-old youth at the time of his arrest. Six years and ten months later, Enkill was now a twenty-eight-year-old man. There were days on the inside when he thought this day would never come. So many men went into prison, never to return to freedom. Some would fatally assault another inmate or become a victim themselves. Others would die of natural causes. Enkill beamed victoriously as he turned in a slow, full circle, taking in the flood of humanity hurrying home from work or shopping tourists popping in and out of the many brightly lit shops lined the avenue.

A young Hispanic couple passed, walking hand-in-hand. The beautiful woman and Enkill's eyes met. She gave him a subtle once over and smiled… a naughty pucker of orange gloss and a sparkle of white teeth. He gave her a sly smirk. Meko's favorite saying came to mind, "Women with

wandering eyes, make excellent hos... but terrible wives."
Enkill always listened to Meko. On the inside, Meko's
encouragement kept him from losing what was left of his
sanity. He had plans to catch up with Meko a little later.

Enkill strolled in the windless winter evening, uptown
towards the flashing lights of Times Square. He stopped
before a small, low-budget electronics store, a fixture
designed to take advantage of naive tourists. The display
window held an assortment of gizmos: from video game
consoles to cameras, and sleek-looking laptops that he'd
never seen before save in the pages of magazines, to car
stereos, and shiny micro wonders of technology that
connected one to the Internet, played music flat-screen and
even served as cellphones were laid out neatly among a few
flat-screen televisions. His attention became drawn to one
such device, a 62-inch color model that displayed the exact
spot where he stood.

Following his highly vain nature, Enkill critiqued his
digital image and was delighted.

For all his emotional shortcomings, physically, Enkill
was a handsome man. Standing a little over six feet with 225
lbs. packed on a muscular frame, Enkill Jones was hard to
miss. Like a dark knight, he was entirely clad in black, from
his leather pea-coat and turtleneck, slim-fitting down to his
slim-fitting jeans and motorcycle-style riding boots. When
loose, Enkill's fashionably neat locks hung down the center
of his back; tonight, they were braided into three separate
tails and pulled back into one. The skin of Enkill's oval face

was like dark rust. He squinted an almost contemplative expression. Lips pressed tightly, Enkill stared into his own eyes.

Eyes that were intelligently cold and of the darkest brown, full of suppressed pain and steaming violence, gazed back, hooded by a tangle of bushy brows. They scrutinized the world with the heartless rationale that only gods and the truly mad are capable of. Running his fingers over the multiple closed piercing holes, he added them to the long list of things he must get done.

He stepped out into traffic at a corner and hailed a cab. To his surprise, a yellow taxi pulled in almost immediately Enkill stepped inside and gave the Middle Eastern driver directions to 59th St. and Lexington Ave. He instructed the driver, "Hey, turn on some music for me." The driver did, and even though his musical taste was diverse, Enkill quickly realized the bubblegum pop that dominated the airwaves was not for him.

After station surfing for a few minutes, he told the driver with an irritated wave, "Um, don't worry about it. Turn that off." Opting instead for silence. With a careless shrug, the driver obliged.

His thoughts traveled along the ride as he observed the Disneyland transformation of Times Square. For years he dreamed of the moment when he'd be free; now it was here. The world was in front of him to do that which he pleased. Enkill believed in no law save his own and had been so since losing his parents to the crack wars ravaging the inner city ghettos of New York since the late eighties.

A most disturbing memory emerged from his subconscious. He was in the first grade. School had just let out for the day; like most boys his age, he was rushing upstairs to watch Thundercats. When Enkill reached the second-floor landing and pushed the door to ring the bell, and the door opened slowly, he knew something was wrong. Slowly, he entered his apartment, calling for his mother. When he pushed open his parents' bedroom door, he found them. The next day, the headlines read, "Alleged Drug Lord and Wife Murdered and Tortured".

Enkill went to live with his father's mother in Spanish Harlem. While his grandmother tried to instill the values of honest living and God in the troubled child, the allure of the streets would prove vital for the troubled youth and his fierce heart of fire. Enkill committed his first stick-up at the tender age of thirteen, and from there, his criminal career was birthed and escalated.

Finally, the images faded, and Enkill returned to the present. At that moment, nothing mattered to Enkill but getting what he felt was rightfully his. And that meant anything he had the power to take. He didn't care that there was a black President in office. He didn't even consider politics. In his mind, unemployment, terrorism, or religion - were the fears and worries of the sheep. Enkill was not one of the sheep – he was a wolf, and the world was his to devour.

Enkill paid the driver from a thick wad of bills. It was a small sum he'd saved in the penitentiary from various unscrupulous hustles. On the inside, he experimented with everything from dealing to extortion. Enkill darted across the street into a small leather boutique on the corner. The floor was hardwood and the air smelled of new leather. Enkill loved that smell. He'd been into leather and suede since an early teen. He still remembered his first Eightball jacket.

The store was a short rectangle with rows of displays on both sides and a short row down the middle. Enkill passed the register and sunk into its welcoming confines. His attention was drawn to an exquisite piece hanging along the back. It was a cranberry blazer of soft suede.

"Would you like to try it on?" He heard her before he saw her. Her voice was like a slow love song, full of allure.

And then, she appeared. She was beautiful, of average height, with the skin of the smoothest caramel. Curvy, under a one-piece black jumper, her hair was spiked and punk – a newer style he'd observed traveling through the city that hadn't changed but was now alien to him.

"Hello,' she said and giggled. It was the sweetest sound. The type of sound that a man who'd been locked away for as long as Enkill could almost forget existed.

That was when Enkill realized he'd been staring. Taken aback, he tried to gather himself offering a teenage boy's clumsy smile. Suddenly he learned all he'd missed in the past years. He extended a hand and introduced himself. "I'm Enkill, and your name is?"

She sized him up in the split-second ability that only women possess. "Charise,"

Trying to keep his calm composure, he asked, "Charise," he paused, pretending to consider the jacket behind her, "Think you can get me one of these in a 5X?"

She made that sound again, the liquid laughter quickly enchanting him.

"If you give me my hand back, I would love to."

The entranced man didn't even realize he was still holding it. He was too busy watching the shiny, blood-red glossed lips he considered all too kissable as she spoke. "Oh! I am sorry," he said, faking embarrassment. With a giggle and a shake of her head, Charise picked up a hooked reaching stick from behind a rack, retrieved one of the coats, and gave it to Enkill.

Running his hand across the smooth material, Enkill paused and tried it on. It fit as perfectly as it felt and looked. "I'll take it," he said, handing the coat back to the salesgirl.

As he paid, Charise stood at his side, smiling...staring. It was a strange gaze, and her brow's slight tensing made him uneasy. It was as if she was trying to figure out something important. He relaxed when she reached up, touched one of his locks, and said, "I like your locks; they're all nice and neat. How long have you been growing them?"

"Thanks... about six years," he replied, trying to match her flirtatious smile.

He could tell the woman was interested, so they walked a little out of earshot from the register, where the cashier was watching them like they were a soap opera. He walked her between the hangers and racks, stopping just before he opened the door.

He asked, "I'm wondering, can I take you out sometime, maybe tonight?"

Charise eyed him with sudden seriousness, shifting her weight to one side, hand on hip, she asked, "Why?"

"You might enjoy yourself."

"I don't think I'm your type," she said with a self-assured roll of her eyes.

"Why don't you let me be the judge of that," Enkill was determined not to be discouraged by what he deemed hard to get active. Excited by the thrill of the chase, he pursued. "Listen, one date, one night. If we find no mutual interest and are incompatible, we go our separate ways. No one loses, even though I know that's not going to be the case," he told her in a smooth, frank tone, flashing a half smile that Charise found almost as intriguing as his confidence.

"Okay, one date, tonight… but I choose where to go."

"No problem," 'he said, not caring where they went as long as the night ended between her legs.

"I will give you my number - call me around eight. We're going to a party to meet a couple of my friends." Charise then added with a mischievous wink, "A vampire party. Are you still interested?"

Wow, she's gorgeous but a little strange. Enkill paused. He had heard of such affairs before; a bunch of adults playing dress-up, high on every possible drug known to humanity, drinking chicken's blood, and engaged in group orgies. First day home, hell yes! "Yeah, I'm still interested. I'll be looking forward to it."

"It's a date then...tonight," one of her fingers trailed his chin as she smiled – it was an expression full of possibilities.

For the time being, Enkill was staying in the east uptown district of Manhattan, Spanish Harlem, or 'El Barrio', as it was known to its residents. With the aid of an acquaintance, he'd rented a room in a five-story walk-up from an elderly lady Mrs. Perez, whom to Enkill seemed nice enough. It seemed like her main source of activities was cleaning the small tidy apartment and watching Spanish soap operas.

Sticking his key in the front door of an apartment felt liberating beyond words to Enkill, even though he rented a single room. He preferred it any day over the metallic clanking of the closing cells he'd grown accustomed to.

"Hello, Mrs. Perez," he said, entering the apartment into the living room of plastic-covered furniture.

From a small rocking chair, Mrs. Perez waved and smiled. She was engrossed in some Spanish program, as he left her earlier this afternoon. To Enkill, she looked just like a traditional grandmother in her floral housedress sitting with her small, wrinkled hands holding a newspaper in her lap. Mrs. Perez was a petite woman with skin like a vanilla blast sprinkled with nutmeg. He could see the narrow veins working under the surface of her skinny neck.

Mrs. Perez had two physical features that Enkill found remarkably interesting. The first was her eyes. They were wise eyes, dark wells of brown almost like his, but aged by life's experience. The second was her hair. It was a soft thick mass of silver. He couldn't tell exactly how long it was, but from the big bun falling down her back, he figured it was very long

After a few more polite words that didn't garner the old lady's interest in her program, Enkill smiled inwardly as he grabbed up his bags and headed down the hallway to his room.

It was a modest set-up: on a bare, carpet-less wooden floor sat a bed, dresser, and a little wooden chair that looked like it had in better days belonged to a dining set.

Flipping on the light switch on the wall, Enkill dropped his bags by the bed, stripped, and took a long shower - his first as a free man. Afterward, he devoured a greasy fried seafood platter he had picked up from the Chinese spot on the corner.

Refreshed and fed, sitting on the bed in his t-shirt and boxers, Enkill dug out his first piece of modern technology. A small black iPhone he purchased earlier and made his first call.

After a few rings, a male voice answers, "Hello." Recognizing the voice, Enkill said with the fake cadence of an Italian gangster, "How you's a doing? I'm looking for Meko."

Smoothly, the voice on the other line replied, "Enkill, it's good to hear your voice outside those walls."

At that moment, the joke was over, and Enkill smiled, genuine contemplative gratitude trickling over his face.

"It's good to be out. But I got a question, how's freedom been treating you?"

Seldom did Meko get visibly excited about anything. Only the pitch of his voice changed, like now, "It's been treating me real good, and now that you're here, it's about to treat me a whole lot better."

Meko and Enkill met about three years ago on the inside, where they were both enrolled in one of the prison's industrial work programs. Their abnormalities - like an interest in current events and history, and a disdain for how most prisoners spent their time; sports and idle talk — drew them together. There was also a darker side to their attraction. Both men, in their way, wanted to make the world pay for their pain.

They also shared similar ideas concerning rehabilitation and recidivism. They simply believed in neither.

With no plans of ever spending their lives enslaved to what they disdainfully mocked as 'the system,' the two men would spend the next two years mentally laying the blueprint for their intended enterprise. This usually happened during long spins around the recreation yard, where Enkill would often say, "I'd rather rule in hell than serve in heaven." Meko would respond, "In this day and age, monsieur, there's no difference between the two - both are made by men."

Meko was released a little less than a year before Enkill. For the next ten or so months, he would keep his newfound comrade-in-arms posted on developments on the outside via letters and calls while he prepared and eagerly awaited Enkill's arrival.

Finally, the day had come.

After the two men got over the initial shock of Enkill being home, their chatting would take on a more severe tone concerning the immediate future. Meko would tell Enkill, as he already knew, that things were already set in motion, and he was only waiting for him to get something rolling in an undetailed lingo because you never knew who was listening.

After Enkill told Meko about Charise and his plans for the night, they decided to meet up the next day. Enkill had just got off the phone with Meko and was admiring the fancy black face of his new timepiece. It was a little after eight o-clock. Enkill reclined back on the small bed, clearing his throat, eyes on the grey ceiling above with the phone to his ear, retrieving one of the only numbers stored in his phone's memory.

It rang once, then twice, after which a familiar voice picked up, "Hello Enkill."

CHAPTER 2

It was about 10:30 pm when Enkill stepped out of a cab on the corner of W.14 St. and 7th Ave. Winter seemed to take a recess, and the temperature was slightly less than fifty degrees. The bright streets of Greenwich Village were vibrant with life. The neighborhood was a cultural melting pot, where people of all ages, nationalities, and walks of life came to enjoy the company of their social circle in its assortment of trendy bars, intimate lounges, and underground clubs.

Enkill wasn't a stranger to the often, festive spirited area. In his early years, Enkill used it as an escape from the more violent social atmosphere of East Harlem. He would journey downtown into the Hard Rock bars and party with the scores of college kids and late twenty-somethings that frequented them. Those were always good nights. Even if he went back uptown alone, as sometimes happened, he still enjoyed the experience.

With those memories in mind, his expectations were high. Enkill looked, spoke, and moved as such when he was in the hood. But once he left its confines, he abandoned the Ebonics for a more proper cadence. Wearing a maroon suede blazer, black suede slacks designed to look like jeans, a striped black on burgundy silk dress-shirt, and a pair of black on burgundy triangular-toed dress boots, he looked like a model. His edge-up and light goatee were perfectly trimmed, and his locks were pulled back in one long braid.

Believing that personal style should be unique and a direct reflection of one's personality, Enkill had even reopened all his piercings. He filled them with three pairs of tiny studs, one diamond, one onyx, and one ruby—too many people dressed like their favorite celebrities: copies of imitations.

An ebony image of self-gratifying physical perfection, Enkill posed under the shelter of a corner phone booth across from a bar, where it must have been goth night. A couple of its heavy mascara-wearing patrons, with their artfully paled faces, stood out front under a sign of flashing neon having a smoke.

A hippie-looking, thin, middle-aged man strolled past with a foot-sized spotted dog, holding the hand of a smiling woman in a long worn wool coat. She waved a friendly hand of long electric pink nails. Enkill smiled a polite nod in exchange.

A masculine-looking Hispanic woman passed arm in arm with a pretty, hip-switching Latina with a red mohawk. A group of harmless young males - probably not yet out of high school - followed, making silly, lewd comments that the women ignored.

To Enkill's right, he heard hissing kisses that accompanied the approach of a small bunch of attractive young women.

"You're cute," said one of the women to Enkill. A Hollywoodish blonde with round blue eyes who was visibly intoxicated let the soft caress of her hand trail down the side of his face as she introduced herself " You're hot! What's your name?"

Before Enkill could say a word, another voice chimed behind him, "Sorry ladies, he's with me." Like a mocha-latte lioness, Charise parted the group of women gathered in front of the booth.

Entering it and slipping an arm around Enkill's waist, she claimed him. A lite blood-red kiss on his lips marked him.

At the taste of his first kiss and the feel of her soft, scented, leather-encased body pressed against his, an exciting heat instantly spread through him.

Charise was smooth. Enkill was impressed. He hadn't even noticed her arrival even though he'd been watching. She must have come from across the street behind me, he thought.

Like a man seeing the sun for the first time, Enkill drank in the beauty that interrupted the pursuits of his would-be suitor. Charise's stylish wild curls shone with a salon-perfect sheen. The hanging side curls were tucked behind her pierced earlobes, which Enkill hadn't known before. Each lobe was adorned with five identical, sparkling diamond studs. The hot weather allowed her to sport her waist-length black leather zipped only halfway, revealing a black lace bra top that looked more like lingerie than a blouse, displaying inviting mounds of cleavage. Claw-like slashes in the leather ripped down her thighs, giving her form-squeezing pants a dominatrix, costumed look. This was enhanced with a pair of black ankle boots with shiny six-inch silver heels, which elevated Charise an inch over Enkill's brow. Her manicure was the same blood red as her lips. On the ring finger of her right hand sat a thick gold band on top of which rested a radiant, iced cluster.

The blonde – who had introduced herself as Michelle looked momentarily lost under the self-assured gaze of the caramel amazon. Quickly pulling herself together, she gave a friendly apology and started to walk off with her friends. She then stopped in mid-stride and glanced back over her shoulder. Giving Charise a provocative smirk, Michelle asked, "Sure you don't want to share? He looks like enough for all of us!" Her comment bought a nervous round of giggles from her friends.

Charise just gave the group of women the back of her head. Lifting her hands to Enkill's face, her tongue invaded his mouth in a lusty kiss. Charise then turned to the staring woman and said in a prolonged and sexy tone. "After I am through with him, nothing will be left!"

One of the women said, "They are so hot, I'll take 'em both!" Again the women burst into a fit of giggles, giving the joker high fives.

At that moment, Enkill's ego was on super-high. Inwardly, his smile was never-ending. It had been a decade since Enkill was this close to a woman, and his blood began to rush.

Charise laughed lightly and winked at the competition as she led Enkill away.

An almost full moon accompanied the couple as they went a block further downtown and made a right on 13th St., heading west down a few darker, more residential blocks away from the crowds. As they walked, cuddled in each other's embrace, they passed a few exclusive high-rises - mostly brownstones and townhouses – home to the neighborhood's sometimes celebrity. Still, there were always wealthy residents, and Enkill enjoyed Charise's company. She became a conversationalist with a real, sharp sense of humor. There were few things Enkill hated more than a woman whose presence he couldn't stand, save in the bedroom.

They walked further on until they entered an area Enkill was unfamiliar with named: the Meatpacking District. He'd heard this was where many of the city's more exclusive clubs were located. For the briefest of seconds, he wondered where exactly she was taking him, but that was soon swept away under her soft ministrations.

Charise stopped in front of a tall warehouse-like structure, standing on the corner under a single streetlight. "This is it," she said.

"It is?" Enkill asked, looking a little skeptically at her, then at the single black door sitting between a pair of long, dark tinted windows. He at least expected a line, maybe a cluster of cars, a small crowd hanging out front, the echo of music from within, but there was nothing. The street itself seemed dead. Enkill gazed around. They seemed to be the only two people out in the whole world.

Up towards the building's roof, the silver flares of the moon seemed to be fighting a losing battle with the darkness for space. The shifting shadows and tricks of light were like an evil sorcerer, conjuring in Enkill's mind strange images of dancing devils.

Charise led Enkill by the hand through the black door into a twisting semi-lit hallway of red carpet. The smooth black finished walls vibrated lightly with fast, heavy drumbeats - what to Enkill sounded like modern techno.

They walked in silence. The music was getting louder. The hallway twisted one last time and ended spilling them in front of two colossus-sized men in black muscle shirts and slacks; one black, one white. Both towered over Enkill by about a foot and outweighed him by over a hundred pounds. He hoped this wouldn't be one of those nights where he ended up tangling with security because the grim-faced duo looked like they'd be more than a handful.

The brother was bald, with no facial hair. Dark sports shades wrapped around his coal-black face. Enkill wondered how the man could possibly see out of them in such poor lighting. His pierced nostrils puffed like a bull's as he robotically gazed down at the couple like he was just noticing them, though they'd been waiting patiently for the last ten seconds. The only reason Enkill said nothing was because he was following Charise's lead.

The black guard then exchanged a glance with his partner, a long-haired blond with a handlebar mustache and python-like arms covered with so many tattoos the original skin was no longer visible.

Without a word, the two guards stepped aside, revealing a black door with a handle of reddish metal that Charise twisted and pulled, emitting them into an extended tube-like lounge area.

Everything was bloody red and black: onyx caged red bulbs lit the room in a vermilion shadow. A couch of -scarlet leather lined the perimeter of each wall. Fancy high-back chairs sat at ruddy tables of pure glass. The walls were even blood red. The floor was a glossy black -with red paint splashed about to look like spilled pools of blood.

The music was louder here, but nobody danced. About forty people were scattered about, drinking, smoking, and chatting. Charise was leading Enkill past a pair of exotically beautiful women, their hair long black strands with blood-toned streaks, in scarlet nightgown-like dresses. Upon seeing Charise, they looked up from the showering of their attentions on the powder-faced man in the frilled black blouse, who was sandwiched on a small sofa between them.

The two women greeted Charise. Enkill felt Charise's hold on his hand tighten as she returned the greeting. His attention was captivated, not by Charise's little show of jealousy, but by the similar color shades that everyone wore. It was just as she told him it would be earlier. Everyone, no matter what they were wearing, be it sports jackets, gowns, boots, shoes, head wraps, denim, or leather, every article of clothing was either black or any of the many shades of red, matching the club's decor, creating a sea of two-toned tides.

Another thing he noticed was there was no other sign of the establishment's employees as she led him forward to a thick crimson curtain hanging at the end of the lounge, towards the music's source.

Enkill had stepped in many clubs in his lifetime, but nothing quite like this. A nervous excitement surged through his veins. The place was packed with gyrating bodies hypnotized by the loud trance-inducing techno. It was dark, with that same reddish tint of the lounge they passed. Lasers constantly flashed overhead and into the frenzied crowd. The beams were every possible spectrum of red. From a visible second level, large cages hung filled with practically naked people engaging in various sexual activities.

Enkill watched one such cage unbelievingly. Housed inside was a big-breasted blonde. She was naked save for a pair of red stilettos and a matching thong pulled over to the side, exposing her shaved goodies to all. The blonde was bent over performing fellatio on a naked tattooed male with snarling vampire fangs. In contrast, two other naked men, one black and a mohawked Asian stood on both sides of the blondes' backside, masturbating like they were in a race to see who spilled first, gritting fangs.

The plastic vampire teeth Enkill saw many of the crowd wearing were the last thing on Enkill's mind. After seven years of fantasizing about paper women, the real thing had him on the verge of going ballistic. It was an actual exercise in self-control for Enkill to contain himself. It was like one big room of hedonistic lust. Everyone was either half naked or in the process of becoming—black coffins with soft red velvet interiors scattered about the dance floor. People were either on them or limbs hanging out from within, like the pair of voluptuous tanned beauties before Enkill, laying entangled on a closed death box. Skirts hitched above their waist, tops open busy hands wandering, sharing deep kisses lost in their lust, oblivious to everything else.

The music then took a sharp twist, becoming faster and more challenging, more rave-like. Screaming guitars blended with gothic-like hymns against a backdrop of fast crashing drums—the perfect definition of organized noise. Being a closet metal head, Enkill was feeling the element. His head and shoulders began a rhythmic bounce to the drums.

They were snaking through the crowd; Charise seemed to be looking for someone when a topless, slender white woman approached them with a head of long fire red locks. Both nipples of her perky, relatively small breast bore shiny quarter-sized silver skulls. Crazy tribal ink ran from both her upper arms to her narrow shoulders. She wore a pair of tight red leather pants that sat low on the curve of her boyish hips. The dark-eyed woman stuck out her pierced tongue like a sensual vamp. Opening her hand, she revealed an assortment of little colored pills with micro letters and cartoon-like characters that Enkill assumed was Ecstasy.

Charise took two of the pills. After popping one in her mouth, she attempted to place one in Enkill's. Brushing her hand lightly aside, he declined her with a finger. Enkill didn't care for drugs of any kind save for an occasional drink. He considered them an escape for people who couldn't cope with reality or lacked self-confidence and needed a boost to become the person they desired. Charise, not sharing his judgmental sentiments, merely shrugged her shoulders, popped the other pill, removed her jacket, swinging it overhead she began to dance.

CHAPTER 3

Three drinks and an hour later, Enkill was leaning back on one of the closed death boxes; shirt unbuttoned, flying open, he couldn't remember where he put his coat, but it didn't matter. The music had invaded his alcohol-hazed mind. He was captive to the sensation of a topless Charise licking down the center of his chest while one of her hands worked inside his pants, massaging his stiffness. Another woman - a bronze beauty with shoulder-length honey golden locks so neat, they were more like twist-sucked at his neck. She wore a flaring gown of raven silk over outrageous curves. The top portion of the gown was pulled low and tucked under her heavy bosom with studded tips.

Minutes later...

One of Enkill's hands slid down the blonde's back to the tender softness of her behind. Her tongue, wet and slippery, moved like a nymphet eel over his.

His other hand was in Charise's hair, at the time on her knees, giving Enkill the most intense oral stimulation he'd ever received. Her mouth was so wet and warm. Enkill felt her try to consume him entirely, her tongue gliding under the sensitive underside of his shaft.

Enkill heard himself moan. He tried to catch himself, not wanting to blow his masculine cool, but couldn't. Again, the passion surrendering sound came forth. Little lights were flashing before his eyes; this was feeling too good. Thinking the women must have slipped him one of those Ecstacy pills,

Enkill let his eyes wander across the crowd self-consciously, hoping he wasn't the center of some spectacle. All the partygoers seemed focused on their affairs, not minding him in the least.

That was good for Enkill until he came upon one set of floating eyes. Eyes that seemed to hold his and shine with a greenish glow amidst the shooting lasers. Now Enkill is sure the women slipped him something. Charise felt so good! But he couldn't seem to tear away his vision from those unblinking eyes. The longer he stared, the Enkill began to make out a face. A laser hit the front, making it completely visible in the reddish haze. It was a man's face. What appeared to be a short Caucasian man with a lot of hair. Maybe the man was some kind of weird voyeur. They were definitely scattered among the crowd. Two lasers crisscrossed mere inches before Enkill's line of vision. He blinked. When he refocused, the eyes were gone.

Enkill's complete attention was drawn back to the two women in his grasp. As the blonde's kisses moved to his chin, down his neck, Charise rose to her feet, and the two beauties switched positions.

Nibbling his earlobe and taking vamp-like suction bites that made Enkill's entire body tingle was Charise. Devouring his solid manhood with porn-star talents was the woman that, in the last twenty or so minutes, he'd named Goldy.

She was unbelievable. Her skills surpassed Charise's. Goldy's technique was perfect. To Enkill her mouth was better than the act of penetration with some women. The moderate speed she glided her warm and slick oral tunnel over his cock, was just how he liked it. Full of the greedy but tender passion, as if she was trying to make him feel as good as it was to her. And she was enjoying it, he knew; he could feel her passion.

Again Enkill heard himself. So good. He had to watch.

Goldy was performing, eyes closed, gripping his thighs, inhaling him in and making his bushy pubic brush her lips. The combined stimulation of the women was almost too much for him to bear. Enkill crushed Charise to his side.

It was happening. Heat swelled in Enkill's groin, the sensation spreading the complete length of his shaft, gathering in the head. Enkill tensed. His body jerked. He was erupting, his first real non-self-induced climax in years. He hadn't touched himself in over six months. What an eruption it was. Up to this point, Enkill had women do all kinds of things at this moment in the past. Some pulled it out of their mouths and started gagging and spitting, spilling his seed. Some took it on their faces or breasts, smearing it in their hands. Goldy did none of that; she was Enkill's favorite kind of woman: a swallower.

When Goldy felt the warm fluid shoot on her tongue, a type of almost orgasmic high came over her. Between her legs was soaked. She reasserted herself to her task with fresh vigor, sucking, pulling, and emptying him.

Squeezing Charise with one arm and steadying himself on the coffin with the other, a shut-eyed Enkill released a loud primitive shriek like the first man being born that, thanks to the music, went unheard by anyone in earshot. After he finished, Goldy held him in her mouth for a few more intense moments. With a speeding heartbeat beginning to normal out, Enkill was a little puzzled as he watched Goldy vanish into the red and black sea. He and Charise were dancing, and the woman decided to join in. One thing led to another. No words were ever spoken. He didn't even know her real name. This was his kind of place. Just then, Charise whispered in his ear, "Welcome home."

He wanted to ask her how she knew but thought better of it. Enkill knew that some people could always tell when a man returns from prison.

Some people called it the glow.

Charise was nowhere in sight. Enkill found himself sitting on a stool at the bar, which was, in reality, ten elevated coffins set in the shape of a pyramid. A glossy black bar of mirrors stood within the triangle, from which the topless male and female bartenders served drinks with names like Virgin's Blood and Oblivion in large plastic cups made to look like golden and silver goblets.

Enkill had tried to tip the bartender n a show of courtesy, and the d-cupped blonde refused with a smile and bounced away. It then dawned on him that not once did he see any kind of financial transaction the entire night. Not at the door, the bar, or for the seemingly limitless supply of party narcotics floating around. Being on parole, the sobering thought of the place being subject to some unexpected midnight raid crossed his mind. But the thought kept going until it disappeared as he looked around at the truly racially diverse crowd gathered. This wasn't the kind of place that got raided. Nor was this the kind of place a person simply wandered off the street. No. The place had exclusivity to it: invite only.

Enkill sipped a Virgin's Blood. From what he could tell, it was a red vodka concoction mixed with something else he couldn't place. Taking casual sips, not wanting to push his limits, Enkill let his eyes roam as he wondered who these people were. These weren't your average blue or white-collar workers who took a night out to play dress-up and indulge in whatever fantasies their perverse minds could conjure because that wouldn't explain the near physical perfection of everyone in attendance.

No one present looked a day over thirty-five though some looked much younger. To Enkill, it was like being in some erotic melting pot. As if someone gathered the most beautiful people from every nationality all over the world, dressed them in red and black, worked everyone up into a substance-induced sexual frenzy, and voila! This is what you would have.

To Enkill's right, for a few seconds, he observed two blonde males in fancy black suits with long red ties inhale line after line of a white powdery substance from a small mountain on the bar that he assumed was cocaine. From their wide-eyed glances around them and their up-tempo body language. He watched the two men's carefree indulgence until one of the gentlemen with a black card pushed a thick finger-sized line in his direction. Enkill declined the man's offer with a slight shake of his head. The man then, like Charise, gave no further encouragement and vacuumed the offering up his nostril with one great whiff.

Not wanting to give the man the wrong impression because it was that kind of crowd, he saw a couple of same-sex male acts on his way to the bar. Enkill looked away to the left of him.

A large Indian-looking man in a red cape, and a headful of long, dark, femininely styled hair, hammered away into a petite Asian female from behind. Her short black skirt was rolled over her hips, with her knees in the stools pillowed center in a manner that had to be an incredible feat of balance, for the man's strokes were powerfully wild. His hair thrashed about his face. Her little jerking body looked elfin in the giant's grasp. Her bouncing hair hung down her face in dark, sweaty strands. She turned and looked at Enkill with dark slanted slits, cranberry around the edges. Black mascara streaked her round powdered face. The foundation mixed with perspiration gave her face a weird muddy look. Enkill felt the bar vibrating with the couple's passion. Watching Enkill, she inserted two fingers between her small pouty ebony lips making the fingers disappear slowly into her mouth repeatedly up to her knuckles.

Enkill entertained the idea of placing something else between those lips when he felt a soft hand on his shoulder from behind and heard the sweet whisper of a nymph in his right ear.

"There is someone who'd like to meet you, Enkill."

Enkill turned away from the bar to be greeted by an olive-skinned woman with model-quality beauty. Thick black waves of hair fell down her shoulders. The eyes under her thick curve of lashes were serious and sparkling emerald green: so green; they didn't look real. They were like the eyes one would expect to encounter in some fantasy art poster, depicting some enchantress Witch Queen, not in an underground club in the Village. Enkill was going to inquire how she knew his name when Green-Eyes summoned him forward with the long curve of a rose nail before turning and heading off into the crowd.

Leaving his drink at the bar, curiosity sparked Enkill felt compelled to follow.

Taking three fast steps, Enkill caught up to Green-Eyes, placing his hands around her waist from behind, a bold gesture. Not that he needed to in order to follow her lead, it was simply a need to touch. To see how she'd feel in his hands. One of his hands slid down the curve of her hip, riding the rhythm of her strut. She made no protest. Her hair brushed his face, and he inhaled a scent so sweet he wanted to smother his face in the plush fall of her soft locks. They were halfway through the crowd heading for the back of the club when Enkill realized that Green-Eyes was dressed exactly like Charise. That he figured was how she knew his name; little did he know it wasn't.

Green-Eyes led Enkill past the pressing mass of bodies to the far wall in the back and entered a maroon door that looked so much like a part of the wall that he would have missed it without his guide.

Then up a short flight of stairs with black walls, lit only by two candles on golden hooks at the top of the staircase. After walking through a red-walled hall, illuminated by a dim light with drapes of scarlet silk hanging from the ceiling, they came to an entrance shielded by a thin red curtain that, from behind, Enkill could hear voices and see moving shadows. In this area, the music from the dance floor was just a low rumble.

Following his escort behind the curtain, Enkill was surprised to find a lounge identical in design to the one he and Charise had passed earlier downstairs, except somehow, this one gave Enkill a more intimate feel. Something was different. He found that difference when he realized that, unlike the electrical lighting in the other, this one was lit by a hanging row of blood-red perfumed candles. Their scents reminded Enkill of fresh apples. Small golden hands suspended in a line across the ceiling held the candles.

"Ah, Enkill, I thought I was going to have to come to you," said a short, smiling, green-eyed white man that rose from among the couch's clutter of chatting females offering a hand adorned with thick golden rings and various-sized bloodstones.

While looking at the man, something clicked in Enkill immediately. He recognized those eyes. Intense cruel eyes that invoked the image of fire, like burning jade. Those were the same prying eyes from the dance floor.

Taking the man's hand, yet saying nothing, Enkill assessed the man with the plastic smile who spoke his name with such insincere familiarity.

The man's grip was remarkably firm for such a small man. It felt like iron. Enkill always believed you could tell much about a man from his handshake. Unnecessary shows of strength were often signs of insecurity or subtle tools of intimidation used by one trying to establish an unspoken dominance over another.

Enkill figured the man to be between five-five and five-seven. A young man no more than thirty, no less than twenty-five, with a slim athletic build as if he spends some time on a weight bench. That was obvious because of the three buttons he left open on his fitted raven top. For some reason, Enkill didn't think the man was American. It was more than how his slacks fell over a pair of two-toned high heels that came to such a sharp point at the toes. They looked like they belonged in the wardrobe of some Vogue model. Nor was it the strange accent the man spoke with. It was the man's face, feminine but masculine, clean-shaven, and the perfect curve of his nose ended in a sharp point. The thin pink line of lips and thick mane of black hair curved to and fro around his neck was like one of those pretty foreign film stars. The man could have been a Greek or maybe a Roman.

The man saw in Enkill's eyes the snug disdain with which he viewed his ensemble and took a spinning step with a grand wave of his hands as if he was leading an orchestra. His first high, pitched word silenced all conversation in the lounge, "You know, I killed the man who made these shoes! Oh yes… You know why?" he asked, pointing to his shoes. "For he had reached the pinnacle of his craft! Any thought that he could reproduce such a work of sheer brilliance is to ponder nonsense. So to save him the humiliation of a tarnished image and ensure him a place in the halls of eternal glory he so rightfully deserved for such craftsmanship. Yes, he did, Yesss! For I Niccolo declared it so, Koon, fi I koon, be, and it is!" the man said, leaning in a little too close for Enkill's liking. Lifting his pants leg with a wicked smile, Niccolo asked, "By the way, do you like them?" In his eyes, a faint alien light sparkled that Enkill saw and dismissed at once, attributing it to one too many Virgin's Bloods.

Unfucking believable, he thought, this guy can't be for real, and if he is, then he's fucking crazy. Or maybe he was drunk and acting out a character from his favorite vampire novel.

Just then, Niccolo dropped his pants leg with a short high laugh. "Enkill, I don't do impersonations, nor do I read vampire novels, for they are full of fiction." Niccolo then spun away from Enkill, resuming his seat.

Enkill knew he didn't just voice that out loud, or did he? If he didn't, then the man just verbalized his thoughts. Confused, alarmed, and off-balanced, Enkill stared sharply at the man who called himself Niccolo, sitting with his hands folded in his lap like a scholarly student watching him.

"You didn't?" Niccolo's face held a questioning expression before melting into a character smile, "I am sorry,

41

Enkill," he apologized, bringing a hand to his heart."Do forgive me. I haven't even offered you a seat. Where are my manners? Please, there is so much for us to discuss, yeh!"

Enkill had been in the lounge for a couple of minutes and had sized it up upon first entering. Yet as the Middle Eastern beauties made sitting room for him on one side of Niccolo, he saw things that he missed earlier. This area was much smaller than the other, less than half the size, and besides him and Niccolo, they were the only males present, surrounded by twenty or so females. About half of them were dressed identically in their black leather get-ups. The whole scene had a strange feel to Enkill, like some cult. Niccolo was the master of all. Even Charise, who took a seat on the other side of Niccolo. Trying to make eyes with him-something he saw and ignored -was enthralled.

Alright, he was game for now, Enkill mused silently as he sat in the space cleared for him, which was a little closer than he would have preferred to Niccolo. His green-eyed escort, who forced the harem-looking beauties further over, then joined Enkill. Green-Eyes was sitting so close to Enkill with her bosom pressed against his arm that not only could he feel her body heat and smell her perfumed scent, but in the silence, he could hear the whispers of her breathing in his ear. She then grabbed hold of his upper arm, squeezing, letting her other hand glide down the ends of his locks in a gesture so intimate, that he was forced to look at her. And when he did, he saw a dreamy sensuality floating in her eyes that beckoned him to consume her right there. A thought he considered but thought against. Seeing this, Niccolo told Green-Eyes.

"Stop it, Natasha. You're exciting him and distracting him. I need all of his attention. For this is the single most important night of his life!"

That statement got all of Enkill's attention. He wondered just what this strange man could want with him. Though he wasn't feeling the man's eccentric style, Niccolo reeked of money, and money was one language Enkill always had time to speak. Enkill then decided he'd hear the man out, and if it weren't what he wanted to hear, he'd just cut the little chat short. "Listen, this place is alright and all, but I am not really into the weird shit! You got something of practical importance to talk about. Let's talk." Enkill stated with a dead stare.

A couple of the women losing interest in the men, began talking among themselves in low tones.

Placing a finger to his chin, after almost five seconds of nodding, Niccolo figuratively said, "Enkill, you would think, a man of your background would be one of great patience, yeah."

"Niccolo, patience is something I have in great reserves, but a tolerance for bullshit is what I lack."

Niccolo smiled before speaking in the stop pause fashion that was his way. "Enkill, I want no," he shook his head, "I am going to make you a God. A dark, handsome ...God!" Afterward, he busted into a nervous little laugh that contaminated the women with giggles.

Enkill seemed the only person not amused. Even when Natasha kissed his cheek and whispered encouragingly, "You're going to be perfect, you'll see!"

What kind of silly games were they playing? Definitely, the kind he had no interest in. Irritated and feeling the alcohol a little more than he would have liked, Enkill stood, giving Niccolo a cold, slow roll of his eyes, to which Niccolo just smiled.

A knowing smile.

Enkill was about to ask a docile and strangely passive Charise for his coat when she pointed behind him. He turned to see Natasha holding his coat out to him.

A little startled, he took it, thinking how weird it was that he didn't see, hear, or feel her move. Either he was a little too buzzed, which he guessed, or something extraordinary was happening. What actually made him consider the latter was that everyone who heard Niccolo's little announcement didn't respond like it was out of the ordinary in the least. They seemed to look at him like he was the psych-patient.

Donning his coat, Enkill turned to leave when Niccolo called his name. The hard seriousness in the man's tone froze him in his tracks and forced him to glare back over his shoulder.

"Enkill, I'll be seeing you later."

To what he viewed as an open threat, Enkill matched the man's tone, "Physically, that's not in your best interest." Enkill warned, seeing the tensing in Niccolo's posture and the violent shade that darkened his eyes.

Seeing nothing in the small man that he couldn't handle, Enkill laughed, a patronizing sound.

CHAPTER 4

After his exchange with Niccolo, a slightly peeved Enkill didn't stop moving until he finally emerged from the club. The crisp winter night's air was a contrasting change from the humidity of the club that he welcomed with a deep breath. Already he felt better. His head clearing, looking back at the house of Gomorra, he sought to put as much distance between it and himself as possible.

Enkill felt like walking, and since it was such a nice night with only the occasional breeze and bright moon overhead, that's just what he did. The streets of Greenish Village were not as busy as before. The crowds had thinned. Most of the seekers either found what they sought or decided to shut it down for the night and try again tomorrow. Checking his watch, he found it was a little after one thirty in the morning. He hadn't realized so much time had passed.

Strolling at a casual pace, Enkill made his way westward, up to 14th St., and crossed the multiple-laned street that made up the Westside Highway over to the pier. Before his incarceration, Enkill used to walk the pier about once every two weeks: just him, the night, and his thoughts.

Standing by the thick silver railings that separated him from the gloomy restless waters of the Hudson River with his sights aimed at a sleeping New Jersey, Enkill remembered something he'd forgotten. It's always so much colder by the water.

Buttoning up his coat and flipping up his collar, Enkill looked up the pier at all the unoccupied benches that were visible for about half a mile due to the countless shining street lamps that lined the pier. In the past, when he strolled the pier, no matter what time of the night it was -especially in the summer-he always came across other lone nightwalkers, the homeless, or couples cuddled up on one of the short benches, talking, enjoying the night, or engaging in activities that should best be kept indoors.

Not tonight.

Besides for him, the pier seemed deserted. For that reason, Enkill always thought the lights were a nice comforting touch. Because without them, the pier would be dangerously dark and isolated, even with the highway a mere twenty feet away. In his younger years, when he used to commit random street robberies, what some called muggings, he would have loved such a place.

All grown up, Enkill's criminal taste had also matured. Just how much he planned to show the world very soon. He'd been walking for almost ten minutes with his head down, heels clicking on the cemented walkway, thinking about what his meeting tomorrow with Meko would produce when something told him to look up from his thoughts. In doing so, he saw the first other human presence since entering the pier, a lone figure sitting on several benches up ahead.

As Enkill got closer, he made out the figure to be a man. A small man dressed in black. Since the walkway was between the silver railing and the benches, all Enkill saw was a profile view of a thick head of dark hair falling into the man's face obscuring his features. The man was hunched slightly over. He figured the stranger to be either Hispanic or Caucasian. The man's hands were folded in his lap, from which small sparkles danced like light catching precious stones.

Enkill squinted. For some reason, the man seemed familiar. Suddenly, Enkill became aware of an ominous blend of sounds that he now wished he could quiet. He heard the tapping of his heels, the rolling waves of the Hudson River, and the roaring of revved engines speeding along the highway. It sounded like the asthmatic breathing of a monster.

When Enkill was about fifteen or so paces away, the figure stood. It was like a blink. A movement so swift, it caused Enkill to question his eyesight.

The figure that posed before Enkill made his heart skip a surprising beat. Now Enkill knew why he thought the man was so familiar. It was the same little man from the club: Niccolo.

For a moment, Niccolo was a framed image in Enkill's mind: black strands of windblown hair beating at a handsomely demonic face. A face that peered at Enkill with eyes of green fire!

Then the picture spoke. A voice that boomed so loud and clear over the waves and traffic, Enkill swore it was coming from within his own head.

"Enkill, I've been waiting for you; we've been waiting for you," Niccolo held open his arms like one would catch a child running into one's embrace. He then laughed the deep laugh of the genuinely amused, flicking a handful of hair from his face like Enkill had seen countless women do in the past.

So surprised was Enkill that he didn't move nor speak. His heartbeat began to quicken. In his belly was the queasy feeling one gets before the first punch in an anticipated fight—his tensed limbs filled with adrenalin.

Niccolo took slow, deliberate steps towards Enkill as he asked the startled man, "What is it you desire most? Tell me...What is it? Money...Power...Recognition...Influence...The slavish adoration of women so beautiful, their pleasures normally reserved for kings?"

Niccolo's words seemed to ride the winds themselves, blowing into Enkill's eardrums. Filling them, besides Niccolo's voice, he heard nothing.

"You don't strike me as the wife, picket fence, and two kids type. No, not you." Niccolo shook his head, then pointed an almost accusing finger at Enkill, "You're a man who lives outside of society's restraining norms. Finally free from your imprisonment, what is it you now feel? What song does the core of your essence sing? Do you listen to the cords? I have! It sings a melody of retribution and revenge on a world that shuns you like a leper, trampling on your dreams at every opportunity. Yeah! It sings a melody of

49

rage, murderous rage! For you are a killer Enkill Jones, I smell the dried blood of the dead upon you, yeah!" Niccolo, rubbing his hands together, inched closer.

"Murderous rage!" Niccolo rolled the words on his tongue, tasting them. So sweet, like fresh blood. "I am going to give you a channel, a means of release. A freedom unlike any other you've ever experienced! Freedom, none will ever be able to strip you of, save death! And if you're crafty enough, and I think you are, you'll be able to put that off for a few millenniums and maybe even become a king among the Kingu. Yes, I have plans for you, Enkill, the Dark God. That has kind of a sublime ring to it. Yeah!"

Enkill watched as Niccolo did a light chuckle and examined his shoes. Something about the man just isn't right. Enkill couldn't explain it. Maybe it was how his mind felt a little foggy, like he was just awaking from some trance-like state. Now once again, he could hear the river and the highway.

He may not have wanted to admit it, but Niccolo's words rung truth until he started going on about channels and putting off death. That was when he convinced Enkill that he was truly insane. And Enkill wanted nothing to do with any crazies. That was also when Enkill overcame the initial surprise of running into the man.

Inside, Enkill grew calculating malice. He quickly scanned the pier, making sure they were alone, as he considered dumping Niccolo into the Hudson.

So engrossed was Enkill in his malicious thoughts that he didn't take the time out to ask himself. How'd the man know his last name? He didn't tell Charise. What was the funny light in

the man's eyes when he first came upon him, or how'd he get on the pier in the first place? Up ahead of him at that, when he left him back at the club. Enkill asked himself none of these questions. The only question he pondered was if the little man made him do something fatal, could he get away with it?

Only a few feet separated Niccolo from Enkill, who said, "Listen and understand me, you little weird fuck! You're right about one thing; I don't know how, probably a lucky guess but your right, I'm a killer, "Enkill stated. His dark eyes were set like stones. "I've killed in the past, and I plan to do so again in the future unless you want that future to become the present. Step. The Fuck…aside'!"

Making a ticking noise by hitting his tongue against the roof of his mouth, shaking his head, no, Niccolo stepped in closer to Enkill. "Enkill your fate has already been written. I am sorry, the ink is already dry!"

Not believing Niccolo's reaction, Enkill asked himself. Why was the small man so cocky? Did he have a gun? To neutralize any concealed advantages Niccolo may possess, Enkill shot forward, swinging a hard straight right!

Instead of leveling the little man, Enkill hit nothing but air. He heard Niccolo's taunting laughter behind him.

Impossible!

Enkill didn't see the man move, but he had to. He was simply no longer there. Enkill questioned just how many drinks he had consumed earlier.

Quickly Enkill spun to face the laughter. He saw Niccolo, about ten paces away, going through a series of mock stretches, then cracking his knuckles. Niccolo's movements were humorous. When the little man next spoke, his voice was deadly, joker-like smile vanishing, "You challenge me, ummm, Enkill, I am going to make you a god. Not The God, but a god nevertheless!" The baritone of Niccolo's voice deepened as his eyes faded into two complete forest green pools illuminated by pupils of torched jade spheres.

"Oh shit!" was the only two words an astonished Enkill could muster

"Enkill!" Niccolo's voice drummed, "Know that I am your alpha ...and your omega...Your beginning and your end. The one that gives you life, and if you ever betray me in action...or thought, I will be the one that gives you death."

With no logical explanation as to exactly what manner of creature Niccolo was, Enkill banished the fear from his mind that threatened to chain his limbs as he prepared to face off, if need be, to the death. Because somewhere inside, Enkill understood that if he lost this encounter, he would lose something he'd never regain again.

Like any predator in his situation, Enkill did what came naturally: he attacked!

Running forward with a cocked fist, at the last instant, Enkill danced to one side, seeing the small man weaving to avoid his charge. Enkill launched a speedy hook, which Niccolo swatted out of the air, and with the same hand, delivered a sharp smack to the side of Enkill's head, spinning him off balance down to one knee. A dizzy Enkill didn't see the blow that hit him. All he knew was a terrible ringing inside of one ear and that he had to get up.

Before he could stand, he felt Niccolo's hand closing around the front of his neck, lifting him.

Enkill couldn't believe it. He was being held with one hand. His feet weren't touching the ground. The man's grip was like steel, ungiving, squeezing. It was becoming hard for him to breathe.

Gagging, spitting streams of saliva in the air, Enkill rained down with all he had, delivering a series of blows to the top of Niccolo's head.

Enkill might as well have been punching a brick wall. His assault did nothing. Niccolo's hold simply tightened. Trying not to panic, a wild-eyed Enkill attempted to pry the man's fingers loose to no avail.

Seeing Enkill's feeble attempt at struggle, Niccolo burst into a short fit of psychotic laughter, spun, and drove Enkill down into the pavement, knocking what little wind Enkill had left from him.

Enkill's head bounced off the walkway. A sharp pain shot down his spine. He couldn't move. Everything spun in front of his eyesight in bright flashes of light.

Niccolo gazed down at Enkill and did a demonic giggle as he straddled the man's chest, yanking a handful of locks. Niccolo pulled Enkill's face to his, forcing him to see him for what he really was.

When Enkill's vision came into focus, Niccolo's face was only inches from his own. What Enkill saw sent a chill through him colder than the pavement beneath him.

Niccolo's hair hung down into Enkill's face shielding the majority of the pier's light. In the intimate shadow was the greenish glow of eyes framed in a Hadean face with enraged nostrils and lips twisted back in a tight, evil grimace that showed Enkill something that made his heart threaten to escape free of his ribs.

The man's teeth were a perfect pearly set save for a pair of blood-streaked canines, abnormally long with curved tips. They reminded Enkill of a wolf's or a...vampire's fangs.

Enkill felt his head being forced to one side. He heard material ripping then there was a cool breeze on his bare neck and shoulder. The chill only lasted for a second or two. It was replaced by the heat of Niccolo's breath, the touch of warm lips against the skin of his neck.

When Niccolo's teeth penetrated him, Enkill's body stiffened as he cried out in pain and disgust, for there was something uncomfortably intimate about the creature's embrace. His strength was beginning to return, and with it came back the feeling in his limbs. Enkill grabbed weakly at the creature but couldn't free himself from it and the sucking noises.

Again, Enkill would feel himself fading. The world spun above and beneath him. The river, the highway, it was all becoming so distant. Even the city's beautiful skyline became a weak flickering like broken Christmas lights. Each flicker threatened to be it's last. Soon, Enkill would feel or hear nothing. Not even the creature. Just the silence of complete darkness.

CHAPTER 5

Earth. the bitter rigor mortis of life.

Earth. all glitter, the whore has per plight.

Cum cum, towards the light,

For your delight.

Killers, love Devils with all of your might!

It's not like you're going to fall for what is right.

Dad! Dad! I hear the call of the night…

Opening his eyes, trying to make some sense of his situation, Enkill looked into the glowing eyes of his attacker, then at lips stained red with his blood. He saw the calculating resolve in Niccolo's face as he released his hold of Enkill's hair. Then rolled up the sleeve of his jacket up to the elbow, exposing the pale skin of his hairless arm.

Satisfaction trickling over his face, Niccolo bit deep into his wrist, then made a fist and held his gashed wrist over Enkill's face, letting the thick, dark red supernatural elixir drip of his veins pour onto Enkill. As he did, he murmured, "Enkill, choose life or death. The life I offer is a power that, in humanity's immense multitude, only a few have known. The death I offer is just that, death; the ultimate finality. So drink of me and live, be great!" the kingu hissed.

Those words said Niccolo cradled Enkill's head, crushing the dripping wound to Enkill's mouth, forcing upon him his offering. Niccolo watched in amusement as Enkill at first tried to reject this gift. The blood spilled over his lips.

Niccolo then squeezed Enkill's jaws, forcing open his mouth. Niccolo laughed at Enkill's resilience as he let the blood pool in his mouth until it overflowed out the corners of his chin. That was until Enkill coughed and digested some. Niccolo observed the spark in his spawn's eyes as the hunger's first signs surfaced. The clumsy, frantic working of Enkill's inexperienced mouth pulled in the kingu's blood in great, hungry gulps. Suddenly, Enkill reached up and took hold of Niccolo's arm with both hands. Niccolo smiled, remembering his first taste of the blood over 1800 years ago. That first intoxicating taste of power that once tasted was always craved.

As each wave of blood hit Enkill's tongue, the one before poured down his throat. It circulated, changing him forever. He felt energy invade his entire being; a titillating fire consumed every limb, organ, and nerve fiber. His body then suddenly began to twist and shake. Niccolo floated up, allowing the convulsions he'd seen before, yet never like this run their course until Enkill went still, and his eyes rolled up in his head, leaving only the whites. They soon returned to gaze unwaveringly at Niccolo.

Niccolo's brow wrinkled in confusion as he gazed down into the ebony irises of his spawn. For a split second, the intimately familiar dancing of bright silver specs before Enkill's lids lowered in the changing sleep.

Enkill's physical body slumbered on a chilly pier in Manhattan, but not his essence. Enkill slowly regained consciousness to find himself sprawled on a bed of leaves and dirt under cover of the darkest night's sky, littered with the brightest constellations he'd ever seen. In the distance, he heard the loud crashing waves. Carefully he stood, checking himself, feeling a foreign strength within his limbs. He remembered his current predicament – as he did, his hand shot up to his neck. To his surprise, he found no wound. He felt his hair resting on his shoulders, a breeze across his bare chest, and leaves between his toes. Looking down, he saw a faded pair of blue jeans that sagged off his hips.

He somehow knew he was very far from New York. He'd been all over the country, and no place he remembered felt even remotely like this. It felt as if he were standing amidst the primordial origins of humanity; with this thought, Enkill became aware of the slow, heavy, gravid rhythm of beating drums.

Though he heard water, there was none in sight. He was in some sort of clearing, surrounded by gigantic tropical trees. Their under barks were tall and full of thick, sprouting branches that hung over, with red and green leaves brushing the almost red earth. Bathed in the flickering light of two massive fires, Enkill could feel no heat. He turned, spinning full circle, noticing he wasn't alone.

By the edge of the clearing stood a mature man with deep cocoa skin and dark eyes that appeared black in the fire's light. He was dressed in all white, wearing a buttonless shirt with no collar and loose flowing slacks that moved with the night's breeze. Barefoot, his complexion was that of a mulatto. His shiny black hair was twisted in several thick plaits and pulled back in a long warrior's tail coming over one shoulder. The man's grave face was hairless, except for a pair of thick, highly arched brows. Wordlessly, he held up a hand with long hooked nails of ivory. On one of his fingers rested a platinum ring with a glowing red stone, which moved, beckoning Enkill forward.

The white-clad figure turned and walked into the dense darkness of the jungle. Enkill followed, trying to keep sight of the man like a child behind a parent in a crowd, stepping quickly over the scurrying rodents, insects, and snakes that lived on the forest floor. Something huge landed in a tree ahead of him, its weight-shaking branches causing leaves to rain down. It appeared to be some sort of golden-eyed wildcat. The creature let out a fierce growl that seemed to shake the jungle; feathered wings flapped loudly as primates harped in recognition from their treetop homes. Somehow, Enkill didn't feel threatened - he passed, accepting it for what it was... a greeting.

Enkill realized that even though the jungle was devoid of light, the branches of trees overhead intertwined, blocking the sky's celestial radiance. His sight was perfect in the pitch darkness, as was his hearing. He heard the faint rustling of a snake crawling beneath the jungle's vegetation before he glimpsed its orange tail. A formless creature of opal slime slid down a bark. Its glowing marine blue eyes focused on him. Enkill smelled the urine and droppings of the beast that hid, only appearing as a fast-moving shape or a pair of glowing feral eyes at his side for the briefest of seconds.

Still, even with his heightened senses, Enkill seemed to have lost sight of the man in white. He followed the drum's melody until he came to another clearing, where the drums rose in volume and increased in tempo.

A big temple with a circular base rising into a stepped point stood in the clearing. Its stone walls were white - like a dove's eggs - with many evenly spaced, glassless windows around it. Within each window burned a small, scarlet, smokeless flame. Enkill moved in awe around the temple's exterior, his hands caressing the stone in wonder. Finally, he came upon a pair of golden doors. After taking a deep breath, he entered, arriving in a large room. His bare feet slid quietly across the cool marble floor, black and white tiles resembling a giant chessboard. Every piece of furniture in the room was either ivory or onyx,

Enkill looked down to see the white-clad man sitting cross-legged before him as if appearing from nowhere. He focused on a small onyx chest on the floor before him on a short white stand. Enkill sat as the man sat, the chest between them.

Inside the chest, Enkill could see nothing but darkness. Darkness, like a night sky, missing the stars and moon. The man put his hand into the chest's abyss pulling from it a ring that was similar to his own, which he held out towards Enkill.

The ring was a large onyx stone - from its wide platinum band reached four claws holding a stone. The ring looked ancient, magical, like the adornment of a shaman or High priest of old.

The man looked from the ring to Enkill, his dark eyes emotionless. When he spoke, his voice was smooth and confiding.

"The wait for you has been long. Finally, you are here. I am Abu; you are one of my own. This is yours. Claim your heritage!"

Enkill silently reached out, taking the offered piece and placing it on the ring finger of his left hand. No sooner than the ring was in place, a silver glow formed in the black stone's core. And grew until it covered the ring spreading to Enkill's hand, traveling the distance of his entire body. Enkill fell upon his back, engulfed in the light. He closed his eyes, grimacing while his body shook, feeling the invasion of the great dark power that mended his soul to become one forever.

The light around him dissolved like mist. Enkill's body was left unmoving on the marble. His eyes opened slowly. Revealing his once brown irises, now almost as dark as the ring-bearer's who now smiled, a fiendish fanged smile. That ghastly image would be the last Enkill saw before once again he experienced the darkness.

Enkill had awoken more than five minutes ago, though he still lay motionless on a bed that was not his own. He was far from his rented room in Spanish Harlem.

The room was dark, decorated in Victorian decor and he was lying under the foreign comforts of a bed's canopy, trying to put the pieces together from the night before. It wasn't that he had trouble remembering, for everything was clear in vivid detail: from Charise, the club, to Niccolo, to Abu. It was believing That was the hard part.

Maybe someone slipped me some kind of hallucinogenic, Enkill reasoned to himself. But as soon as the thought appeared, it was chased away by the evidence of the present. That evidence came in the form of an alien presence that originated in his core and pulsated throughout his entire body, making him feel in a way he could never recall before. The only word to describe that feeling that came to mind was...Powerful!

He slid off the bed in one motion, noticing someone had removed all of his clothing, save for his boxer briefs.

The room may have been dark, but his vision was perfect. He could clearly see two red oak chairs with fancy embroidery seats and circular backs, which stood on either side of a matching dresser with golden knobs. He could see the carpet, lush red even in the gloom. He made his way over to the room's one large window covered by heavy red and golden drapes. For all the room's gaudy displays of luxury, like the Tiffany lamps on the nightstands by the bed and the human-sized, gold-framed oval mirror standing solitarily in a corner, the room did not feel real. It was like a false replica of a bedroom, devoid of life's fabric like a showcase in a museum. The carpet was dustless, the polished knobs of the dresser untarnished by fingertips. There were no signs of personal occupancy as if the room had never been used.

Enkill fumbled with the drapes for a couple of seconds before realizing they were held together by a heavy zipper, hidden in its creases, running down to the scarlet carpet. Undoing the zipper, he pulled back the drapes allowing the rays of the high noon sun to invade the darkness.

"Ah shit!" he moaned, squinting his eyes at the sudden intrusion of light as a strange, tickling sensation danced upon his skin. The skin on his arms, directly in the morning, burned hotter than the rest of him, and his eyes began to feel hot as if he had a fever.

In need of fresh air, Enkill opened the window and inhaled a passing breeze as he scanned the block both ways, taking in the tightly parked cars in front of what looked like a never-ending row of two-floor brownstones. From the looks of things, he figured his location to be a residential block somewhere in mid-town. All of a sudden, Enkill gripped the windowsill, then slowly brought one hand up to his ear.

"Unbelievable," he whispered, backing away from the window. Then hesitantly reproaching, he stuck his head out into the afternoon. He could hear everything with almost preternatural clarity. Everything, from the traffic that jammed a nearby avenue to the fragmented conversations and miscellaneous sounds that made up the city's soundtrack. Though he heard everything as if it was taking place right in the room with him, this burst of sound wasn't cluttering or overbearing on his senses; his brain seemed to differentiate the sounds naturally.

"Incredible," was all he could manage to say. One level below the basement of the townhouse in an earthen room of stone, another stirred.

Niccolo's eyes shot open in marvel as he lay in the protective confines of his coffin.

"Impossible! The sun has not set. A newborn Perus. Such a thing cannot be!" He said aloud to the walls of his coffin. His mind raced, searching for a plausible answer. For in his almost 1800 years of existence, never had he seen one such as this. He sent out a mental probe only to find it violently rejected. A door slammed in his face.

The shock caused Niccolo's eyes to become glowing green spheres."Such power!" He uttered through trembling lips, for excitement and fear pulsated within him. Reluctantly, he closed his eyes and waited in anticipation for his mistress: the night.

Upstairs, Enkill was like the Greek Narcissus, marveling over the physical perfections of his proportions when his chain of thought was momentarily broken by what he could only describe as somebody trying to peer inside of his head. He evaded this unwanted intrusion by mere force of will, accompanying it with the mental message, "Get the fuck out of here!"

Seconds later, he would return his attention to the physical changes brought about by last night's incident. His once dark brown irises were now as black as the void. Identical to the stone in the ring on his left hand, save for the specs of sliver circling his pupils, giving his eyes the appearance of a mini cosmos. He then took in his torso - though it was already in superb shape, the now muscular definition was so outrageous - it resembled something from a comic book. Still, the most fascinating aspect of his change was his arms. Last night there was only one tattoo on his upper right bicep: a skull.

Now the skull was gone. Both of Enkill's arms, from wrist to shoulder, were covered in an array of black symbols that could only be described as tribal. Circles, long lines, short swirly lines, triangles, and other geometric shapes flowed into one another, forming a strange pattern he couldn't decipher. Below one of his elbows, a line of symbols that looked like some ancient arcane writing twisted to his wrist.

Looking at the ring in the mirror from every imaginable angle as he turned and twisted his hand, Enkill told himself he wasn't going to try to figure this one out. He would have sworn his meeting with the dark-eyed Abu was of a dream nature. Yet still, the heavy stoned ring sat on his hand. A dilemma whose answer he figured would be made clear at a later time.

Enkill then dropped his attention down to his legs and was satisfied that his bottom half matched his top. Because nothing Enkill thought looked more ridiculous than a man with a muscular torso walking on the legs of a twelve-year-old. He snorted with laughter and stretched.

Feeling he needed to freshen up with the sour taste of sleep still in his mouth, Enkill ran his tongue along his upper gums to be met with sharp points he didn't have before.

Holding a snarl of sorts, Enkill lifted the corners of his top lip to find his canines were abnormally long and curved into points, about half an inch longer than the average person's. Just then, Enkill felt a pulse of energy move within. If one could feel one's own soul stir, then this was it. The pulse originated in the pit of his core: hunger. He watched in amazement as the surface of his eyes swam and wavered like an onyx pool as his mouth filled with bloody saliva, caused by his canines growing a full inch longer. A burst of adrenalin shot through him as he tensed his muscles, squeezing until he shook, admiring his sinisterly evil appearance in the mirror. A line from an old movie ran across his mind.

"Wait until they get a load of me!"

With a newfound power that gave him a sense of invincibility, and a strange hunger calling that he instinctively knew how to satisfy, Enkill exited the room.

The bedroom opened into a long dim hall with thick burgundy carpeting, so thick it absorbed Enkill's steps cushioning his toes. His eyes ran over the hall. Even in its dimness, not a spec of the magnificence present was hidden. Tones of blood poured down the wall, finished with ebony trimming. Under a mirror with bronze figurines was a short table of smoked wood. Within the wood's polished luster, he observed the swirling patterns of its texture within the wood's polished luster. Enkill could see his shadowy reflection down to the minuscule detail on the surface in the shaded gloss of a golden candleholder.

Enkill passed two other closed doors that he had only to pause by to know they were empty of human life. Right before the hall ended, Enkill stepped through the open door of a carmine-tiled bathroom so immaculately kept that it made Enkill wonder had it ever been used. Tediously, he washed his face, scrubbing away the effects of sleep, and doused his locks with a light sprinkle. The water was refreshing. Checking the mirrored medicine cabinet over the sink, he found what he was looking for: toothpaste and an unused toothbrush. Enkill then quickly washed the bittersweet taste from his mouth, all the while never tearing his eyes from the reflection staring back at him. As he watched the bristles glide over the tips of his fangs, Enkill couldn't help but ask himself, what is happening to me? Or better yet, what had happened to me?

Even as he posed the question, the dark magic that now animated his being gave him the answer in the form of a jolt that cramped the walls of his abs, bringing the feeling of eerie hunger new.

Through his mind swam graphic visions of blood and lust, some so perverse the average person would have been repulsed.

Not Enkill Jones.

He was above average in his pain tolerance and appetite for inflicting pain upon others. Two traits he admired in himself. Unbeknownst to Enkill, in a way of ways, it was these same traits that led him to this moment.

Leaving the bathroom, Enkill cleared the hall and paused at the top of a spiraling stairway. The hunger was becoming stronger by the second. His eyes narrowed in the gloom and stared absently at the ceiling as he picked up a feminine scent that tinged the air, painting in his mind the image of a certain green-eyed enchantress. At once, he was twisting down the stairs, not touching the smoked banisters. Not realizing it, Enkill was practically running as he tracked the feminine allure that extended to his hunger, a soft-spoken invite of promise. Everywhere he looked, the Victorian burgundy and black decor had stretched its two-tone tendrils. Not even the wooden panels that separated the walls in half were exempt.

The scent took Enkill through a short hall lined with paintings and an assortment of vanity plates to a closed pair of doors that Enkill forcefully pushed open and entered into a very spacious living room that was strangely different from the rest of the house. Life-sized ivory and onyx-toned statues of demons and angels greeted him with lustful stares and devilish grins. He gazed upon an ebony statue of the Black Madonna: Isis and a baby Horus, which looked divinely sculpted and out of place among the perverse stone figurines.

Up from the dark leather of a sectional in front of a large flat screen jumped a startled green-eyed woman, her black hair pulled back in a ponytail. The olive-skinned woman wore only a black tank top and panties. Instantly, Enkill recognized her as his escort from the club... Natasha.

Natasha stood frozen, open-mouthed, staring unbelievingly at the man who'd just burst into the living room. It wasn't just the man's near nakedness that spoke to her body in an arcane lust, bringing about her sudden arousal. It was his eyes... spellbinding orbs of onyx seduction. She'd seen others Niccolo had made, but never one like this. Niccolo didn't even do this to her.

They never had this effect on her. Last night, she was toying with him. The attraction he may have imagined, a game for her own personal amusement. It was different now. Natasha was having a hard time thinking straight. Just his presence birthed a longing within her that tingled in the moistest of her confines. Her heart pounded mercilessly. And when he smiled, flashing the ivory tips of his fangs, and she saw the sparks of lightning that danced in the darkness of his pupils, she almost lost it. Natasha gazed through dilated pupils at Enkill, nearly overcome. It took all her self-control not to consume or be consumed by this handsome creature.

Natasha gathered herself, stuttering husky words over the chatter of the television, "Something is wrong, you are awake! You're supposed to sleep until tonight. The sun, the sun!" she repeated nervously, pointing to the window behind the T.V. that was letting a thick slash of light which cut across the living room's gloom.

In less time than it took to blink, Enkill moved from within the statues into Natasha's personal space. They were so close that the supernatural energy Enkill radiated fell over Natasha like a hot flash.

"What are you worrying about the sun for? You got more pressing matters to attend to," he said slyly, grabbing his almost erect organ.

Natasha searched her mind for an answer to her present dilemma. On one hand, she wanted nothing more than to answer the desire inside her for the beautiful vampire before her. On the other hand, could she really risk Niccolo's disappointment with her?

In the past six months since she'd met Niccolo, Natasha kept her promise of not giving herself to any other male in the hope that he would keep his promise and make her as he was; a kingu.

He never used the word vampire. It was beneath him, for those unattached to their heritage. Niccolo only gave her small doses of his changing blood, but never enough to bring her over. Just enough to keep her enthralled - an addict to her drug of choice. Before today, she never even considered breaking her bond. For no mortal, no matter how physically alluring, could reproduce the promise of sexual fulfillment, the kingu's embrace flaunted. Not even Niccolo's guards - kingus themselves, who he made sure to keep thralls distanced from - had this kind of effect on her.

When Enkill grabbed Natasha, wrapping one arm around her waist, pinning her to him, the sensation made all other thoughts vanish as she surrendered herself with a soft sigh.

He kissed her roughly, palming her shapely rear. While Natasha's hands roamed across his chest, over his shoulders, down his back, and finally down around to the bulge in his boxers poking into her belly, and pulled it free.

Natasha got a sharp charge, running her hands up the full length of his hardness. A current that made her love moist and her knees tremble with passion. Wow, Niccolo is good, but nothing like this, wow!

Enkill was ready to release over six years of caged-up sexual frustration. Last night with Charise and Goldy was on the money definitely, but that was just oral satisfaction. What Enkill craved was the warm, wet penetration of a woman. The energy pulsating from within his essence was a feeling of power that was both alien and familiar because, by some encoded instinct, he knew this power was his to command, heightening his arousal aggressively.

He rolled up her top, allowing her soft, perky breasts to smash against his abs. Enkill's other hand was between her legs, rubbing the moist lips hidden within her damp panties, bringing a soft song of moans from Natasha as she held his neck with both hands, lightly biting his chest, tangling her fingers in his locks.

The two bodies found the back of the couch; Natasha removed her top, letting her eyes linger on his erectness. She licked her lips and purred playfully as, with a feline arch of her back, she leaned on the cool leather. Enkill stepped out of his boxers. With a steadying hand on her stomach, and the other in the waistband of her panties, Enkill yanked, ripping them forcefully from her body. A gasp came from her lips, and a look of wonderment and excitement took residence in her eyes. Grabbing her ponytail, he spun her around and bent her over the couch's back. Steadying himself behind her, with one powerful thrust, he entered her.

Natasha let out a series of short yelps as Enkill pumped into her. Filling and emptying her again and again, drilling into her wetness. With every thrust, a sound escaped her mouth as the hard flesh of his thighs collided with the soft flesh of her rump, producing a clapping sound that echoed over the television.

Enkill hammered into Natasha relentlessly, thinking only of how good she felt. All the years he'd spent fantasizing failed in comparison to this moment.

They were covered in sweat, him on the verge of climax when Enkill felt strange. It was as if his body had reached its limits of containing the energy, and now it was threatening to burst free. If a person were watching this scene from across the room, they would see the black smoky mist escaping from Enkill's pores and beginning to cover them like an incorporeal blanket.

To Natasha, it was like she was being consumed by pure passion. An orgasmic heat burned inside her. She'd already climaxed twice; her legs were weary, and only the couch and Enkill stopped her from falling to her knees.

Enkill now entered Natasha with frantic urgency, a primal lust. He was almost there; he could feel the buildup, ready to release. Enkill unconsciously sent forth a burst of the energy housed within him into Natasha, bringing her every amorous zone to life at once. His thrust became deeper and harder as if that was possible. Natasha was making a clenched teeth sound that was a cross between the bearing of intense pain and blissful pleasure. Her song urged him on in his frenzied pursuit. Almost there, he told himself as his gums began to bleed and his fangs grew another inch dripping his crimson fluid down the crevice of her sweaty buttock.

Enkill buried himself deep within Natasha as he spilled forth his seed. Simultaneously he yanked her ponytail back, exposing the flesh of her long swan-like neck. Enkill made a sound, a war cry of sorts, as the instinct of his new being took over. He bit deep into Natasha's neck under her chin. Piercing the vein, he began to drink.

Below the house's basement, Niccolo's eyes opened in a shocking flash. He saw the events as they transpired, feeling the power that he knew shouldn't have been, bet it was. A newborn should never be able to break the hold of one such as he on a thrall. At that moment, he knew he'd lost Natasha forever. A somber mood overcame Niccolo as he sent a mental message upstairs to the kingu, whose embrace she'd given herself over to.

Enkill was literally floating on cloud nine as the incoming blood flowed throughout his being, creating a feeling of blissful fulfillment he never knew existed. He now knew his strength and exactly what he was. The feeding intensified the orgasm; Enkill's virgin vampiric mind was reeling when he heard a distressed voice in his head, "You're killing her. You must stop now!"

Obeying the voice, Enkill released his hold, leaving two deep puncture wounds and a few minor ones on Natasha's neck as she slumped, unconscious to the floor. Enkill knew she wasn't dead because he could hear the weak flutter of both her heart and pulse. He also knew that Natasha would die if he continued the feeding.

"You must feed her!" the voice said in Enkill's head that he now recognized as Niccolo's.

The exact nature of vampire genetics is unknown, for the magic of the blood, like a mutating virus, reacted differently in each host. In Enkill, it gave him a scribe of encrypting data that, with time, would instruct him in its usage. So even without the assisting voice, Enkill knew what he must do. It was second nature. All she needed was rest and a little taste of her new master… him.

Taking up Natasha's nude body, he placed her gently on the sectional. Cradling her head in one arm, he bit into his own wrist until he tasted blood. Holding her mouth open, he pressed his bleeding wrist to her lips. The touch of his blood on Natasha's tongue worked like a shock to her system. Natasha's eyes sprung open.

She allowed the blood to gather in her mouth before swallowing. As she did, she felt the blood's magic replenishing her exhausted body. She swallowed again and again, feeling a new strength entering her, filling her up. This was different, unlike any feeling she experienced with Niccolo. It was like comparing a mild buzz to being drunk.

Every sense in Natasha's body suddenly flared to peak awareness. A jumble of sensations she could smell, hear, and feel all came to her.

It was happening; finally, it was happening to her!

Natasha began drinking with new, excited vigor, gratefully accepting the gift she was being given. She'd been with Niccolo for the past half a year, only being given little tastes of the blood from time to time: just enough to keep her enthralled, to keep her wanting more. Living with a craving eating her insides that she couldn't satisfy. Niccolo cruelly dangled his gifts before her and the other girls, visible yet out of reach. Now, at last, she had that which, due to loyal servitude, was so rightfully hers. Fuck Niccolo was her last oriented thought before the changing furnace of power that was Enkill's blood burned her anew, and the darkness overtook her.

Enkill felt his essence traveling into the woman. He watched in awe as her eyes began glowing like burning emeralds and then faded to normal, leaving her pupils dilating with a glossy sheen. Maybe he'd given her too much. He thought, pulling his wrist away as he tried to steady her, for she was shaking uncontrollably, and her breaths were coming in ragged gasps. There was no maybe about it, he told himself. Not having a clue what to do, he let it play out its course until her breathing returned to normal, her fits ceased, and her eyes

closed in a peaceful slumber. Like a parent holding a child, Enkill gazed down at Natasha's sleeping form in his arms. His blood stained her lips, dripping down her chin. The wounds on her neck looked like old scars, practically invisible. Something happened just now, something he didn't intend. Natasha looked different but the same.

She'd changed. He felt and saw it on her.

The feeling of her flesh, the deepening of her features. It was as if she'd been remolded in an image of her perfection. In her changes, he saw his own. The tie of her ponytail had come loose. Smoothing out her tangled hair, Enkill contemplated the effects of such a change on his future.

CHAPTER 6

Night found Niccolo in a state of quandary as he emerged from his sub-basement lair. Sporting a white form fitting sweater, slacks and loafers, his hair in a loose tail, the vampire in white smiled as he mentally opened the living room's doors to greet his latest creation.

There was Enkill, seated nonchalantly on the sectional, looking dapper in a money green knit, copper tone jeans, and a pair of Gucci slip-ons. Natasha under one of his arms, and Charise under the other, tracing her fingers over the stone in his ring, just like she'd been doing for the past five minutes.

Three sets of eyes turned on Niccolo as he came around the front of the couch stopping before his guest with his hands folded behind his back. His attention on Enkill, "I see you've made yourself at home," Niccolo said, casting a distasteful glance at the women.

"Just trying to make the most of the situation," said Enkill.

"That's what you call it eh, making the most? I bring you into my home, give you a place to sleep, relax... perfect hospitality. I sleep and you defile what is mine," Niccolo cut an eye at Natasha. In response, her hold turned clamp-like on Enkill's arm.

"Making the most, yeh!" Niccolo said dryly.

"Enkill smirked, "Hey, the ladies have chosen. Now to avoid situations like this in the future, you should either tighten your game or don't bring your women around a man with so much more to offer than you have."

The two women giggled. Niccolo took it in stride, taking a seat at the far end of the sectional on Charise's side. Crossing his legs, he smiled as he pointed a ringed finger, a slight fire in his eyes. "Enkill, you trying to antagonize me, yeh?"

"Nah not antagonize…more like provoke," Enkill said, leaning out of the women's embrace. "Call it a hunch, but the way I see it, I know you can't repeat the events of last night!"

Charise shifted uncomfortably in her tight blue jeans, crossing her arms over her halter-topped bust, and tapped the thin heel of one shoe nervously. Burdened by mixed feeling, Charise felt an attracting pull from both vampires that left her confused. Her head was beginning to hurt. She knew Niccolo was doing it to her. It hurt the same way as it did in the past, whenever Niccolo felt she was out of line. Suddenly, she wished she wasn't sitting between them. Her heart skipped a frightening beat when she looked into the dark violence of Enkill's eyes.

A confrontation at this time was not what Niccolo wanted. For he knew Enkill was powerful, more so than he should of been. He had to figure out why. Springing to his feet, he approached, Enkill with open hands, "Calm down, my apologies to you Enkill, I am just teasing. We have some very important issues to discuss. Yeh! You've fed already, so I'd imagine you know exactly what you have become. The blood has a way of making one… very aware of its nature."

Niccolo said reclaiming his seat, before continuing seeing the sudden interest in Enkill's eyes, "You are now what our kind call-kingu-or the what the people of your time call, a vampire..." Niccolo waved his fist in the air, "Now one of the world's immortal blood-drinkers. An honor has been showered upon you. To move from among the countless ranks of man, up into Godhood! We have existed forever alongside what you call society; a separate entity, with our own culture. Our own laws, and our own hierarchy - an empire headed by a King!"

"A king?" Enkill repeated and then asked, "You mean like your king?"

"No, I mean like our king, our absolute ruler, who can decide that you are unfit for a chance at immortality and destroy you!"

The whole thing was stretching the limits of Enkill's rational, yet still he knew this thing was all too real. The proof was the present. So life, whatever kind it was to be, he cherished, and didn't make light of threats to it, because it was his one and only. With a slow suck of his teeth he said, "Listen man, I'm not into that bullshit. I was born in America and I don't abide by their laws! I may be one of you, a kingu or whatever you call it, but understand, I don't serve anyone! No king, no nothing. I don't give a fuck about no king's laws, no American laws, no laws but my own!"

"Ah, we then have something in common, yeh. I too don't care for the King of the Kingu!"

"So let me ask why. 'A minute ago, you were talking about your privileged society. What gripes have you with your King?'" asked Enkill suspiciously.

"The answer has all lies in the past. First, you must understand who our King is, yeh".

"So shoot, who the fuck is he?" "His original name far as known to me is, Inkosi, addressed only now as, King Anu. Some say he is over 3000 years old, and comes from old Ethiopia, what was known as Abyssinia. Others say Upper Egypt, where as a mortal he wielded influence over the Delta, as a high priest for the Pharaoh Amenhotep the Third. No one knows his origins for sure, yeh. The only thing that is known for sure is that he was ancient before he came to power. And we are like wine, the kingu get better with time. So one can only imagine the power he wields!"

"So what's he like, the oldest of us?" asked Enkill.

"No Enkill, and that's the strange thing. There are still... a few older than him. A few...Left," Niccolo's voice became a whisper as he shook his head towards the tiles.

"Hold up what's all that?" Enkill asked. "You mention a few left, looking all crazy in the face, like you lost a family member or something."

Niccolo's eyes flashed a glowing rancor, his voice rising as he hammered a fist through the air, "I lost her! Ishtareena - my maker - to King Anu's madness. You follow! About 2000 years ago, Anu felt the need to reaffirm his powerbase so he began slaughtering anyone, he perceived a threat! With the aid of his Nosfers, he hunted and destroyed any elder he could find. Any he felt he couldn't bend to his will. Ishtareena was one of those, unbendable."

Niccolo's eyes became distant, like the slow tone he spoke in. "She was beautiful; to this day, I've yet to see one who could rival her in physical form. She came from the desert... Babylonia. Smooth sun burnt skin, thick black hair flowing below her waist, fanning behind her like a cape when she rode the night's wind—delicious full lips, like the sweetest blood. Long lashed almond-shaped eyes of fire and passion that faded from dark amber to black when aroused, much like your own. But that wasn't it, no. She was so much more. Small, what you would call petite, but she was a giant in stature. To be in her presence was to share the companionship of a Queen.

"Wise and beautiful, wielder of a power matured beyond her years and respected by all of our kind throughout the world. To Anu, she was a rival, one he could do without. Especially with the whispers of a planned usurp circulating at the time. His head is not right!

"Paranoia, and his love for carnage got the best of him." Niccolo, stood and shouted, "His head is not right! His sanity, a forgotten memory!"

"Carnage amuses him, remember Shaka Zulu, let's just say he was the spear that Anu used to spill the blood of a nation. He befriends mortals under many guises. Remember Adolf Hitler and the rumors of his spiritual guide, and occult practices? I wouldn't be surprised if when Jesus went to the mountain, it was Anu himself, who tempted him. Yeh."

Enkill was actually intrigued by the vampire's tale. When he went silent, Enkill lifted his head from his promethean pose and asked, "Niccolo what's up, go on and tell me everything I need to know. Not to sound self-centered and shit, brushing off ya lost and shit. But for example, what are my mortal enemies: is it like the movies, fire, stakes sunlight, what? And I thought vampires slept in the daylight hours. It's evident you do, but why don't I?"

The two men's gazes locked. Niccolo nodded, an admiring expression turned up the corners of his mouth as he thought to himself, so many he'd created over the years were intoxicated by the new power, blind to its dangers. But not this one, "Ah, the similes and the differences, for surely you are one of us but different, unique yeh. The answers you seek lie in the completion of my tale. Where were we? Ishtareena and Anu. You see, Enkill, there are many other beings in this world besides the ones you can see with your physical eyes. Every culture, every religion all over the world speaks of the unseen. Is a people's religion nothing but a reflection of one's cultural ideals, beliefs, a people's place in the world, an answer to the hard questions? Yeh"

" A comfort zone is what I call it " added Enkill.

"Yes and no. You see Enkill, though many people believe many things that hold no credibility in the factual world. Many people have placed limits on what the factual world really is. Our existence alone should prove that to you. But off track I get...know as we exist, other forms of life exist. Your new heightened perception is not just physical, it's also if I dare say, spiritual. The next time you see an apparently insane person walking the street talking to him or herself. You may also see the other participant of the conversation that would normally have been invisible to you. One night you may walk through a crowded street, and make eye contact with an individual. The two of you will immediately know each other for what you truly are. Sometimes it will be others of your kind, other times it may be spirits, or what you call demons in human guise or anyone of the countless different species of were-beast. Other times it will be a special human, trained in the arts, or with a natural gift who'll just know. What you call psychics, and witches, and warlocks."

A small laugh came from Niccolo as he paced before the - trio. Gesturing with his jeweled hands, excitement gripping his voice, "You see, Ishtareena was one of those special people. So when she became one of us, the transformation enhanced what she already possessed, creating a power!

"She told me her power was manifested the first night after the change. Her eyes glowed with a fire like the moon, then a lightless black, just like yours!" Niccolo pointed at Enkill, "You see, only one other had eyes like hers, her maker: the one simply known as Abu, an Arabic term for, father. Now he, is somewhat of an enigma, more ancient than Anu, some say he's wore many different names in different times and places. Yeh, they say he was worshipped as a God, and the inspiration behind a few legends of old.

From Thoth, to Aesop, The Phoenix, Loki, but that's another story for another time, yeh. Again Abu, was another one of the special people. A power before the blood of our kind flooded his veins!"

Shaking his hands above his head, Niccolo began dancing around, his eyes wild, "For he controlled the elements! He could summon rain, thunder and lightning, crushing winds, and freezing waters, bringing snow to people who had never seen such before. A human, a mortal! Yeh, it's really no surprise he was worshipped" said Niccolo Calming himself he took a seat by Natasha. The kingus leaned away nudging closer to Enkill.

Niccolo told her, "You used to love my touch." reaching for her hair, only to have her smack his hand away with an irritated look.

"Yo, easy," Enkill didn't feel like playing.

"Okay, okay," Niccolo laughed holding his hands out in front of him. "Where was I, Abu yeh? You see his eyes were not always so, after the blood for centuries, they say his eyes were either brown or green. I myself have never seen them or him, but legend has it that after he became a kingu he continued with the arts, for they were an innate part of him. Yeh, they say he use to wander off, and no kingu would see him for centuries, then one night he would just reappear. On one such of these journeys, they say he stayed in the heartland of what is now called Africa; places with names now lost to modern man. Dark places of magic. For over three hundred years he was gone, upon his return he was changed. They said, to look into his gaze, was like viewing the omnipotent cosmos, the primal matter of Nutt. This symbolized the power of his evolved spiritual essence, yeh. No one knows for sure these days, this is the stuff of legend. I suppose the truth is buried somewhere beneath the myth. Who knows?" Niccolo asked with a shrugging wave of his hands, as if dismissing the seemingly impossible to figure out.

"I got a question," said Enkill "Where is he now, and why is he not king instead of Anu?"

A few seconds pass, Niccolo silently transferring his gaze to each one of his guests. His face as expressionless as a corpse Niccolo finally answered," He's dead. Anu killed him, and took my maker as his own holding her in a state comfortable captivity. She was miserable. Ishtareena existed in a state of never-ending mourning, for her love for Abu was too great. She refused to defame his memory by giving herself to his murderer. It was during this period, I was created."

Niccolo paced in small circles, his steps hovered six to eight inches above the floor. "You see Enkill, Ishtareena often spoke of her and Abu's hopes to once again walk in the light of the sun. For all of Abu's abilities, the sun was still his mortal enemy!" Niccolo's voice rose as he faced Enkill, hovering perfectly still.

"Fast forward two thousand years to you, Yeh," Niccolo slowly pointed a finger, "You appear with his mark, the eyes, and you walk under the sun, inconceivable. Yeh!" He paused again, before continuing. "You see one of the other reasons Anu murdered my beloved maker, was because she showed signs of becoming a Perusu: a kingu that does not sleep every time the sun rises. One that can move about quite naturally, as long as she's protected from the sun's rays. And some need no protection at all!

"The only Perusus left save Anu, and he is not a full Perusu: that is that I am aware of, are the remaining Elders who have pledged their eternal allegiance to the Empire. And understand, not even all of the Elders are Perusu, and Anu can only take the sun in doses."

Slowly Niccolo descended the forest green glow of his vision reflecting the intense emotion of his voice, "Enkill, not even all of the Elders are Perusu! Understand, it is a talent that some develop, and some don't. It does not matter if a kingu is one thousand years old, or two thousand years old. We do not know exactly what prerequisites makes one a Perusu, we just know that the Perusu is a very rare creature. Yeh!" Niccolo laughed softly, a strange sound given the circumstance, it was like a joke shared between cuddling lovers.

"Now you show up like this, Ishtareena's ideal manifested in the flesh...You're such a wonder, if only you'd understand. For the past ten years I've traveled all over America, and before that the world spawning more of our kind. Not once did one become as you. Do you know why I made you?"

With that question there was silence. So caught up in the how's, and what's, not once did Enkill ask himself why? But now that the question was posed, its answer he desperately craved. In the room's calming quiet Enkill realized just how enhanced his senses had become. The two young women passing outside the window chatting about their boyfriends, Enkill heard their conversation as if he walked at their side. A taxi driver shouting an obscenity at a biker, a key being inserted into the door of the brownstone next door. The nervous beat of Charise's heart; all he had to do was relax and focus.

Enkill's mind had drifted momentarily; it was bought back by a tapping sound Niccolo was making with his shoes. An inpatient gesture. The devilish wrinkling of Niccolo's brow, the cracking of his knuckles by squeezing his hand in a tight fist was as if releasing some inner tension. A flash of pain and vengeful anger painted his eyes, leaking out into his voice as he told Enkill, "I made you for the same reasons I made the others. You see, the King has declared me an outlaw; to be destroyed on sight!"

Niccolo laughed nervously like a madman, watching his guests' puzzled expressions of amazement.

"Why does he want you dead?" Enkill asked after waiting for the vampire's nervous laughter to calm.

"He claims I was involved in a blotched assassination attempt on his life, and claims, I was involved in a prior conspiracy to oust him from the throne. Can you believe it? The nerve of him, me and assassinations. Ha!" Niccolo giggled lowering his gaze to his shoes. When he raised his line of vision to Enkill his smile was devious. He then spun in wild circles, waving his arms like the room was filled with unseen spectators as he shouted, "I...am Innocent!" before bursting into another fit of maniacal laughter.

Enkill was now thinking that Niccolo was involved in some next-level political mess, and he wanted absolutely nothing to do with it.

And he felt like Niccolo, was trying to manipulate him into just that. Not to forget he also figured Niccolo to be a bit deranged. So sarcastically he told the smaller kingu, "I don't know what to make of all this yet, but you seem quite capable. You only sicced your girls on me, followed me from a club, and attacked me on the Westside Highway damn near ripping my throat out. Then this morning, I wake up in a bed, in your house wearing nothing but boxers. Hey, I think you're just about capable of anything."

Composing himself, Niccolo winked pointing a finger at Enkill, "That is a very good observation yeh, don't ever forget it. But my capabilities are the least of your worries."

"What the fuck do you mean my worries?" Enkill asked not liking the vampire's sudden ease, knowing he would like his answer even less.

"You see, when one is declared an outlaw, that one is not allowed to create others like I have: And if the outlaw does, all it creates will also be outlaws, hunted for destruction. Like you are now! For it looks like one is trying to build some kind of rebel militia to undermine the Empire's power," snickered Niccolo.

Dumfounded Enkill said nothing. He simply listened as the outlaw went on. In the past ten years I've created over two hundred and forty spawns. Only forty are left, maybe now even less! The King has his own army of enforcers, if you will, to ensure his every wish is obeyed. For what good is a law, you lack the power to enforce."

"Enkill!" Niccolo pleaded, seeing the anger hovering beneath the surface of the newborn. "I've made bad judgments in the past when it came to creating more of our kind. Some did not come out as strong as I expected. Some, strong physically but weak mentally. Physical strength without competent mental faculties are useless, save to move furniture, or guard doors."

Enkill's mind caught the image Niccolo sent of the two hulking bouncers from last night.

"You!" Niccolo pointed into Enkill's chest. "You, are my crowning achievement. You, have greatness written all over you. I know you will exceed, my most vast expectations. Strong in body, in a way I can't begin to fathom… a Perusu!" Niccolo raised his fist. The mad fervor returning to his eyes. "Strong in mind, I felt your strength of will at the club when we spoke. Tasted the blazing inferno of your spirit when I drunk from you...After all the heartache and lost, still you are whole, unbroken! Yes, yes, you will be one of the men of renown! A giant among our kind that others will seek, some for perverse and selfish reasons, others for the security you'll be able to offer, once you accept who you are completely!" Niccolo rubbed his palms together greedily, like one unpolished in social etiquette anticipating a greatly desired gift about to be bestowed.

Enkill got up and began pacing in slow circles, his tense gaze never leaving Niccolo. Above all things, Enkill hated feeling like he'd been manipulated; played like a fool. Many times in the past those who evoked this feeling in him, found themselves on the receiving end of a loaded barrel. Tonight he felt powerless, like he had no say in the course his life was taking. He wasn't buying the whole savior bit that Niccolo was trying to sell him. Nor did he care for the man, whom he knew he couldn't trust. How could he, when the man just thrust him head first into what was looking like a very dangerous situation, without the least bit of consideration for how he'd take this? And to make matters worse, he knew beyond a shadow of a doubt that he was only receiving half the story. Under different circumstances, he would have done everything in his power to kill Niccolo. But at this moment, that wasn't an option; at least not yet, because Niccolo was the only hopes he had of understanding the complexities of his new life. So he tried to curb the distrust that was so apparent on his face, it caused Niccolo to say.

"It doesn't matter if you believe or not. Yeh, for the truth is the truth, wether one person believes, or a million believe, or no one believes. Just inquire among the so-called leading minds of today's world about the kingu's existence! Yeh,

90

we'll be dismissed as folklore, rooted in uneducated pagan superstition, only believed by those with mental shortcomings. Yeh. But that mind-set is necessary for our survival. If too many believed, they'd hunt us by day, raiding our lairs, casting us out into the sun to perish. I am sure you've heard of Europe's Dark Ages. That was a joyous and terrible time for many of the kingu. Does the name of Vlad Tepus, or as you call him, Dracula ring a bell? A stronghold in the Carpathian mountains, reduced to a burned out shell by the hands of frightened peasants; more than a few perished during the period.

"Still many of the kingu, you'll come to find are arrogant with very little respect for the mortal man: the Goyem. Not humble like myself. Many feel we are the great immortals!" he shouted in mock bravado. "We should rule over man, for they are naught but the food supply, Yeh. We...the top of the food chain. The kingu should be revered. The mere mention of our names should strike fear in the hearts of goyem! Niccolo calmed, "Such fools, for they understand not what a great motivator fear is. For all the years they've spent on this planet, some are mentally no better than when they were mortal. A good example you can relate to, is a man who goes to prison say, twenty years of age and is released at thirty years of age. Ten years have passed, but still he thinks and acts as he did ten years ago."

Enkill stopped directly in front of Niccolo. He waited for a few seconds riding the other man's pause before asking,

"Doesn't Anu deal with this kind? I'd imagine that kind of mindset, wouldn't be good the kingu's future longevity."

"Hah," Niccolo laughed dancing away putting a little distance between them, "Like I said, you have a good mind. Anyhow, most of those I speak of are the King's favorites- I told you he is not right; the empire is in shambles. There are tales of our kind that live in remote jungles among its more primitive residents where their worshipped as gods! Gorging on the simpletons, who ritually offer their blood in sacrifice, to their greedy gods!"

A picture then jumped into Enkill's mind, of a short dark chestnut skinned woman her long flowing locks adorned with bones.

The night was behind her. She was naked, save for a short cloth tied around her hips, where from underneath an assortment of tattoo like markings ran down one of her toned legs. She stood on a primitive altar of stone with her eyes closed illuminated by torches burning nearby. Pressed to her voluptuous bosom was the limp form of a man bare as his day of birth. His head hung at a broken angle and blood ran down one side of his neck. As she raised one arm casting her face to the sky, Enkill saw the wild sensuality of her beauty. It quickened his heart. Her luscious lips smeared with blood parted in what one would dare interpret as the clutches of ecstasy. It was the way she her fangs pierced her lips as she tossed the body aside. But what sent an almost orgasmic sensation through Enkill, was not the many linked silver necklace with the black stone centerpiece she wore, no, it was when her eyes opened, and they were two dark mirrors of his own. The ring on Enkill's finger suddenly vibrated with an energy that shot up to his brain, then evaporated taking with it the vision.

Niccolo and the women had now retreated to a far wall. Enkill's eyes had darkened completely, onyx pupils swimming in a blackish mist of platinum voltage. His feeding fangs revealed themselves in all their macabre glory and a dark mist rose from his pores. Two statues laid toppled along with the sectional, now ten feet from its prior spot.

Niccolo was mystified. Never had he seen a power like this. The only thing that was even remotely close was when he shared the presence of King Anu himself.

Enkill's body told him that anything was possible; all he had to do was conceive it. The power within him gave Enkill a new level of awareness. He now knew why some of their kind believed that mankind should serve them. The rush intoxicated Enkill as he gazed over at the three figures against the wall, and began to read them. Under the scrutinizing pressure of his stare Natasha lowered the jade glow of her eyes to the floor in a gesture of servitude. It was then he realized that even though she was now a kingu, she was also his: she would be useful.

Enkill then turned his sights to Charise. The young woman seemed caught between wonderment, confusion, and fear. She was enthralled to Niccolo, but somehow Enkill knew the short vampire's hold would be nothing to eliminate. Because his power was greater than Niccolo's, he saw it in the man's eyes. So Enkill guessed that Charise's mind and body was trying to make sense of this new attraction. She would be his if he wanted her. All he had to do is beckon her. Enkill's smile was dark and alluring. Raising his ring hand he summoned Charise, his voice caressing like a seductive spell. "Come here."

Charise crossed the room obeying the being who commanded her. In her mind, she saw Enkill as the focal point of some great lifelong desire about to be fulfilled, all she had to do was surrender to his dark embrace. In a moment of frenzied passion Charise removed her top, the black lase of her bra barely containing her as she rushed into Enkill's arms craving what they promised.

The dark eyed newborn squeezed Charise tightly around her lower back, his other hand in the seat of her pants. She moaned as if penetrated clutching his waist, grinding on his hand in a slow dance, arching her back offering her neck. Enkill looked upon the offering imagining its sweet taste.

To an observer he'd appear to be lost in the moment, but actually he was paying very close attention to what was transpiring. His first observance was that unlike with Natasha, he wasn't erect but still excited. So every feeding wasn't sexual. He now felt more in control of the energy radiating within. To test the theory, a focused thought shot a burst from his fingers into Charise. Her body quaked in orgasm voicing lustful melodies as her knees gave way. He held her up. Interesting, Enkill said to himself and lowered his fangs to Charise's neck in a deep bite. Her hold on him tightened as Enkill did that which his nature commanded: he drunk, the blissful sensation of her life liquid flowing into his veins. He let his eyes wander over to Niccolo and saw what he swore was envy. As the two kingus gazes met, Niccolo smiled weakly, confirming what Enkill suspected.

Swooping up Charise's unconscious body in his arms, Enkill held her while to his surprise, Niccolo righted the sectional into its previous position with a casual wave of his hand. Seeing Enkill's puzzlement at his display of telekinetic ability, Niccolo winked, "You can do it too, and probably much more. Who do you think downed it in the first place? "Niccolo told Enkill as he laid Charise on the couch. Natasha came and sat by her head, a hungry look animated the emerald glow in her eyes as she ran two fingers over the puncture wounds in Charise's neck, pressing, producing a slow red leak. She stared at her bloody fingers for a quick second, before looking up at Enkill, who watched her with a unreadable indifference as her tongue seductively glided across her fingers.

"She needs to feed. Soon Yeh," Niccolo said.

"I know," the dark eyed kingu answered. The mist had begun to evaporate, but the room still cracked with his invisible signature.

Niccolo stood defiantly before his mightiest creation, "Enkill from how your eyes observe me, I know I am not high on your list of trusted ones, Yeh, but your personal opinion of me means nothing! Take the knowledge I share with great heed. From now on Charise will be bonded to you; a servant if you will, Yeh. You'll come to find her mind will be more yours than her own, as long as you–feed from her from time to time, and give small infusions of your blood. When separated her eyes will be yours to look through, as they were once mine. From the moment I came upon you in the store, I knew there was something different in you, just how much, I'd never imagine. I just knew you were perfect for the blood."

"So you invited me to the club, not her."

"Precisely so", Niccolo smiled. What Enkill would view as his first genuine expression of the night, for it softened the devious corners of the small vampire's eyes, as he had a quick thought revelation. For all the things Niccolo knew about the drama of his maker's existence as he retold the tale as it was told to him, Niccolo realized how many pieces were missing. Such as, why he never saw an image of Abu's face. Kingus can mind-link and show images difficult to convey in words. So why hadn't Ishtareena ever shown him Abu's face?

Why hadn't he ever asked to see? Was he so lost in his maker's affection that he didn't care for such an image? Because he was actually trying to replace Abu's face in her heart with his own.

Maybe.

A half-truth, not a lie, just a half truth. Kind of like now, Niccolo could have easily mind-linked with Enkill and shown all he'd said so far with words in a matter of minutes. Maybe it was just Niccolo, knowing he wasn't the most gifted telepath and didn't want to risk revealing something he would have preferred keeping to himself.

Keep private...private. That was probably the same way Ishtareena felt when viewing him. No parent tells the child everything about them. The mystique is part of the allure. Feeling his thoughts traveling to an unneeded destination, and the eyes of his guest on him, Niccolo turned to more urgent matters, "Enkill listen, the hunters will come to destroy you, just like they have been trying to do with me!"

The grave pleading of the vampire's tone commanded the newborn's attentiveness.

"Create an army, you'll need one," Niccolo advised. "In the beginning they may come alone or in small groups, but when they discover you are a formidable opponent, and they will. I have faith in that as a fact! The King will send more, and more skilled adversaries. There are many different kinds of beings in this world, unknown to you at this present time, but very soon you'll be familiar with them all!"

"You say all, all like what?"

"For one there are the Nosfers, Yeh!" Niccolo paced a few steps away once again gesturing franticly with his hands. "A different type of kingu, bloodthirsty, they view all others not as powerful as themselves, prey! To be used for their own sadistic, macabre pleasures. The nosfers are shape shifters, a rare talent among our kind, it's what sets them apart, Yeh. The majority are over one thousand years old and very seldom do they spawn. Nosfers are the right hand of the King, his private guard, his executioners. You see, normally

97

a kingu who kills his own without just reason would be punished, possibly destroyed. For Anu is somewhat of a nationalist, but not when it comes to the nosfers. In exchange for their loyalty, he allows them to feed their perverse desires as they see fit, save it does not personally go in counter accordance with the King's!

Then there are the many species of were-beast scattered all over the globe. They are not Kingu's, just shape shifters. Normally they take the form of large predatory animals. In places like Africa, you'll find were-lions, hyenas, and apes. In India, tigers, in Europe and The America's, wolves and maneless cat beasts that resemble cougars and panthers, even a few bears. At times territorial, living in tribes, other times they roam as rogues. Most of these kind act as mercenaries selling their services to whoever can afford them. Savage in nature, they often wage bloody wars on one another. Their life span is not as long as ours, but it's not unusual to come across one that's close to a thousand years or older. Know when you come across such, you face an accomplished killer, a seasoned warrior, male or female, who has probably killed more than a few of your kind, and their own, yeh. Physically their often large and ugly. Monstrous, some in beast form stand over seven feet, their strength is legendary. They've been known to decapitate enemies with a single bite, then feast on the defeated enemy's flesh. Unlike many of us who possess mental talents, and the power of flight, their strength is purely physical.

Niccolo's face swelled to a predatory state, his eyes burning with rage under his swollen brow. His fangs hung in sharp curves from his protruding jaw as his nails became curved claws. A transformation that the two newborns found remarkable. Niccolo's body shook, his voice a dark growl, "I fear them not! I've killed many and will kill many more, but even I would flee if given the opportunity, rather than fight a pack and taste certain death," Niccolo slashed the air with blinding sweeps, before balling his hands into fist pressing them to his temples. "I've lost many dear to me, to them! Curse Anu 1000 times!"

A somber silence settled on the room like dust after a passing

wind. Both Enkill and Natasha could feel the deep extent of Niccolo's pain.

It was the compelling knowledge that another faced the same trials he had in the past that made Enkill speak, "I always knew hate was a strong emotion. At times not even second to love. I've lost more than a few. That pain, I understand," Enkill's voice held empathy as his eyes took on the remote glaze of resurfacing memories.

Unclenching his fist, Niccolo slowly nodded, "Let's just hope this particular pain is not one that one that one day, you too will feel."

Inside Niccolo knew he hoped in vain. For life is pain, a kingu's more so than others. The other man knew how in vain it was. For in Enkill's short years of life, he'd lost much. Both parents murdered, Enkill was raised by his grandmother, whom passed away on the first year of his last prison stint. He'd lost comrades even a girlfriend; Jessica, she was murdered right next to him-before his eyes–on the heartless streets of Harlem. She died in his arms. What ate Enkill since, was the guilt of knowing she died in his place that day.

The bullets were intended for him.

Enkill was no stranger to death and loss. He was a man with no family and one friend, scarred by the grave realities of urban life. Enkill accepted and expected lost, for him, it was the natural order of things.

"I have told you much Yeh, now share something with me Enkill. Tell me about the markings on your arms, and the ring? How'd you come to possess it? The last time I'd seen such, it was on my maker, Ishtareena."

Instinctively Enkill lied, "I don't know, when I woke up, this is how I was. I was hoping you could tell me."

Leaning against the television, Niccolo stroked his chin. He knew Enkill was withholding something. Magic of some kind was amidst; he could feel it. The echo of words long spoken whispered across times gone came and vanished before Niccolo could catch them. His mind tried to remember in vain as he supposed, maybe the new-born didn't really know. Or, maybe he did. Either way experience taught Niccolo patience, so he didn't push. All in due time. Time: the great revealer. All Niccolo said was, "Now that is strange indeed, yeh."

"There's a lot of strange shit in life, but on to more pressing matters, everything you've said tonight I'll take into consideration."

A surge of anger shot through Niccolo like a live current springing him off the television, "Take into consideration," Niccolo erupted. "Oh you take this all too lightly. This is a matter of life and death. Not just your own, but also the two under your trust!" Niccolo pointed to the women.

Cutting the smaller vampire off with a casual wave of his hand that seemed to aggravate Niccolo further, Enkill entered Niccolo's personal space pointing a finger that the other attempted to smack away but couldn't move, His tone was smooth and cold like an assassin's blade, "Calm the fuck down! And at this point I got this, shit ain't really that complicated. Anybody, I don't give a fuck who you are: King or not. You violate mine, and I'll violate you to the fullest!" Enkill's laugh was chilling. "And when I violate a motherfucker, I really violate a motherfucker!"

"But the hunters!" shouted Niccolo.

"Fuck the hunters, you've survived this long with them on yo ass, I know I'll be good," Enkill laughed taunting the small kingu, "I am stronger than you, I can read it in ya eyes, ya whole vibe. Now since you feel like talking so fucking much, tell me something. Mortal enemies, who, or what?"

"Fire, decapitation, and sunlight, but since you are perusu, I am unsure of the last. But for her, I am sure,". Throwing Natasha a look.

"Enkill, feed much! You must be strong at all times!" Niccolo stressed, "Build an army, it is the only way to defeat Anu. Others will join you."

"What others?"

"Outlaws!" said Niccolo as if revealing the universe's mysteries.

"Fuck out of here! I ain't taking on no more problems."

"You are so very arrogant, a major character flaw, yeh."

"Niccolo, there are two types of people in the world, hunters and prey, or masters and slaves..."

"And you are a slave to your own ignorant arrogance!" Niccolo over talked his spawn, dancing away. "Did you know that King Anu's Palace lair is located in Ethiopia? Huh, Yeh, no you didn't, "Niccolo shook his head pitifully. "Did you know that he has embassies on every continent, from which he dictates his degrees handling the empire's affairs Yeh. And from these embassies, ambassadors who are representatives of the empire are spread out to every major city, where they assure that everything is has it should be. As their King commanded!" Niccolo's voice rose. "The embassies and the ambassador's lairs, serve as places of gathering, where one can keep abreast of the kingdom, feed and congregate among one's own kind. Yeh, did you know, did you!? Of course not!" Niccolo laughed, his madman's rant, "Did you know that these embassies exist on every continent save Australia? Do you know why? Did you know that the island continent is off limits to our kind, and to the were-beast. If any of us step foot on the island continent, and are spotted, we run the risk of being executed on the spot! Yeh, do you know why?" Niccolo stared at Enkill with the blank expression reserved for dummies.

"Of course you don't," Niccolo giggled. "So let me tell you. Australia, is home to the Rangi! An ancient order of sorcerers, and sorceresses: powerfully talented humans, who've vowed make the world free, of what they coin, the creatures of blood magic yeh. After the last war, which I myself took part in, "The outlaw grinned," an uneasy treaty of sorts was reached. They have Australia, and we the rest of the world. Yeh, but they cannot be trusted! Even as we speak, they conspire to devise a way to destroy us all, banishing the kingu to the pages of yesterday's lost. Do you know of the Dravidians of India?" he whispered, then cackled out loud.

"Demons, who pose in the guise of beautifully enchanting women. They exist by feeding on the supernatural male essence. Kingu, were-beast, demon, even Satan himself if such a creature exists. It doesn't matter, as long as it's male." Niccolo giggled, an almost feminine sound. Gliding over to the couch he took a seat crossing his legs. His hand playing on the lower half of a now semi dazed Charise's legs.

"I am really going to miss her you know, the things she could do with those lips. A true talent!" Niccolo, again giggled turning towards Natasha, noticing the rebuking scorn in her eyes. "I'll miss you too, you tried hard,

103

always willing, yeh," features melting back to a resemblance of normality.

"At this point and time playboy, you should choose your words a little more carefully," said Enkill.

Niccolo just did a school-girl's giggle.

"Enkill, pay our little friend no mind. He's just upset because he fails miserably in all comparisons next to you, "Natasha with the scorn that only a woman was truly capable of.

"Enough games! It would do both of you great benefit, to respect me especially in this house. Yeh." Warned Niccolo with the growl of a guard dog before it attacks.

"Or what?" Enkill challenged folding his arms across his chest as they started to tingle with a strange heat along their new markings.

Something he tried not to show.

"Perhaps, you forgot our little conversation on the pier. Perhaps I should remind you, Yeh!" Niccolo came to his feet, the emerald fire returning to his gaze.

Enkill matched the outlaw's stare, "You could try. 'You're welcome to. But things are different now. Very different. So different, you no longer hold the upper hand. That's why you got your little security waiting on the other side of the door. What you fail to realize is, if I decide to get in your, ass. The only thing ya little man's are rushing in here for, is to pick you up, or lay next to you." The dark intensity in Enkill's eyes, added a menacing volume to Enkill's words that Niccolo didn't really care to question. He had enough problems, but his expression didn't change, save for a half snarl: an attempt to keep face. But under Niccolo's icy facade, he wrecked his mind for answers he couldn't find. Why was this one so different than the rest, a Perusu, powerful beyond understanding? A fragmented piece came to him. The kingu that relayed the message to him claimed, they were his maker's last words and was not present when they were spoken. The one who told him feared for his life, for the King declared death to any who dared repeat them. So all Niccolo had was a piece of a piece, something about Black eyes and blood flowing in tides! Why did Enkill conjure memories forgotten by the passing of centuries? Why?

Enkill watched as the contemplation in Niccolo's eyes relaxed the tense aggression in the smaller vampire's body language. Sensing the threat of confertation fading, he figured now was a good time to leave. He didn't really at this time want to do anything drastic to Niccolo, because he was his only source of information, even if he felt some of it was shaky. Half-truth, is better than no truth he reasoned.

"Hey, it's time for us to be getting up out of here; I got a lot of shit to take care of. If I need you, I know where to find you," with that he told Natasha, "Bring little miss." Natasha lifted a groggy Charise in her arms carrying her with the ease of a mother carrying her baby. As they made their way out the room, Niccolo called behind them, "Enkill, I'll be seeing you soon, try to stay in one piece, yeh. Head on shoulders." In the hallway, Enkill paying close attention to the two guards standing on each side of the door. Vampires, both of them, whom he recognized as the bouncers from the club. They were now dressed in some kind of Dark Age looking leather uniforms with metal breastplates. Each was heavily armed with long broadswords hanging more than five feet in length held in leather scabbards on their waist. Strapped across their shoulders were long assault rifles. Their faces were emotionless, save for the glow that burned an ominous warning behind the dark tint of their shades.

CHAPTER 7

Meko sat up in the bed and looked around. The first things he noticed were not visual, they were internal: the dark power of his altered essence flowing within him like fried lava, an assuring power that stroked his ego mercilessly. It was in the totality of his being, a strength new and foreign that spoke to him with a fanatic's conviction telling Meko every dream, no matter how extravagant he harbored for the future, he now possessed the power to bring to fruition. The details of Enkill's conversation with Niccolo ran a lap through his mind bringing from him the utterance, "Forever young, Forever young," gazing down into his fist.

"Yo this is fucking incredible, incredible," a hazelnut glow lit Meko's eyes as he surveyed the loft trying to figure where exactly he was, resting his vision on Charise.

Seeing her for the first time, Meko absorbed the simple features that made up the complete package of the visually pleasing female that sat playing cards by herself at the table. Her style was a little too eccentric for Meko's taste but physically everything about her form seemed near perfect, and she radiated femininity in even the smallest of gestures; the flick of her wrist as she turned over a card. The way she tucked a stray bang behind her ear. Tuning in a little more, Meko heard the rhythm of her heart and he could smell the scent of dried blood lingering under her perfume. A glimpse of Enkill feeding on the woman earlier materialized in Meko's mind causing him to wonder what it would be like to take her. As if he spoke his thoughts aloud, Charise suddenly looked up from her card-game at him with a perplexed look that faded into a smile as she announced in a little girl's voice, "Everybody look who's up".

Snapping out of her reflective trance, Natasha came up from the couch. Maybe now she could finally feed. She had already debated leaving twice. It's not like she needed them anyway. The only reason she tormented herself and waited was because she knew Enkill expected her to. Even being a driven, young independent woman, Natasha never lost sight of the fragile nature of the male ego, and since he'd assumed a role of leadership, she'd respect it, unless he proved unworthy of that respect.

In a movement so smooth and swift, like she rode the air itself, in less than two seconds Natasha hovered over the fifty or so paces that separated the couch and the head of her bed. The green eyed vampiress gazed upon the awaking kingu with silent interest. Meko noted not only the woman's seducing aura, in her emerald orbs he saw something so chilling, he almost voiced it aloud. Instead Meko said, "Why are you looking at me like that?"

" Why not?" Natasha asked. "Don't you like when women look at you? Most handsome men do", she said riding the curve of his sideburn with a finger.

"I am not most men."

Natasha laughed, a sound honed to perfection, " So you're different, hmmmm. Maybe sometime you could show me just what makes you so different."

The flirtatious advance of Natasha, made Meko uncomfortable. He looked to Enkill hoping to find a hint at the true nature of the relationship between his friend and the kingus. Meko found no assistance in Enkill's blank expression.

He took the hand she held out to him and slid out of bed, "You're a wild one huh!"

"I can be... Do you like wild Meko?"

Again Meko looked towards his friend for some sign of suggestion

to a course of action, in which to proceed, again finding none. "What's your name, Natasha right?" He asked clumsily trying to change the direction of the exchange.

"Right, Na-ta-sha," she pronounced her name softly. The words dancing to the sexual rhythm of her voice as she took in her hand the diamond bullet attached to his necklace.

"Oh, ya'll on some freak shit?" Meko asked incredulously stepping out of her reach.

Meko's, minor perplexities were eased by Enkill's playful laughter who now stood next to Charise enjoying his friend's uncertainty.

"What's really good up in here? " Meko asked giving Enkill a sly smile, but it was Natasha who answered him.

"Whatever he wants to be," she said moving past Meko with the same grace and speed she exhibited earlier, clearly relishing in her new found abilities throwing her arms around Enkill's waist.

"You really like the boys huh," Enkill teased, dropping a hand to back pocket of her jeans.

"You have no idea," Natasha said with a flash of fangs nibbling on the base of his jaw.

"I'm getting jealous," said Charise releasing a loud sigh, puckering her lips in an exaggerated pout.

Enkill, wrapped an arm around her and pulled Charise to him. Charise brushed against Natasha. The kingus cut an eye. Enkill kissed Charise's lips lightly telling her, "It's no need for that."

Adoringly Charise gazed into his eyes, laughing that laugh that still made Enkill's heart speed.

"Damn girl, he got you wide open," Natasha teased.

"Look who's talking," Charise retorted, and both women laughed. Meko from across the room watched the exchange smiling to himself. If this is what it's going to be like, I could definitely get used to this.

Through with the games Enkill left the women and beckoned Meko over. When Meko took a seat at the dining table across from him, he said, "You're looking good, I could feel the change on you. But how do you feel?"

"I am alright besides the craving: it feels like being hungry, yet it's more than that. It's like something I feel really deep, deep down!" Meko said, trying to describe the blood hunger that was spreading through him, begging to be sedated.

Enkill took Meko's words into consideration, thinking if he's hungry already, Natasha must be suffering. From the corner of his eye he watched her briefly. She was talking to Charise by a bookshelf. He couldn't detect a sign of discomfort, save for what looked like an involuntary tensing and relaxing of her brows.

"Alright, we got some important things to discuss. One, ya'll got to feed, and the night only got like maybe four hours left. Two, we got to secure this place so you two can sleep undisturbed. Three, we need some burners, don't forget the outlaw thing. And I want to start working on progress immediately,"

"True indeed, true indeed," Meko nodded catching his partner's drift. "Alright guns, I got that covered. Remember sun, you seen in the flicks I sent you. The flicks from Vegas, with the chubby bald cat in the limo."

Doing a split-second mental search Enkill said, "Yeah, I remember him".

"That's Ty-born, he can get us anything that we need. From hand guns, machine-guns, to motherfucking grenades as long as the papers right. But don't stress that, I got a little stash set away.

"And if you need any additional assistance, just let me know and I'll arrange something with my bank. That's if you need it," Natasha offered, causing both men to look up to see her standing over the table.

"Thanks, we might," Enkill said turning back to Meko. "You know we got to build this team, what's up with Ty? That's the same cat from back in the day you was telling me about?"

"Yeah, that's him."

"He's riding?"

Meko leaned on the table, his chain clanking as it hit the glass, "No question, I told him about you, and our intentions. He's just waiting in the background right now. I know a couple of the rules or the terms of the game been changed, but not the game itself. He's gonna play, trust me. You gonna see, I was just waiting until you came home to set up a little sit-down, so everybody could just vibe and what not. You're going to feel him, he's decent. Besides,

on some next shit, can't no man that's really about what we about resist what's being offered at the table." Meko leaned back in his seat, wrinkling his grill continuing. "I don't see it, dudes ain't turning this down. We just got make sure they right though. I can't see nothing stopping this, no king, no police, no nothing!"

Enkill shared his comrade's confidence, " My sentiments exactly." "I have a question, "said Natasha.

" Speak what is it," Enkill said pushing a handful of his locks over his shoulder.

"Not to be a downer, but. I understand the ineffectiveness of the police in dealing with us. We have guns, they have guns. We can kill them with our guns, they can't kill us with theirs. But where does that leave us with the King and the nosfers? We can't use our guns."

Natasha's inquiry caused the loft's occupants to exchange silent nods of agreement, searching each other's faces for a suggestion until, at last, all eyes focused on Enkill.

"Decapitation, that's what Niccolo said right?" Natasha stated more than asked.

"You are very correct," said Bnkill who was going to speak on it first. "I am glad to see you pay attention to the fine details. I have a feeling that those details, are going to be what determines our survival." Enkill paused briefly, when he spoke again, irises that had lightened a few shades to a very dark brown, instantly blackened to the tone of his pupil. His voice sounded sure, yet distant like one recalling a memory, "Sunlight and fire both destroy our kind. The only problem is both might prove to be difficult agents to harness without putting one's self at risk. Now destroying the heart, and draining the body of blood immobilizes a kingu giving one the opportunity to remove the head; something that's easier to do before the body rejuvenates itself. Normally at what speed a kingu's body rejuvenates is determined by its individual ability. Most of the time the kingu would rejuvenate enough to feed, but the stronger of our kind can rejuvenate to greater degrees without an infusion of new blood. Now the damaging and destroying of limbs also weaken, because they create open wounds from which blood exits the body. Now the best way to remove a head, would be with a sword or any type of blade. I'd imagine that's why Niccolo's guards were armed so.

"With that said, it's going to be necessary for all of us to become familiar with using some kind of blade. As for the guns, they won't kill, but the right-sized bullet should slow them down, say a .50 cal. But to be real, I had other

113

intentions for the guns, like our line of work, dealing with human adversaries and were-beast!" He paused, letting that last word hang in the air like a dark phantom, "As Niccolo said: physically strong, but an animal. They're vital organs. If you can get to them-a remarkable feat in itself makes them vulnerable. Once you get through all the muscles, claws, and teeth, they're just flesh and blood. Blood that means they're edible." Enkill broke into a devil's grin.

"Excuse me, but how do you know all of this?" Natasha questioned hesitantly. "Niccolo didn't tell you this in such...detail."

"Niccolo, didn't give me the ring either. Certain shit I just know it, as it comes to me. Sought of like instinct."

"Where did you get the ring from?" Natasha asked peering deeply into the black stone. She'd seen precious stones of all kinds in her life, yet never one such as it. Natasha could swear she saw something move inside of it.

"Everything in due time," he told her flatly.

"You don't think now is the time?" Natasha pushed.

"No, I don't." Enkill said giving her a look, that forced her back a few feet from the table. Natasha didn't know why she backed up save for the reason, Natasha saw something that made her uncomfortable in Enkill's eyes. Something cold and merciless, something that for the first time since they met, actually frightened her.

Meko too felt the lethal change overcome Enkill. "Natasha, be easy," he said seeking to calm things. "Let's handle the most important things first. That's my sun, I trust

him with my life, if he say it ain't the time...it ain't the time."
With that Meko produced a Blackberry from his pocket and
made a call.

Lowering her head like a chastised child, Natasha began,
"I meant no offense..." Her maker's stern voice silenced her.

"None taken. Listen, everybody here has a role to play.
How well you play it, will determine if you live or die, or
one of us lives or dies. You play your position and I am
going to play mine. Understand?"

"Yes," Natasha looked him squarely in the eyes, trying
not to show her unease.

Enkill didn't want to be hard on Natasha, but he needed
her to accept his decisions in doing so respect his authority.
On the other hand, he didn't want spineless sheep, or yes-
men around him either, or those that felt they could question
his decisions too freely. He did plan on telling them about
the ring, the dream, and the vision: all three he knew were
somehow connected. It was just going to be when he was
sure of their meaning, because he didn't want to appear
confused or lost, burdening them with any more
uncertainties than need be.

Meko had finished his conversation and begun filling
Enkill in on the details; pointless since the dark eyed kingu
heard every word on both ends. He was to stop by Ty's place
tomorrow; everything was set up. Charise had just emerged
from the bathroom, and Natasha went into freshen up.
Fifteen minutes later, along with Charise, the kingus left the
loft filing out into the night seeking to satisfy the thirst for

115

the substance that made their potentially immortal life's possible.

Amidst the F.D.R. Drive's light traffic Natasha whipped the B.M.W. east, further downtown, and exited on Madison St. She parked at the end of a long block lined on one side with double parked cars across from a small club. In front of the club, a large man in black with a clipboard was conversing with two women in their best short and sexy outfits.

The sights of the car's occupants was not on the trio standing in the bright light of the club's entrance. It was concentrated further up the block where underneath one of those protective wooden structures put up by construction crews to prevent falling debris from landing on passing pedestrians, stood a young couple. From the car, Enkill and company could smell the traveling odor of the weed the couple smoked. The three kingus could also smell something else over the scent of designer body fragrances diluted by perspiration. Something that called in an arousing whisper. They smelled blood!

As two hunters of the night, Natasha and Meko exited the vehicle sliding down the street's narrow gloom towards the couple, leaving Charise and Enkill to watch with morbid fascination.

Enthralled by the hunger, Meko walked not even feeling his boots against the sidewalk. All he felt was an empowering jolt of adrenaline. Meko tasted blood as his gums split in anticipation. There was no fear or nervousness, just an eagerness to satisfy a hunger that intensified with every step closer to his prey.

Meko glanced over at Natasha. She slipped her arm in his, and leaned into his shoulder sliding her other hand inside his coat around the front of his waist creating the surface appearance of an affectionate pair of lovers out for a late-night stroll.

Meko was admiring her astuteness to himself; when Natasha looked up, "Thank you handsome." He was surprised she read his mind yet too engrossed in the coming act to show it. Natasha just smiled. In her smile he saw the cold, calculating cruelty of the kingu.

They were now upon the couple, a bald and stocky, rather short young man garbed in a snug fitting navy-blue sweater and jeans. The female was the exact opposite, if one would dare say. Tall for a woman, a little over six feet with a fair complexion like nutmeg and milk. From her head tiny braids hung like a tight tangle of black vines over the shoulder straps of a pearl white spandex body suit that really flattered her voluptuous curves. The high-heeled woman giggled and hit the man playfully with her purse.

To Meko, the woman looked like a stripper. The couple's attire seemed a little too light for this time of the year, so he assumed they just stepped out from the club to catch a smoke or two. He looked into the short man's red rimmed eyes, and nodded. The man returned the nod and put the thick weed filled cigar to his lips and inhaled deeply holding it for a few seconds before exhaling a large grey cloud. Natasha inhaled the air as they stopped, "That smells so good!"

The couple exchanged glances and giggled. The male extended the cigar towards Natasha and asked, "This that gas. What's up, y'all wanna hit this."

Natasha answered him in a husky voice, "That is not what I was talking about." The couple once more passed baffling glances, giggling clearly feeling the effects of the drug. " So what are you talking about'?" asked the man with an amused look.

In a fleet fleet-footed movement, Natasha left Meko smacking the cigar from the man's hand, and snatched his wrist, pulling him into her embrace.

"What the fuck! Get off me!" The man yelled struggling surprised at the woman's strength, before swinging a fist into Natasha's face.

It had no effect. She laughed as she held the man by his wrist and waist.

They looked as if they were dancing, and they were; the tango of death.

"Get the fuck off of me!" The man's protesting pleads were met by Natasha's deep demonic laughter as she threw the struggling man to the ground like he was a mere child.

Watching the scene unfold, Meko couldn't believe it; she was actually playing with him. Meko glanced over at the female who held her face in clear disbelief at what she saw: a slim white woman, manhandling a much bigger black man. Meko snatched the tall woman by her braids.

"Help!" She screamed, only to be silenced by a vicious backhand to her mouth that sent saliva and blood into the air. The woman's knees failed, but her fall was prevented by the vampire's hold on her hair. Pulling her back to her feet, Meko squeezed her chin in his hand and forced her to watch Natasha and her companion.

Natasha knelt on top of the fallen man with a knee in his back, and a hand clutching his bald dome stretching his neck at an odd angle as if to break it. Natasha's eyes shone with a jade glow as she opened her mouth wide to reveal long fangs with curved blood-streaked points. She growled and bit like a wild beast into the man's neck ripping free a chunk of flesh that she spit to the sidewalk. Blood squirted up from the wound like a fountain into Natasha's face. The man made a gagging noise.

The woman in Meko's grasp was too horrified to do anything but burst into sobbing tears, her body shaking uncontrollably. The man tried to put a hand on his neck. Natasha pulled it away, snapping it at the wrist, and drove her fangs into the gushing wound. This time she didn't pull up. Natasha drunk: feeding the hunger.

A dark amber inferno blazed in Meko's vision as the woman shivering as if suddenly frozen, mumbled something incomprehensible between her sobs. He yanked her braids giving her neck a violent twist. Meko's embrace was like the coils of a boa, his claws dug into her back as his fangs struck above her collar. The taste of the blood introduced to Meko a satisfying sensation unlike any other: Kingdome Come,

Utopia, almost like an addict's first high. Through the blood, the killer's mind and the victims were linked. Realizing the dying woman was praying for God to spare her life, he sent her the mental message, "Your prayers are in vain bitch, no one can save you!"

The two vampires left their victims in bloodless heaps upon the pavement. On their way back to the vehicle, they shared a single thought that they both found comforting: Ah, the first of many. Meko looked on as Natasha cleaned the remains of her meal from her face by sensually running her elongated tongue over her cheeks and chin, as they strolled arm in arm like two lovers on a winter night.

Racing against the coming dawn, the foursome went back to Natasha's place to retrieve some of her belongings before heading uptown to Meko's pad to crash out for the sunlight's hours. They all agreed it felt better having a sanctuary that no one knew of, not even Niccolo. Meko's Harlem apartment, since he lived alone would serve that purpose just fine for now.

Natasha and Meko were secured together in a spare bedroom with two small windows that they covered completely by moving the living room's wall unit into the room, just in case the added drapes and comforter they hung over the windows wasn't enough. Enkill snatched up the duffle bag given to him by Meko, and left with Charise.

Enkill pushed the sedan through the deserted night, stopping at a 24-hour diner to pick up Charise a meal of barbecued ribs and baked macaroni that she devoured down in silence before they even made it to her place. Watching her eat, he made a mental note to be more conscious of her human needs.

CHAPTER 8

After dropping Charise off at her upper-eastside apartment to get a few hours of needed rest before they tackled the coming day, Enkill decided to leave the car parked just where it was and strolled on foot down the side street, pass its sleeping clutter of short apartment building. With about a hour of night left, and his rented room less than fifteen minutes away, Enkill wondered just how much of the city he could see through his new eyes in that time. It's not like he was hiding from the sun anyway; after all, he was a Perusu.

Enkill hadn't seen a single soul as he came to the corner of the block putting him on 94 St. and First Avenue. Before him stood the huge grey monoliths of twenty stone buildings called Issac Newton's Housing, he knew the area from his youth; a predominantly white, working class community with a scattering of Blacks and Latinos. He'd passed through here a couple of times in the past to visit a female friend or two. After losing his parents, life wasn't easy, but he and his grandmother made the most out of it. There were some good times, reminiscing bought a rare nostalgic smile to his lips.

Standing under a luminous yellow shower of a street-light, Enkill

watched as two jeeps screaming loud reggae music sped up the avenue.

He heard other vehicles zooming along the F.D.R. behind Issacs, and the deep rumbling of the East River's dark waters like a million whispering souls. Enkill also heard something else. The instinctual voice within him, who's command he obeyed.

Enkill's eyes were like pools of murky ink swimming behind his specs as he lifted both arms overhead in a closed fist gesture to the heavens like he was challenging the Gods themselves for supremacy. An inner volt seized him tensing his frame. By sheer force of will, Enkill defied gravity, his rigid body rising into the night's sky. Higher and higher he rose, pass the project's roofs. The heavy thud of his supernatural heart echoed in his ears. Still higher he went, until the winter winds snatched his glasses, blowing his loose locks about like a nest of aggravated vipers, lashing through his clothing, and beating against his skin. To a mortal it would have been a most chilling experience. Not to a kingu. The oppressing discomforts of the elements were nothing to his kind. So the cold he didn't feel, only an exonerating sense of freedom and invincibility as he hovered in the vast nothingness of sky.

From his vantage point, Enkill could see the entire island. Matching locations to visible landmarks, he spotted the burning torch, a beacon of democratic liberty hoisted high above Elise Island. The bright beam of the Empire State Building summit, way uptown to the snaking lights of the George Washington Bridge. Peering down at the rooftops of the city's colossal high-rises, the countless blinking streetlights under which a few automobiles snaked through the Manhattan urban maze, Enkill knew a feeling he could never again imagine his life without. Scattered groups of people were still journeying to and fro at this hour, oblivious to the dark agent of death hovering above, watching with the unblinking eyes of a predator.

The newborn wanted to soar the entire city, seeking its hidden wonders, riding the winter winds like some arcane archangel, yet he couldn't, responsibility called and he felt the earth moving beneath. Dawn was a short time away and there was so much to do tomorrow. Enkill willed his body north heading uptown, moving at a speed so great he couldn't fathom, the city underneath appeared like the viewing of a film on fast forward. If one can be so amazed as to be intoxicated with wonder, then that one was Enkill. Like a snowflake on a pillow, he descended to the pavement. A rather long dark side street lined with umber brick tenements, and economy-efficient parked cars two blocks from his rented room. It was the kind of street that made the lone female clutch her purse tightly, holding a high pitched scream on reserve in her lungs, to be used at the first warning of danger as the woman sped pass its dark confines of hidden hazards, some imaginary, some real.

Tonight was no different, yet Enkill did not hurry along suffering the effects of self-imposed paranoia. He strode confidently with his chin high. The effects of his first flight a stimulant in his veins. So as he neared the corner towards an all-night bodega bathed in the silver beams of a street-lamp and saw two males suddenly emerge from a parked car heading in his direction, it didn't dampen his stride in the least.

Now Enkill was judgmental, but he didn't stereotype people. Especially not his own; still he was not naive either. The men moved like trouble. The good thing was they were amateurs, they hadn't learned how to mask their intentions. Both wore the inner city uniform of puffy coats, jeans, and boots. The only difference was that the Latin looking male wore a black do-rag. The other, a dark-skinned black male, wore a skull cap pulled low to the top of his scheming eyes.

A heated tingling ran up Enkill's arms along the markings. Both of the hoods were assessing Enkill. Both of the hoods were already assessed by Enkill. He could taste the ardor tinged adrenaline rolling off them like the unwashed stench of the homeless. It came as no surprise when instead of passing the doo-ragged man stopped directly in front of Enkill, and his partner stepped to the side producing a long black automatic pistol from his waist gritting chipped teeth, "Yo, you know what this is, run everything!"

Two buildings separated the encounter from the bodega. Enkill nonchalantly gazed down at the gun, pointed in his kidneys, then up into the eyes of its possessor. In a motion that neither of the men actually saw, he reached out grabbing the gun's barrel in his ungiving grasp-twisting-while simultaneously thrusting his other hand, tipped with sharp saber like nails deep into the unexpecting man's chest shredding flesh, smashing bones until they found the object

125

of their search, pulling it free from the body in a bloody fleshy mass. The man fell without a sound releasing his hold on the weapon. Enkill turned to the other man displaying the organ in his hand, squeezing, he converted it to a bloody pulp of gore that oozed from his fist.

"Jesus Christ!" the man screamed with trembling lips, eyes bulging, paralyzed by shock and fear.

Enkill swung the gun in a vicious arc, hitting the do-ragged man in the side of his head with the gun's butt so hard that not only did he open a large indent in the man's head, fracturing the skull, the blow spun the man completely around snatching all consciousness. Before he fell, he was in Enkill's grasp. Holding the comatose man from behind by his neck, placing the gun in his own waist, Enkill then ripped off the man's coat by the collar exposing the back of the man's bare neck as a small cloud of white feathers floated about like fairy dust.

The dark eyed kingu tasted blood as his jaws dislodged and stretched to accommodate fangs that were now an inch longer than when he bit Meko and the girls earlier. He closed them like a bear-trap on the man, and pulled ripping the neck bone, and a portion of arteries from the body. Spitting the tangle of bones and veins to the pavement, Enkill dropped the corpse as its heart beat its final beats spilling scarlet nectar onto the sidewalk.

Enkill was standing with a bloody smile admiring his work when he heard a sound like a gasping for breath. Somebody was watching. He turned looking up the building behind him, his enhanced senses working in perfect union. His eyes made contact with another's. The figure quickly withdrew from the open window, fading into the darkness of the apartment's shadow.

Too late, see ya babe, Enkill laughed to himself springing upwards to the open window two floors above. Climbing into the dark room of the apartment, his' eyes shining with the maniacal blood induced lust of his kind, were on the trembling figure by the far wall. With the bravado of a cinema villain, he said, "Hoped you enjoyed the show!"

The room was small and cluttered with few pieces of worn furniture. A queen-sized bed sat in the middle of the room taking up most of the space, along with a dresser and desk. On top of the desk was a small television next to a stack of books. The desk's chair was pulled up to the window next to an overturned ashtray.

"Just having a smoke huh?" Enkill asked looking down at the spilled ashes, then at the alarmed brown skinned female, who was practically naked in her red thong, and short matching tank top.

"How old are you?" he asked, realizing that she looked kind of young.

"Eight-teen." the frightened young woman muttered back.

Feeling another presence in the apartment, Enkill inquired, "Who's here with you?" in a smooth conversational tone like they were two friends shooting the breeze. Like he wasn't standing there with his lips and hands covered with the blood of the two men she'd just witnessed him kill. Like there was a logical explanation for how he'd got from the sidewalk to her window, or the blood-streaked fangs he flashed every time he spoke, or the supernatural glow in his eyes.

"Just my mother," she answered clearly trying to get a grip on herself figuring panic would get her nowhere. Enkill was amused by her attempt at calmness. He wondered how long could she keep it up.

"So tell me little lady, what's your name?"

"Meka."

"Meka," he repeated taking a seat on the edge of the bed, where he began licking the blood from his fingers, his eyes never leaving Meka's in an attempt to unnerve her. To his surprise, Meka held up watching him with an awed interest. Enkill felt the blood lust passing as his teeth retracted a bit into his gums.

Finished with the finger theatricals he introduced himself, "My name is Enkill. Come here," he said patting his leg, motioning for her to sit in his lap. Meka strode to him in a confident manner, her light brown eyes full of curiosity.

Meka stood around five-foot-five, pretty by any standards with smooth dark nutmeg skin. She was what you would call thick; big breast that thanks to her lack of a bra bounced with her every step. Thin in the waist with wide hips and meaty legs, she was built like one of those dancing video vixens. Tonight her freshly permed shoulder length tresses were matted to her scalp under a red scarf, a shade lighter than her manicure.

Enkill was physically impressed by Meka's attractiveness, as was most men. The fresh berry scent of her body wash hung in the air under the lingering cigarette smoke. As she sat in his lap unable to rip her eyes from his ebony orbs of intrigue she asked, "What are you?" to the being her nervous rational mind screamed wasn't human, beckoning her to run, but she couldn't!

"You not scared," he commented ignoring her question, listening to the inner language of her body. A language he was beginning to find quite desirable as she fidgeted in his lap. Her soft femininity awaking the feeling within him that always waited just below the surface. The hunger.

Meka's voice had a sway that Enkill found surprisingly sweet when she spoke, "All you could do is kill me, and if you was going to, I think you would have done, done it already."

"So logical, even in the face of potential danger, I like that. It's an admirable trait owned by a few, but desired by all," he said tracing the line of her pouted lips with a finger. Looking into her dreamy eyes, he realized that he'd beguiled her somehow; she was in his power to do with as he pleased.

Enkill lowered his face into the valley of Meka's neck, licking as his hand gently explored her bosom. The pulsating energy of his essence was a living intangible being that entered her, and erotically caressed her senses, forcing her body into a state of arousal. Meka moaned, a soft lust induced tune. From the firm tip of her nipple, the kingu's hand made its way down her soft belly leaving a faint silverish energy trail that glowed and vanished. Knowing his intentions, Meka parted her legs to give her seducer's wandering hand access to her wet spot. Pushing his fingers inside her panties pausing briefly playing in the soft curly tangle of her bush, further down his charged fingers traveled to the thick lips of her wet opening.

Meka gasped, throwing her head back as Enkill's fingers entered her. The sensual joy inflamed her like none before. She became nearly delirious with passion, when Enkill started working his fingers in and out of her in a smooth rhythm, shooting a steady stream of erotic current. Her moans became strident cries of lust. Climax gripped Meka, her body convulsed, as with Natasha earlier, this was the moment the kingu waited for. Enkill sunk his fangs into Meka's jugular, taking back that which he'd given. In the vampire's rapturous embrace of sensuality, Meka surrendered her consciousness. Enkill didn't kill Meka, he just took enough to mentally make her his. Tucking her into the bed, he stood over the sleeping woman wondering what purpose she would serve. He still had to give her an infusion of his blood to make the connection physical like Charise's. He could always leave her and never return, but no. Enkill knew he would be back even if it was only for pleasures of the flesh. He needed to build a team, this the kingu was sure of, and this feisty woman might prove useful later. Making up his mind he slashed one of his fingers with a nail, and placed it in the sleeping woman's mouth. A gift that some part of her subconscious greedily accepted, her eyes fluttering briefly, but she didn't wake.

About two minutes later the tranquil of the room was shattered by the sound of sirens coming from outside directly beneath them. Enkill didn't need to see the flashing ambulance and police-lights to know there were four police cars, and two separate ambulances. Or to know the first two officers who arrived on the scene, summoned by an anonymous call had nearly lost the contents of their stomachs upon first viewing the bodies. Enkill laughed deviously to himself, First kill in over seven years and a double, what a life!

The kingu stood in the open doorway and casted his vision upon the sleeping woman branding in her mind the mental message, I'll be back for you soon!

Pulling the door shut behind him, Enkill moved swiftly down a dim cramped hall, past a bathroom, and a small picture of a black Jesus with both hands folded in prayer. As he came upon the closed door of the apartment's other occupant, it suddenly opened. A black woman stuck her scarfed head out, "What are you doing in my house? She snuck you in here didn't she? Imam a fix her little fast ass, and you look a little old for her anyway. And what's wrong with your

eyes, are you on drugs?" She asked feeling an immediate sense of alarm she couldn't explain, as she glared into the

131

man's dark glare which seemed to reflect light where there should be none. "If I was you, I'll be leaving before I call the police. They're already outside you know," she said.

The woman pointed down the hall towards the front door, as she clutched the front of her scanty night-gown which didn't hide the fact from Enkill that she was naked beneath. Enkill had an idea, with a wicked smirk he shoved the woman by her face back in her room and entered behind her closing the door.

The woman was visibly angry, her eyes dark slants under arched brows, "Nigga, I don't know who the fuck you think you are putting your hands on me, but you got about five seconds to get the fuck out of my bedroom and out of my mother-FUCKING house!"

Enkill acted as if he didn't hear her looking around at the inexpensive yet well-decorated bedroom. Everything was coordinated in tones of lavender and black, from the drapes and carpet to the puffy comforter and pillowcases. A porcelain vase full of scented violets sat on the nightstand giving the room an intimately womanly feel. He then turned his sights to the fuming female. A short, dark umber woman of thick curves; a splitting image of her daughter only older. Enkill figured she wasn't a day over thirty-five but could have easily passed for a late twenty-something; she must have had her daughter young.

"Oh, you think I am playing wit cha ass? I work at One Police Plaza. You don't want no problems with me!" she advanced on Enkill, pointing a candy apple polished nail in his face, twisting her neck in what could only be described as that feminine, don't fuck with me ghetto attitude. "NOW get...the...fuck...out-"

Before she could finish her sentence Enkill's open hand struck out with a dizzying speed across the lady's cheek sending her spiraling to the floor. "Don't you ever talk to me like that again, you uppity bitch!" Enkill growled.

Selena looked up into her intruder's eyes and knew a terrifying fear. It wasn't his tone or words because she'd been called worst.

It wasn't the fact that he struck her, because she'd dealt with violent men in the past. It wasn't the dried blood that stained his sleeves, for it was too dark and she couldn't see it. It was the inhuman hue of his eyes, which she had mistaken for drug abuse that struck a chilling cord deep within her soul.

"Stand up!" he commanded. She obeyed, making an attempt to cover her near nakedness pulling the short gown around her on trembling legs. "What's your name?"

"Selena," she mumbled in a shaky voice.

"Selena, what exactly do you do at One Police Plaza? What is your job title?"

"I'm an administrative assistant to the Police Commissioner." Perfect, so fucking perfect, Enkill couldn't believe his luck. "Come here." Selena approached eyes pinned to the floor.

"Remove your gown," he said. Selena slowly discarded the garment letting it pool around her ankles.

"Look at me!"

Selena's eyes held a wild fear, like a fallen gazelle waiting for the lioness to deliver the killing blow. Looking into the swimming cosmos that was Enkill's vision, she was consumed by the regret and dread of knowing she had no say whatsoever in the outcome of this encounter. Her womanhood had been violated before. Selena would just add this to her long list of scars; she only wished to survive this encounter.

All of Selena's life she struggled against being victimized. As a single young black mother, she'd taken the worst life had to offer and kept going. From running away at sixteen from an abusive father and an overly passive mother who pretended like Selena's father's perverted habits were non-existent, to hooking up with Meka's' father, an older, womanizing hustler that showered her and Meka with everything they could possibly want materially; but had very little time to spend with his new family. The streets were his true love, and it came as a major shock to Selena when that love claimed his life leaving her alone at-twenty with a three-year-old. With him gone, her life changed drastically. All of life's amiable luxuries that she'd grown accustom to started gradually vanishing as the little money they saved dwindled to nothing.

With no prior work experience, Selena now had to support herself and Meka the best way she knew how. Selena now realized that education would be the only keys to open the doors of a new life. She'd always wished to pursue college, but after finishing high school her pregnancy kind of sidelined that ambition. Figuring there was no better time than the present to get back on track, Selena enrolled in a junior college for a year, before transferring to 4 four-year picking up a Bachelor's in criminology. All the while working as everything from a home health aide, bartender, to a stripper.

Selena had many different men in her life over the years, yet couldn't seem to find that right one. She always seemed to attract the street element type, who'd end up either consumed by the streets or the New York State, prison system. Disillusioned with ever finding Mr. Right, Selena turned her entire focus to building a career only dating occasionally. For the past two years she'd been sacrificing wants, only catering to her and Meka's needs which was hard with a hip, street-savvy teenager. Finally, her plan was beginning to take shape. Last week Selena went to view a really spacious two-bedroom duplex condo in Forest Hills, she was now really considering. With her career on the right track, Meka enrolled in her second semester of college, Selena felt she'd finally beaten her past. Evan if the only thing missing was a good man, she believed she would find one in due time.

Now this happened. Here she is scared half to death, standing stark naked in front of a stranger, whom even though she wasn't religious, she could only describe as the devil. Suddenly her mind filled with concerns for her daughter's wellbeing. The corners of her eyes dampened, she should of left this place long ago. Tears of regret and a life of harbored pains started the slow descent down her round cheeks.

While Selena's turbulent life was flashing before her, Enkill picked up every vivid detail as if he'd shared the experience. This knowledge gave him a newfound respect for Selena. She was triumphant over the odds. He almost changed his mind, but quickly disbanded that sentimental link of thought for a more rational chain. Having someone that close to the Commissioner could prove to be invaluable: an opportunity he couldn't let pass. Therefore his mind was already made up when he gently lifted her chin letting the dark energy that was within him transfer from his body to hers. Snatching away her fears and mental anguishes, he replaced them with a consuming primal lust that tore a sound from Selena's mouth that she couldn't believe she was making Selena tried to fight it. She couldn't, it felt so good… too good. When a heat exploded in her womb that almost snatched her balance, she was sure this handsome stranger was the devil.

Enkill seized Selena up in his amorously charged embrace, and carried her over to her bed laying her down. Enkill ran his thumbs along the arch of her doll like feet with their cherry pedicure and caressed the smooth skin of her legs up to her vaginal crevice, careful not to enter her. All the while Selena gasped in a near delirium of "Oh my God! Oh my God!"

Climbing on top of her, Enkill took her tender breast in his hands, letting his tongue brush her nipples in small charged circles. He licked lower, down to her inner thighs. Her hands tangled in the vines of his locks, as she tried to lead him to her spot. Enkill laughed to himself, there will be time for that later, while he lowered his fangs into her flesh. Just a little drink, just enough to mark.

Leaving Selena in the same state he left her daughter, and with a similar message, Enkill exited the apartment by the front door. Making his way up to the roof, he ascended into the dawn's bright orange sky. Less than one minute later, Enkill landed on the roof of the building his room was in. Quietly he tracked through the neat apartment to his room, where he stripped out of his clothing, wrapped a towel around his waist, and headed for the shower.

As only a kingu could, Enkill listened through the walls to the rhythm of his sleeping hostess's breathing. He really hoped that Ms. Perez wasn't an early riser or had to make an urgent bathroom run. The bathroom was small and paneled with yellow and white tiles. Draping his towel over a yellow wicker hamper, he pulled back the shower curtain and turned on the shower. Hot water beat into the small tub creating a thin sheen of rising steam. Enkill leaned on the face basin and looked from the mirror to the toilet, and realized that he hadn't used the toilet since his change, nor had he eaten, nor had he felt a need to. So many changes, so many changes, Enkill repeated to himself studying the features of the familiar stranger in the mirror, wondering how many more changes did this life have in store?

Knowing he'd have to make the best out of what this life threw his way, Enkill stepped into the shower and let the water beat across his muscles calming the turbulence of his mind, as he mentally mapped out the day ahead of him. Enkill found himself asking a strange, but valid question as his thoughts wavered from his meeting with Ty-born. Was he fatigued? No. If the sun wasn't a mortal enemy, did he have to sleep? And if so, when? The blood he just injected was circulating in his system and to be honest he didn't feel like resting. Yet and all, rational told him until he figured out the exact dynamics of his new state, he should exercise caution. Ten minutes after finishing his shower, Enkill laid restlessly on the cramp bed struggling to calm his active mind. Eventually he did, and sleep clutched him like an owl's talons around a rodent.

CHAPTER 9

Sunset was a little less than two hours away. The remaining sunlight was more than ample time for the two standing outside of Niccolo's brownstone lair, watching its dark windows for any sign of movement to complete their grisly task.

Rejis and Maleeka were dressed identical in long sweeping black trenches with the collars pulled high around their necks. Their hair fell in long concealing waves over their faces, which with the aid of tinted spectacles, helped to obscure the assassin's features from identifying eyes. A precaution against later confusion. Besides for Maleeka's high heels, and Rejis's slip on loafers, they wore not another single article of clothing. In one of Rejis's pockets were two lighters, under his right arm a large sport's bag. The kind athletes carry to a game, but instead of a uniform or a change of clothing Rejis carried three gallons of gasoline.

The two walked arm in arm up the steps of the brownstone's porch, smiling, exchanging pleasant nothings like the loving couple they were. At the top of the stairs, Maleeka leaned her back against the front door, pulling Rejis in close to her quickly scanning the near empty block. Placing a hand on Rejis's chest, in a conspiratorial tone she whispered, "Do you think we should ring the bell, maybe he's expecting us?" Then, she laughed gleefully, like a little girl playing with her favorite toy. Not the murderous assassin she was, who intended to kill everything that lived in the dwelling.

"He's probably sleeping, why wake em? " Rejis's reply came in a deep gruff voice. The change was already upon him, an azure flame glimmered behind his shades. Maleeka giggled loving his dry humor as she placed an arm around his neck, and took the gym-bag with the other as he gripped the doorknob, rested a flat palm on the top far corner, and pushed!

The steel reinforcements of the door's frame were nothing against the supernatural strength of the werewolf that pushed the door completely off its hinges.

To any who may have witnessed the blatant broad daylight break-in, they appeared an excited couple that just couldn't wait to tear into each other as they staggered into the house.

The hall leading from the front door's entrance was as black as a bat's cave, as was the entire house. Rejis positioned the door at such an angle that it wouldn't fall unless touched, and appeared closed from the outside. Rejis and Maleeka, felt this was the best time to engage the enemy; for the sun was ablaze in the sky. The kingus here should either be caught asleep or at least in a weakened state, thus lessening resistance, leaving the main obstacle ahead of their goal the vampire's human thrall security. Still and all, experience had taught them in the past that every kingu who's supposed to sleep in the daylight hours doesn't always sleep. Since they couldn't take the sun's direct rays, they often kept their sleeping lairs in dark underground places, so when rising before sunset, the strong vampire still kept many of its abilities. The werewolves would soon learn this day would be no different.

Hoping to finally bring this cross-country chase to an end, the assassins sniffed the air. Their enhanced sense of smell instantly picked up the distinct bodily odors of the lair's eight occupants.

Five humans: two of them were on the first floor, one was upstairs, and two more were downstairs guarding the entrance of the vampire's sleeping quarters.

Both of the werewolves recognized the individual scents of the vampires, for they'd faced these three before. They knew their strengths, and if they hadn't-Maleeka possessed a talent nonexistent in Rejis. The ability to gauge an enemy's power by its preternatural aura, a mental talent. A rarity in her kind. So today she felt the incorporeal energy reflecting the volcanic rage of the target that she knew all too well. Simultaneously, they both received the mental waves of living fury, and suffocating fear that revealed to them visions of their own impending deaths. Visions, that if the assassins were human, would have scared them witless and sent them fleeing. Or if they were even weak of will, would have shaken their confidence, allowing the crippling disease of doubt to fester. But they were not human, nor easily influenced. They were werewolves, known to some as Flesh-Eaters: 'The Rejis and Maleeka', living legends of carnage among their kind. So the visions did nothing save fuel the rage of the blood craving beast they held within. Beast, that at this very moment they were releasing, as they stood naked, coats at their feet in shallow pools of perspiration. Their bodies expanding, bones lengthening and shifting to accommodate a couple extra hundred pounds of muscle, as they shifted into another form. A form more suitable to carry out the grisly task that lay ahead.

Within the sub quarters of the townhouse, beneath the foundation in a large dark room made entirely of rock and earth sat Niccolo. The kingu sat on the room's only other piece of furniture, a black davenport as he waited patiently for the inevitable. The vampire ran his fingers in glancing repetitive swipes over the seat's cushion. His emerald eyes burned into the sarcophagus positioned in the room's center that served as his resting place.

Two hulking armed guards entered from an adjacent similar room without a word. They'd been with Niccolo long enough to know exactly what was at stake: life or death.

The bald, dark-skinned guard stepped away from his partner into the center of the room. Removing a long broadsword from the scabbard that hung at his side, he commenced to perform a series of overhead sweeps and down thrusts, moving the blade at speed so great no mortal could ever hope to emulate. In the past, he'd killed many with the long iron blade in his grasp. Today he reasoned, he would kill more. His pierced nostrils flared, and in his eyes glowed a topaz pride bright as a high noon sun. He flashed confident fangs at his master, who merely bowed his head in encouraging recognition.

The blond guard did not share his counterpart's confidence as, he combed a large tattooed hand over his drooping mustache. His name was Kenseen. He'd been with Niccolo for close to two hundred years. They'd been hunted for as long as he'd existed, but never could he remember this current level of intensity. Before King Anu would only send one or two attacks a year that they'd fend off, move on and regroup.

Niccolo, would always say, " It's Anu's way of showing us he remembers, yeh!" Now the attacks come barely months apart giving them very little chance to rebuild their numbers. Before Anu would only send Kingus, so the playing field was pretty much fair if one dare say, for the battles always took place at night, when all the combatants were rested and fed.

Things changed when the king started employing the werewolves to hunt outlaws, for they could change form and attack in daylight. And if they found a lair like this one, things could go disastrously wrong as they have in the past. The human thrall security were no match for the beast, no matter how well armed. And to make the situation more hazardous, them being vampires, they needed rest and blood to be at their best, right now, not being perusues, they were lacking in both. His master looked in his direction as if reading his thoughts.

"Fret not, great dealer of death. They are two, we are three. They fight for fortune, we fight for life!" The conviction of Niccolo's words lifted Kenseen's spirits, boiling his blood in anticipation of the upcoming blood-fest.

Niccolo said nothing more as he went back to watching the carnage that was taking place above them, through the eyes of others.

Upstairs, a young thrall was at the top of the winding staircase holding a mac-10, sub-machinegun. Timothy was one month shy of his twenty-first birthday, a tall slim white male with model's features. He was upstairs in one of the rooms lying across his bed, fantasizing

how grand life would be once he acquired the changing dose of his master's blood when he first heard a noise at the front door and received Niccolo's mental message that their sanctuary was under attack and to kill the intruders.

Timothy knew this was the opportunity he craved, to prove himself worthy of the blood that was eternal life. He crept closely to the wall, taking careful steps down the dark twisting staircase. His prior small infusions of the blood enhanced his sight so the dark was nothing. Timothy was coming upon the first turn holding the machine gun tucked to his hip with nervous hands. The gun became heavy in his sweaty grip. His heart beat franticly fast in his chest. Timothy had never killed anyone before in his life, but for the promise of the blood, he would kill anyone.

The first turn brought nothing. Still he knew they were there, he could feel them. With the gun's barrel pointed down at his feet, he cautiously approached the railing. Slowly he looked over, and down into a set of deep eyes that burned with the golden fury of hell. Eyes that belonged to the large black beast, who in the time it takes for a heart to go from beat to beat, had sprung up towards him. Jaws, a pink canyon of spear tipped teeth, whose touch promised pain. There was no time for Timothy to move backwards or raise his gun. The jaws of the beast closed around Timothy's entire head, crushing his skull resulting in immediate death as it pulled his thin body, gun and all over the railing. His body broken by the fall would later be found: his head would never be.

The blond beast that was Rejis. released a blood-chilling howl as he stalked towards the living room's closed double doors. The smell of the two frightened humans inside excited him. Breaking into a full speed run, Rejis smashed into the doors like a charging bull, with a loud crash sending hunks of wood flying into the dark room.

One of the guards, a woman screamed letting off a burst of gunfire at the beast from her position behind the sectional. The beast moved too fast, not a round touched him. Snaking from side to side, Rejis leapt over the sectional landing behind the frightened crouched female. An exotic specimen; flowing carmine hair, fair creamy skin and wide terrified aqua blue eyes. Her delicate lips trembled. Rejis wished he had some more time with this one, such a beautiful creature, she deserved his special treatment, too bad. The woman dropped her gun jaws aghast, raising her hands in an attempt at shielding her face. One of Rejis's paws shot out smashing through her pointless defense, removing one of her hands, opening a pair of gashes in her neck, sending the amputated limb along with pieces of her shattered neck bone and blood floating through the room's darkness into the television set behind, staining its screen, silencing her screams. The only sound now heard over Rejis's heavy panting, was the bubbling of her heart's last pumps ejecting blood from the hole that was once her neck. Regretfully, Rejis took a couple of quick bites. He so wished there-was more time.

There was one more would be guard left in the room hiding among the field of statues. Rejis could smell the fear rolling of the woman like rain drops down a windowsill. Lifting his monstrous-head, standing upright on his powerful hind legs, looking in the direction of the fear, he saw her! Trying to make herself invisible, kneeling behind a 4-foot statue of the sitting Virgin Mother. Rejis threw his head back howling, a terrible sound that filled the room, and echoed throughout the entire floor. A sound that caused the guard to wet herself, closing her eyes. Her gun clanked noisily to the floor, as she clamped her small hands to her ears, as if she didn't hear death it wouldn't come. Rejis smelled the stench of the hot urine, and thought to himself, Golden Shower...freaky!

The blond beast slowly stalked around to the front of the statue separating him from his prey. Resting his front paws on the Virgin's marble head, Rejis pulled himself up leaning over the statue until his head was mere inches over the cowering woman. He called down to her in a raspy growl, " Hey beautiful !"

Tears of self-pity streaked the goth make-up of the small terrified woman, who couldn't believe this was happening to her. Tonight, Magoran and her sister were supposed to become part of the immortal family of blood drinkers: Kingus. Niccolo promised! She always thought the idea so macabrely romantic. Now her sister was lying dead across the room. She heard her dying cries. The victim of some monster, and in her heart, Magoran knew she was next.

Magoran felt the statue she rested against shake, oh my God, she thought, feeling a sticky liquid drip into her long black hair. A liquid she knew was blood from its distinctive metallic aroma, her sister's blood! The thrall now knew the beast was directly above her.

She smelled its wild scent, felt the hot inferno of its breath laced with the stench of raw flesh.

Then Magoran heard it speak to her, for sure she figured this was a delusion produced by the thoughts of her pending death. Struggling to overcome the frightening paralysis restraining her shaking limbs, Magoran looked up towards the voice into the cold ungiving blue eyes of Death. Magoran watched as Death opened its huge jaws. Jaws lined with the largest blood-streaked teeth she'd ever seen this close in the twenty-two years of her life. Death's tongue was unnaturally red, it was coming for her. First Magoran felt its wet caress on her chin, and around the back of her neck under the base of her skull. Magoran saw a suffocating darkness, as she felt herself being lifted by her head. When Death jerked his head upward swinging her body like a rag doll, snapping her neck, Magoran felt nothing, as Death bought her lifeless body down in a violent crash upon the statue's crown breaking her back.

CHAPTER 10

The two werewolves had found the entrance that would take them down under the house into the vampire's quarters. Sniffing the air with a sense of smell twenty times more powerful than any living bloodhound, the assassins were aware that two guards with guns waited at the bottom of the twisting stairs. For not only did they smell the fear induced adrenaline coming from the humans, they smelled the one-of-a-kind stink of lead. And the unnatural musk of the vampires the humans watched over. An ability only their kind possessed.

The two men knelt side by side, bent on one knee against the far wall of the stone room. Their A.K. 47's were pointed at the steps like Swat officers waiting outside a bank's entrance to gun down escaping robbers. Niccolo mentally communed with the men, " Kill them, and immortality is yours ! Prove your worth to be gods, Yeh!"

To the left of the guards sat a pair of sarcophaguses. With steady fingers on triggers, the two guards waited, they could hear the intruders rapidly approaching. When the huge blond head of the beast came into view, they opened fire. But the beast though it was close to 500 lbs, moved with the unnatural speed and grace that was its to command, dodging left then right, faster than the two gunmen could follow, their bullets struck the stone and dirt of the beast's tracks. So absorbed were the guards in its accelerating approach. They never saw the black beast emerge from the staircase darting for them with a speed greater than the fastest cheetah, until she was upon them.

Rejis, using himself as a decoy drew the fire of the guards, taking a couple of nicks, so Maleeka could surprise and dispatch of them.

Before the guards could aim at the approaching black werewolf, death's mistress had them. One flashing swipe of her claws ripped off the closest guard's gun arm at the shoulder. The shocked man watched his limb fall to the floor still gripping the firing gun, he started what would have been a scream when, Maleeka struck again. A mighty bat like swing of her arm smashed her paws into the guard's temple with such force, it removed the man's head from his shoulders.

The other guard witnessing the grotesque decapitation of his partner, in panic tried to turn his weapon on the black berserker. That was the opening Rejis needed. Coming from the blind side, grabbing the man in his powerful jaws by the midsection, scooping him in the air. Rejis standing on his hind legs, commenced to swinging his head from side to side, smashing the man's body against the wall. Continuing to beat the man's body against the wall like a living pinata, in a snarling rage Rejis ripped the guard in two. Dropping to all fours, Rejis let out a haunting howl that shook the chamber.

A concerned Maleeka watched Rejis, seeing blood painting his golden coat, she wondered about the extent of his injuries. Though mere bullets alone wouldn't kill their kind, they could impair. Maleeka glanced at the wooden door in the corner of the room, then back at Rejis. The prize they hunted was on the other side. The other two plus Niccolo, who had proven himself to be a crafty adversary. She would take personal satisfaction in his death. So far he'd killed both a handful of vampires, and weres who've dared to hunt him. This day she promised to end his victorious streak.

On the other side of the door, listening to the thrall's dying screams, Niccolo and his guards waited positioned in a triangular formation. The broadsword wielding guards stood upfront on both sides of Niccolo, leaving enough space between them to swing their iron deaths, yet still close enough to come to each other's aide. Niccolo stood back in front of his sarcophagus with one short katana blade in each hand. They were more like silver daggers than swords, since each of the razor sharp, double edged blades were only a little less than 2-feet in length, including their foot long ebony handles. Unsuited for distanced fighting, ideal for close combat; one of the one-time Spartan's great loves.

The kingus waited, eyes lit with their respective glows in the dark ominous silence of the chamber. With the intensity of a cobra's gaze, they watched the door ready to destroy whatever dared to cross the threshold. Then it happened; the door exploded,and a speeding object flew into the chamber. The bald guard rushed forward swinging his sword in a down swipe, feeling the blade slicing through flesh and bone, he screamed a triumphant fang baring battle cry. That was until he looked down at his feet and saw the armless remains of the thrall split in two at the torso, thanks to him, just like its comrade in the other room.

The bald kingu's eyes widened in confused alarm refocusing on the doorway a second, too late. A snarling Rejis charged like the demonic blond kin of Cerberus he was, cutting the distance between them to arm's length, rearing in a steady advance swinging his claws in three quick swipes. The kingu regrouped, dancing backwards with vampiric agility dodging two of the blows, but the third smashed into his armor removing a large chunk of meat from the right side of his muscled chest, spinning him to the floor on his stomach. Before he could even flinch, Rejis stormed in, wrapping his jaws around one of the fallen kingu's legs crushing bones, with one jerk of his neck he swung the vampire into the stone wall over the davenport smashing its skull and it dripped to the davenport.

The other guard seeing opportunity came up from Rejis's rear with a powerful thrust driving the blade into the blond were-wolf's back out his stomach. A momentarily stunned Rejis howled in pain as the guard wrenched the blade from his body. To attack Rejis, the kingu had to turn his back to the doorway.

Kenseen heard a movement behind him, but couldn't pull his sword free fast enough to protect himself, so he knew his situation was perilous when he felt the weight of the beast on his back; gripping his shoulders ripping muscle and tendons; the beast's jaws closing around the back of his neck and lower skull. Maleeka had such a grip that her top incisors gorged out the vampire's eyes. After over two centuries of fighting, Kenseen knew he would fight no more.

At seeing the sight of the broadsword impaled in her loved one, Maleeka switched her target from Niccolo to the blond kingu jumping on its back, and locking her jaws around his head like a mongoose on a cobra. In an emotional rage she jerked her great ebony head upward, decapitating the blood-drinker crushing its, head in her jaws. Niccolo seizing his moment moved like a blur at the black werewolf as she reared, plunging both of his blades deep into the right side of her chest. The kitanas scraping bones, punctured her lungs. Just as swiftly he pulled them free. The remains that was once Kenseen's head dropped from Maleeka's mouth as she fell forward and landed on the headless corpse; her blood adding to the forming pool beneath her.

Niccolo spun around, right into one of Rejis's gargantuan paws. The blow ripped the flesh clean away from one half of Niccolo's face sending him in a flying spiral halfway across the chamber crashing into his sarcophagus, dislocating his shoulder, as one of his katanas flew from his hand.

An enraged Rejis took two huge leaps, swinging his claws in a downward sweep. Niccolo, rolled out of the furious werewolf's path in the nick of time slashing his katana behind him, slicing the beast's bicep as it landed in the exact spot he was just lying in, but not before one of the were's claws open four gashes down the center of his back. If the blow had been a little deeper, his spine would have been severed.

Niccolo using his ability of flight hovered upward, holding himself flat against the stone ceiling. The remaining kitana, he angled its bloody tip down at the blue-eyed beast.

Rejis and the kingu were now in a standoff. Both beginning to feel the effects of their wounds. Niccolo, held himself still as a corpse. Blood ran freely from his face to the floor, gathering with the blood that now flowed from the wound in his back, running around his waist soaking his shirt. To add to matters he hadn't fed yet, nor was he fully rested which slowed his recuperation process to a halt.

The assassin was also starting to feel the many wounds he sustained, even though his mind was frenzied by the bezerker's rage, it could not cancel out the pain. Gunshots peppered his shoulder, arm and chest area. Thanks to the stomach wound administered by the sword, the gold fur of his midsection and thighs was completely red. Looking over at Maleeka's still frame, the hindering weight of his injuries was suddenly nothing. The threat of lost love intensified his rage, emitting a deafening growl, he sprung himself up at the source of his emotional agony with open jaws and bloody claws. Seeing what wore the shroud of death coming to meet him, Niccolo did not falter. He launched himself like a comet from the ceiling blade first to meet destiny.

The two collided in mid-air, Niccolo's head hit Rejis's stomach, while his katana entered the were's torso disappearing up to the handle. With gravity's aid, Niccolo drove the larger beast back down. The collision was not one-sided, Rejis sunk the claws of both paws deep into Niccolo's shoulder blades. Niccolo screamed in pain as the momentum from flight sent them both crashing to the blood slicked floor rolling over a couple of times, a mast of limbs and dirt clouds. Niccolo not letting go of his blade's hilt; Rejis not surrendering his bone crushing grip as he rolled on top of the smaller man. Quickly bracing his feet wide, Rejis stood jerking Niccolo up in the air by his shoulders. The movement caused Niccolo to pull his blade out of the werewolf, with it a stream of blood from Rejis's chest. Standing upright, holding Niccolo suspended in the air, Rejis's jaws closed on the swarming kingu's midsection, removing a meaty chunk that he swallowed whole, causing Niccolo to cry out in agonizing disbelief, "You fucking dog!"

Rejis's fit of rabid violence swelled to its pinnacle. He pulled Niccolo in for the death blow, bringing his open muzzle towards the vampire's neck. In the next moment, Niccolo did something that would have been impossible for a mere human. Using the sheer will of his vampiric might, he moved the arm hanging limply from its mangled shoulder to shield his neck from the onslaught of the werewolf's jaws. Rejis's canyon of a mouth snapped shut on the kingu's arm crushing it completely. Niccolo screamed, and drove his blade down with inhuman strength aged over a millenium into the top of Rejis's head. The katana's blade penetrated a few inches through the skull before becoming stuck in the thick bone.

The dazed assassin released his jaw hold and swung the vampire in his grasp overhead. The devastating force crashed Niccolo into his stone death box, and not only did his skull crack, but the sarcophagus also slid a good four feet. The werewolf then collapsed to both knees and tried to rise with the aid of his forelimbs, grunting wildly to no avail, as it fell again—this time on his side in silence. The assassin's blood-rimmed eyes blinked rapidly. His breaths came in sharp choking gasps. As Rejis's blood seeped from his body, he had a dispiriting thought. The knife must have hit something.

Across the chamber Niccolo had his own problems. He was struggling to move his battered frame; his arm below his shredded shoulder gushed hanging by a few threads of skin. He knew that though he injured the werewolves with his special blade cloaked in a cancerous spell, he'd purchased from a witch for this specific purpose, they were not dead: not yet. And until the spell had time to marinate in their systems, just like a kingu's, they would heal.

Once again, as so many times before, the urgent necessity of departure overwhelmed the outlaw. He would gather his strength and rebuild to fight another night. In the future it would be harder, this night he'd lost much with the demise of his two guards. They would be hard to replace, especially Kenseen's focused dedication to the cause. It takes time to train minds; time for the blood to age and really become strong. Time, Niccolo knew he didn't have. At least his time spent in this city wasn't a total waste. The creation of Enkill, even if he didn't understand it, Niccolo crowned it a trump card yet to be played. One that bought a self-assuring smile to his once handsome, now deformed face, and a silent curse to King Anu.

Niccolo now directed his attention to the partially revealed iron plate in the ground exposed by the moving of his sarcophagus. His escape route; every lair he had, had one. And Niccolo owned properties all over the globe. And in each one, he built with his own hands such exits. A precaution in case of situations just like this one, secret routes that none but him alone knew. Under its iron disk covering, this particular route led to the maze of tunnels that was the N.Y.C. sewer system, all he had to do was move the sarcophagus a few more feet. A task that would have normally taken a second, not feeding, his wounds, plus the daylight outside all contributed to his depleting physical strength. His telekinesis abilities-which were never very great-due to his current form were practically non-existent. Niccolo reasoned he would have to move it the old fashioned way, and with one arm at that, again he cursed Anu.

Struggling to his feet, something in the air called Niccolo's gaze to behind him, "Ah shit!" he bellowed, "Black Bitch!" The female he knew as Maleeka was standing, and seemed to be undergoing another transformation.

A spellbound Niccolo watched in leary awe. He'd seen were beast metamorphoses before countless times, but none like this. As her limbs shifted, formed and reformed under skin smooth like ripples in a pool, she didn't make a sound, and the maddening golden glow of her gaze never left him. For the first time today, Niccolo truely knew fear!

Maleeka rose to see Rejis unmoving in a puddle of his own blood with one of Niccolo's blades buried in the crown of his head. His sapphire eyes flickering like a windblown shutter. She knew he wasn't fatally wounded, but he was hurt bad, very bad. Seeing Rejis like this brought tears to her eyes, but not tears of sorrowful pity, tears of maniacal rage. Rejis had been the only man she'd ever loved for over five hundred years, he was lover, maker, mentor, friend, and at one time her savior. She couldn't imagine existence without him. So to now witness him in such a state, took her somewhere, somewhere dark. Somewhere, where the repressed memories of her capture, and countless rapes receded. A place she never went, though she'd murdered and mutilated thousands in her lifetime. Most had been business; some had been in compelling surrender to the macabre desires of her bestial nature. But never like this, in the name of personal vengeance. It used to be just another job. King Anu paid a large sum for this one; more than he ever had in the past. Still it was nothing but business; the personal affairs of the blood drinkers were of no concern to her. Unlike now, seeing her champion in such a condition, and the blasphemous leach across the chamber doing what she swore was laughing to himself unaware of her bought something out of her, something new.

With unblinking eyes of murder Maleeka watched the vampire. Her changes were always swift, this day its speed was nothing short of extraordinary. She felt her body cover with perspiration, her hind legs reforming to that of a woman's once more, only packed with more thick conditioned muscle than a 300lb. bodybuilder. Short sleek black hairs covered her thighs and calves, but the hair was so thin, her smooth mahogany skin was still visible. Likewise her torso was a woman's, full breast hanging in Evevonic freedom. Its only hair, a soft bushy patch of down that started between her legs making a thin trail up across the etched ripples of her stomach. Ebony waves of hair dropped from her head like a dark veil across powerful shoulders which sprung muscled arms that elongated, until all five fingers passed her knees. Each finger was human in appearance except for the fact, they were each six inches long, and tipped with dark curved claws of almost double length just like her toes.

Maleeka's face was beautifully hers, only the monstrous protrusion of her jaws hinted at the ivory death within. In Maleeka's mind's eye she saw herself, and felt a power unlike any she'd ever known. What could this savage dominance mean? What was this new form of beast? The answers at press time were of no relevance: they just didn't matter. She would come to love and master this form, just as she did the rest. The wounds in her back had closed during the change leaving only stiffness, and a sticky coating of sweat and blood.

The assassin's pupils flared with golden murder as she watched the stunned blood drinker, who was now looking across the chamber at his fallen blade.

"Go pick it up!" Maleeka spit in her sultry menacing cadence of norm, "For I will afford you the opportunity to die like a man, even though you did not live as one!"

Niccolo tried weakly to match the unshakable confidence of her gaze. Pulling himself over to the katana, gripping its hilt he winked, "Really dear, you're too kind yeh!"

The smile on Maleeka's face was wolfishly all teeth, as she scooped up the headless corpse at her feet by a leg, and flung it at Niccolo. Landing at his feet, its blood splattered his puzzled face, "Daaaarling, consider it your last supper," Maleeka laughed, a sound befitting this dark chamber of death.

The sound chilled Niccolo to his vampiric soul, yet he accepted the humiliating offering of his fallen guard. He had to survive. Staring into her feral madness, the jade radiance in his eyes began to brighten as the guard's blood traveled through his veins replenishing his essence. Though they're few things richer to his kind than feeding on another kingu, it wasn't enough. The body was less than half full, and his wounds were great. Even though Niccolo regained full mobility in both arms, and his face was once again whole, still he required more. Standing, Niccolo dropped the empty remains and gave a taunting bow, "Shall we dance, yeh!"

With a hand of pale claws, Niccolo raised his blade and gave a fanged hiss, as he flew at the assassin, who stood stark still until, at the last second, she met the vampire's approach.

Spinning on one leg, Maleeka flashed a kick to Niccolo's chest that cracked three ribs sending him flying across the chamber, his head crashed against the back wall.

The surprised and disoriented vampire quickly staggered to his feet, bracing for a follow-up attack that never came. Again the werewolf stood motionless. Her fierce gaze focused on Niccolo. He shivered inside, her speed is incredible, the cunning patience she exercises in not attacking. A trait totally unknown to most of her kind, who just slash, claw, and bite, until their prey is no more.

Niccolo decided to use what he considered Maleeka's abnormality against her. He darted to his sarcophagus and pushed it aside in the time it takes to take a breath revealing his escape route, a small hole covered by an iron disk. Wasting no time he yanked off the covering. Niccolo was holding the disk in one hand, preparing to fling it behind him, when suddenly she had him.

One clawed hand penetrated the right side of Niccolo's back, the bloody tips of her claws exiting out his chest. Maleeka then closed the hand and with a handful of innards and bones she hoisted Niccolo in the air. The impaled kingu screeched in pain swinging both the blade and disk behind him wildly, but the length of her fully extended limb made it pointless. All he hit was air.

Maleeka made a rage induced sound of exertion as she drove Niccolo head first into the ground to the right, then scooping him up again, to repeat the movement to her left, then again to her right , then her left. Maleeka continued her pile driving assault until both katana and disk flew from Niccolo's hands, and his screams were hushed by the deafening wet thuds of his head cracking on stone.

Seeing a movement in her peripheral, Maleeka turned in the nick of time to see the black guard up on shaky legs, half of his bald head flattened wielding one of the machine guns. The guard let off

a barrage of shots. Maleeka dropped Niccolo, and picked up the fallen iron disk in the same movement. Using the disk as a shield, she snaked across the chamber in a rapid advance through a series of graceful leaps, zigzagging from the floor to the ceiling, to the wall to the floor. So swift were her movements, the zombie like vampire's aim couldn't follow. His wild shots hit nothing. A swipe of Maleeka's claws severed his gun arm. She then swung the disk into the kingu's neck. The headless guard crumbled at her feet.

Maleeka then refocused her sights on the target. She turned to see a battered Niccolo, his neck twisted at an odd angle trying to make his exit crouched at the hole's edge holding his katana. In a moment of fury and panic that the vampire would escape, she sent the disk spinning through the air. It struck Niccolo hard. He cried out an almost feminine sound as the disk sliced clean through his hip, flattening him over the hole, and kept going crashing into the wall where it stuck. Seeing the assassin coming for him, Niccolo turned his body slightly to the side, and dropped into the hole.

An enraged Maleeka ran to the hole's rim glaring into its darkness. Frustrated because she knew its entrance was too small for her to follow and to put any body part into it would not only be pointless but dangerous. As if to confirm her last thought, the katana flew from the hole's confines striking her above her breast. Maleeka didn't make a sound as she heard the shrill mocking laughter of Niccolo in her head. She just swore a bloody revenge as she removed the blade. Carefully she gathered up her unconscious Rejis, who had now reverted back to human form and carried him outside to their parked S.U.V. Less than five minutes later, she would return and torch the place to the ground.

CHAPTER 11

The night was still young when Charise and Enkill arrived at Natasha's loft to find everybody was already there, including two new kingus, whose presence Enkill picked up outside the front door before actually seeing them.

Upon seeing Charise, Natasha rose from the dining table gliding to meet her, like some seductive ghost in a form squeezing dress of green silk that matched her eyes. A matching shawl with bark brown embroidery was fashionably thrown over one shoulder. Her long hair was pulled back into five black braids that were arranged in a fancy wrap like a princess's crown. She stopped in Charise's path holding her in a wordless scrutinizing glare that Charise matched. Neither woman spoke, the air took on an uneasy hostility until Natasha's rose red lips burst into a smile, and she opened her arms. The women hugged, "Girl, he did it to you…," Natasha's words were an accusation, a friendly one.

"You know he did," Charise blushed.

To Enkill the scene reminded him of a big sister testing little sister. Natasha was clearly the big sister, he watched the pair go slink off into the dining area, Charise sharing the experience of her first feeding while he stepped over to the living room area where Meko was seated on the couch with Ty-born. Ty had a long machine gun resting in his lap.

Removing the carrying case from his shoulder, Enkill let it drop to the floor--where it joined what looked like an army brigade's stash-house. The floor in front of them was covered with firearms big and small. So Ty-born made good on his word, as Enkill knew the man would.

Meko got up dressed in black from head to toe, sweater, jeans, and boots, "Yo man, what's up? I thought you was taking the night off or something, and we was going to have to get this thing poppin' without you," Meko smiled, giving his comrade a pound.

"Never that," Enkill answered. "Just had a little business to take care of. A little expansion if you will," nodding in Charise's direction, then offering a hand to Ty, Enkill continued "I see you been doing the same."

"A - alike, B - alike, C - alike," was Meko's response, an old Five Percenter lingo.

Enkill now focused on the chubby newborn, who was also dressed in black as he put the gun down and pulled Enkill into a brotherly hug speaking in his excited chop, "Yo Enkill, what's good baby!"

"I am real right, the question is how are you? How does the change feel? "Enkill inquired, studying the shorter man seeing what changes he could tell by mere observance. One he noted when Ty embraced him was that the man seemed more solid than before, like the fat was hardening out. Another was Ty's teeth, even though he wasn't in feeding mode, they struck Enkill as small. Much smaller than Charise's and she was a female.

"I am taking this real good. It's like a nigga never felt better in his life. You know, I'm a little fat fly nigga. Got asthma and all that, plus I be blazing that haze, so a nigga used to be a little short of breath and all. Not no more!" Ty's excited animation increased volume. " Yo, like a half an hour ago, I just jumped off a four-story building on some fucking Incredible Hulk shit, picked up a car, and bit a bitch neck off! You ask how I'm feeling. I'm feeling how I am feeling! Like a man's supposed to feel. Like the true and living God and father of civilization, this is real talk!"

Enkill found Ty's expressive little outburst interesting, especially the car part. He never thought to test his own physical limits, Enkill made a mental reminder to do so as he looked over at a smirking Meko, who hiding his downcast face behind a hand, "Yo this cat's crazy," Enkill said with a half laugh. "He's good though, but have you filled him in, "Before Enkill could get it all out, Meko cut in knowing what was coming.

Easy homey," said Meko. "I did all that, I told 'em both exactly what's up. They riding, I got this," Meko gave his partner in crime a suave wink of confidence.

Natasha then shouted from the dining area, " I am not trying to hear this Blackman is god, Whiteman the devil bullshit in my house!" " Easy baby, easy. I got's love for you," said Ty.

"Sure you do! Hate the Whiteman, but you love some white women!" Natasha's unexpected straight-laced comment made Charise and Meko burst into surprised laughter, as Ty stuttered with a dumbfounded look unable to make legitimate sense of his bigotry.

Unconcerned with the debunking of society's left-wing racial propaganda, Enkill watched the new female kingus standing silently at the window, looking up at what he assumed to be the stars taking no part in the current frivolous dialogue. Looking closely at her, the first thing that came to mind was the actress who played Selena in that movie. As if feeling Enkill's inquiring gaze, she turned and faced him. Her eyes were hard hazel diamonds, so out of place in her delicate features. Without asking, Enkill knew this pretty-faced Latina had seen the worst life had to offer and kept coming back for more.

Like two brains sharing one thought, they gravitated towards each other meeting in the room's center. Enkill saw that like Natasha, the short curvy Latina preferred to glide. But unlike Natasha's ghostly float, this woman's body still moved with a feminine swing of her hips, like she danced to a song that only she heard. Enkill then realized she was actually walking, on air. The high heels of her beige pumps stepped a few inches over the floor.

Seeing what was taking place Meko, apologetically said, "Pardon self ya'll. Yo Enkill, that's Marisola. Marisola, likewise. Ty, that's Charise."

Both Enkill and Marisola ignored Meko's late introductorily rambling.

"I am Enkill," he said accepting, her small hand as she introduced herself with the light voiced cadence of an intellectual," It's nice to meet you Enkill, I'm Marisola."

Enkill now took a good look at his team's latest entrant. Marisola stood about five-three. Light skinned with a reddish tint that gave her the look of a South American Indian. Her face was a perfectly small oval with a beauty mark on her lower left cheek that gave character to the flawless balance of features that made-up her subtle beauty. Parted at the crown, an auburn cascade of hair with dark chestnut high lights fell to her chin in a tangle of wavy curls that reached into the plush cleavage of a late blouse, fastened only by two buttons under her -bosom. So when she moved, the delicate material flared open and bared a smooth stomach with a naval ring of gold. Her waist was really small, giving the wide curve of her hips a really dramatic effect that was magnified by a pair of cream slacks that fit like a second skin. Holding her manicured hand, Enkill saw the nice sized diamond set in a cluster of smaller stones on a thin gold band; the fancy glittering tennis bracelet, and the classy golden timepiece on her wrist and wondered how did she get here? What was her story? It was one he was really interested in hearing, but the time seemed inappropriate so he settled for a more presently relevant inquiry. "How do you feel?"

Knowing exactly what he met, because though it seemed like Marisola was staring distantly off out the window, doesn't mean she was, "Like a new woman, thank you," she nodded in gratitude. Enkill saw the barely noticeable tensing in the corners of her eyes, and the tightening of mahogany glossed lips. And wondered, why she was thanking him so he asked, "Why are you thanking me?"

"Because of you, this is all possible," she replied.

Enkill just looked at Marisola and smiled. It was beyond mere curiosity now, who was this Marisola? Not Natasha, Meko, or Charise thanked him, and he'd giving them the blood personally. And here she gets the blood from a second party, but yet expresses her gratitude. What made this woman so different in mind state, yet familiar enough with Meko to receive the blood?

Charise watched the intense look Enkill was giving Marisola and rolled her eyes, "I thought we was starting a army, not a brothel," turning up her nose at Marisola.

The Latina didn't let the childish slight go unaddressed. She retorted, "Funny, from the looks of things, you'd fit right in at a brothel."

"Oh no she didn't," said Charise looking over at Natasha, to find her bent over in laughter. "And what are you laughing at?" Charise shot at Natasha.

Seeing what appeared to be Charise's bruised ego, and Natasha's disregard for it, Enkill attempted to put a stop to the little verbal spat before it escalated, "Okay ladies, that's enough. Let's not forget why we're here, and what we are!"

"Chill kid, let 'em go a couple, you know how chick fights get. So vampire chick fights got to be some next level shit," Ty grinned rubbing his belly. Everybody in the room gave him irritated-grow the fuck up-looks, that made him change his tune, "Okay, okay, it was just a joke," holding up his hands in a halfhearted plea.

Brushing off Ty's antics Meko told Enkill, "Yo on the real, Marisola is good peoples. She has made a lot of power moves possible for ya dude.   She's the truth!"

The truth, Enkill figured that much, "You know I ain't questioning ya judgment. If you bought her here, I know it's for a reason." "Of course, you see everybody's dressed and ready to go," Meko said giving himself an once over.

"I got a little heads up on that move I told you about. Cat gonna be at this little affair tonight. So the way I see it, utilizing the pieces we got here right now, we could move on to bigger and better things."

" Alright I am feeling that, Let's make it happen, say no more but yo, Check this out first," Enkill said moving over to the black carrying case he arrived with. A casual wave of his hand, and the case unlocked flipping open at his feet.

Everybody seeing Enkill's little display of mental ability was a little impressed, but had no time to inquire as Ty, who seemed unfazed by the-small spectacle blurted out, " What the fuck is all that? We got mad ratchets," said Ty referring to their new acquisition of firearms upon seeing the case's assortment of shiny blades.

"I am sure Meko told you, we're right now in the middle of some bullshit, whether we want to be or not. Now with that said, guns a slow a motherfucker down, but they don't kill our kind or were-beast and shit. Only decapitation does that, or fire or whatever. But all we got is these. Now I don't

170

know when it's gonna happen, just that it's gonna happen. And when it does, we're going to be ready. I'll make sure of that!"

Enkill removed his specs revealing darkness; dark has the beginning of time. Turning his address to everyone present, "I know everyone's feeling themselves right now. You could get cha little float on, feel a little strong, could manhandle ya food and all that," Enkill's tone became deadly like sharpened steel against a jugular. " But that ain't about nothing. We're up against motherfuckers that's like a thousand years old. They've been killing before ya daddy's daddy was a sperm-drop. So the little couple of bodies you may have under ya belt don't mean nothing. From this point, you gonna have to step that shit up, self-included!"

"Now y'all", Enkill pointed to the females," Ya'll better get your shit together. No fucking games! We ain't having no...petty...shit! I am depending on you to perform under pressure, and together. So know in all certainty, if anything happens to anyone in this room that could have been avoided, but wasn't because of some trivial shit. I am a drain you, and take off ya fucking head myself! Do you understand me?"

"Yes." The chastised vampiresses answered almost in unison.

"Alright," said Enkill," Since we're all on the same page. From this point on, this is our fucking city! We are at the top of the food chain here," his intensified voice rising as his fangs dripped like bloody knives from his gums, "Anybody who goes against us, be it the police, kingus, niggaz, wolves, I don't give a fuck! They're dead!" Enkill may not have realized it, but like everyone else. He was also intoxicated with the new power that surged through him. But unlike everyone else, his power was a great aged power! Its potential his mind could not yet fathom. So when he finished his enraged, yet inspiring proclaim, everybody else, including a few pieces of furniture were on one side of the loft. And he put them there, but not consciously.

For with every word Enkill had spoken, the dark energy poured forth from his frame. Energy so prodigious, it cloaked him, creating a visible dark misty wall that expanded outward like a booby-trapped room where one wall moves to smash its captive occupant. From his eyes burst of white lightning eschewed, forming spiraling rings that entangled with the darkness producing a crackling sound like a live current. To some of the gathered like Natasha, Meko, and Charise, it felt like a parenting comfort and assurance. A definite in a world of uncertainty. To Ty and Marisola, it was the establishment of dominance, a sinister warning from their maker's maker. The loft's lights flickered ominously, and the dead television sprung to life, switching stations in rapid flashes of light.

CHAPTER 12

The darkness accompanied Enkill like brimstone would a hell-born god. Slowly he stalked towards the group of visibly awed kingus. All of whose eyes shone with their respective vampiric sheens, from their open mouths protruded their fully enlarged fangs, red saliva from the tips. Holding open his ring hand, from within the open carrying case a clanking of steel was heard. A four-foot-long silver battle-ax floated up from the case with gleaming double blades, the length of two feet across from blade to blade. Each one of the four edges came

to a fine curved point. The solid steel handle was thick like the lower half of a baseball bat. It fit perfectly in Enkill's mitts. The ax weighed close to 75 lbs. Enkill would wield it effortlessly, making it his chosen tool of grisly death.

From the case of blades rose a smaller case that could have stored a tennis racket. When it opened, there was no tennis racket; like babes in a cradle of blood-velvet were two shorter, foot-long versions of the larger ax. Laying his ax at his feet, removing his coat. Enkill took hold of the smaller pair and what looked like three long strips of black leather that actually turned out to be sheathed for the smaller blades. Securing them in a crisscross to his back, he took up the larger ax and slid it down the center of his back between its smaller sisters. As his coat floated up into his waiting hand, he told the assembled band, "I suggest everyone find something they can work with and become really familiar with it." Enkill gave the brood his back and strode over to a window taking with him the evaporating dark mist leaving only static traces in the air. Seized by a fit of narcissistic possession, the dark-eyed newborn looked down upon the city. In his mind, as he gazed upon the slow flow of traffic creeping beneath him through SoHo's narrow streets-it was his city. Everything was his.

Everything!

Silence claimed the loft in her intangible hands. The only sounds heard were the clanking of steel and blades cutting the air with inhuman speed as the vampires chose their arms.

Meko selected a set of two blades. One was a long samurai sword, the other a shorter blade. Both had fancy golden hilts with Japanese inscriptions.

Charise took a pair of black handled daggers with foot-long blades, which she positioned inside her leather jacket under both arms. The jacket was too tight, the print off the weapons was too visible.

Ty found to his liking a mid-sized sword with a thick blade and a two-foot-long spiked hammer with a fifty-pound head.

Marisola chose a rather long sword with a curved machete-like blade and a dagger. Its six-inch blade flipped out of the handle, making it easy to conceal. And conceal she did, slipping it into her latte purse.

For Natasha, a pair of matching katana blades about the length of her arm. From the katana's hilt sprung three thin cone like rods of sharp steel, the middle being the longest.

Little did she know, when Enkill chose the weapon he had her in mind. It was ideal for stabbing. For slashing pursuits Natasha took a thin, flat, short blade which came with two straps that allowed her to fasten it to her inner thigh under her dress.

The kingus would listen to Charise's brief description of their new pad, then cover a few last-minute details before leaving the loft to set about tonight's work.

CHAPTER 13

It was a cool February, Friday night in the steel and concrete metropolis known as N.Y.C. Exactly two weeks had now passed since Enkill was released from prison. Clad in black jeans, a black T.X., and a t-shirt with the word 'Narcissus' across the chest in letters of silver lightening, he stood alone on the spacious balcony of their new penthouse. A breeze blew, lifting his lion's mane of locks from his shoulders while he gazed up into the night's sky at the silver crescent that hung majestically, the sky's sole cosmic ornament on this starless night.

Tonight Enkill was doing what he always did, comparing progress against how much time had passed. So far, everything was right on schedule. Their enterprise, as Meko called it, was way ahead of schedule. Shit was pumping! They'd agreed to name their stamp.

Red Rose because the heroin they sold came in clear plastic baggies with the symbol of a single red rose.

Both Enkill and Meko had decided that since Meko had more experience in the chosen field, it would be better if he handled the basic arrangement of the enterprise's day-to-day structure, and Enkill handled the team's overall personal safety.

Enkill was thoroughly impressed with Meko. Like the mastermind dealer Meko had claimed to be, he orchestrated everything perfectly. After setting up a base of operations on an inconspicuous block in the heart of East Harlem, along

Lexington Avenue behind a large supermarket, Meko had covered everything. From the newly made kingu lieutenant Manchild, who handled the often young wild street teams and the two stash-houses, each located in different nearby buildings. One was for storing street-ready products, the other for storing currency. Both of the stash-houses were run by a few of Meko's new thralls who answered to Manchild, who in turn answered directly to Meko. He then personally transferred the day's profits from the stash-house to the penthouse in case of a police raid or robbery-losses would be minimized. But since no humans except the thralls knew the stash house' locations, and they were bound by blood, the promise of immortality, raids, and robberies at this time were both highly unlikely.

Since Red Rose's grand opening, they'd already run through over two kilos, with a little less than one left, and at the ever-increasing rate the product was selling, they needed a supplier: and fast.

A steady supplier was the main factor Enkill was debating when Meko entered the glass doors, joining him on the balcony. Meko sprawled out under a large umbrella roof that covered half the balcony protecting its furniture from the elements. The balcony was furnished with two fancy hand-carved cherry-wood tables with carmine glass surfaces and three matching sofa-sized cherry-wood benches that looked more suited for some upscale living room with their dark scarlet leather cushions.

On one of the benches, Meko sat hunched over, looking like a hip-hop poster child in a blue and white pullover; True Religion blue jeans; and some kind of azure and white striped sneakers that cost close to $400. A long platinum Cuban link hung from his neck. The medallion was a single diamond rose: sparkling red stones made up the rose's petals and clear white diamonds on the stem.

When Enkill turned and looked at his partner, the first thing that took him was the perfect grooming of Meko's face. He looked good, like new money. The two silver bulbs on the wall allowed a bright dizzying sheen to spin through his perfectly trimmed waves that complimented his sharp edge up. From the cocky smirk, Meko wore that said he was above the world, Enkill knew the man was feeling himself.

"What's happening man, how you? Why you always out here by yourself? What's good man, talk to me. It's your boy Meko!"

Enkill laughed, "I see you're feeling real good tonight."

"No question. Life's good, I am making money, buying cars and shit. I am fucking bitches, eating bitches. You know, what more could a man want?"

Seeing Meko's upbeat energy kind of raised his own, but essential matters still had to be checked on, so he said, "Okay, you said making money. So I assume you took care of that little supply problem we had, because if not, we might not be making money for long."

"Come on, kid," Meko said, giving Enkill an unbelieving look. "I told you I was going to take care of it and it's taken care of. That's one of the things I came to get at you about. We got a little meeting set up with ole boy tonight."

"Say word."

"Word, a cat, named Raphael, older dude, a friend of a friend's, you know. We're supposed to meet him at the Marriott later. He suggested we swing by, get acquainted, you know."

"Oh, so you built with dude already."

"A little something. I was with this cat I knew from back in the day. Me and my man K-mac was downtown at this little club the other night, and he introduced me to Raphael. He got a funny little vibe, though. Anyhow, we talking this and that, and come to find out, we was in some of the same places at the same times, even though we had never met. One thing led to another, K-mac holla'd at cat. Cat got back to me. So tonight we see what's what. Yo K-mac is good peoples, and his word is good. He said dude is a heavyweight, big!"

"How big?" Enkill asked.

"Own his own island big. So this might be what we need," Meko said stroking his goatee.

This is exactly what Enkill wanted to hear. He'd done some searching on his own, turned up a few hopefuls. But nothing major that he felt confident about that could deliver the vast quantities that he knew they would soon need, "I've been thinking," Enkill said. "We could get a connect and get some decent prices, or we could get a cat like Raphael, draw him in. Thrall him or put him on the team so we then pay what he's paying, then find his supplier and repeat the process until we find the source: Columbia, Afghanistan, wherever the fuck it's coming from and then, we'll really start generating funds. What do you think?"

Silently Meko processed the idea. His eyes got brighter and brighter as the limitless possibilities unfolded in his mind, "Yo, that right there makes a lot of fucking sense. You talkin' about taking over."

Of course," Enkill responded calmly. "Fuck a block or two from this city; we could supply the whole East coast! I think with our newfound abilities, we could revolutionize trafficking. Fuck a boat. We could literally fly the shit over ourselves. And eliminate all competition in this city, so we'll be the Tri-State's sole supplier. Which in turn will give us complete control of the prices."

"I am with that all the way, let's start with Raphael and see what he's working with. If he's the man we need him to be, then we take it from there. You know something," Meko smiled," You know why I don't beef about you spending all night out here stargazing, looking like some strange black rocker because I know when you come back to us, you're gonna have some good shit."

"And I don't beef about you running around looking like some twenty-one-year-old rapper because I know you're out there handling business." Both of the men laughed, relieving some of their individual pressures.

"You got jokes, huh? This here is my element," Meko smiled, waving a hand over his ensemble.

"Alright, you said there was something else you wanted to tell me. What's up?" Enkill asked.

Like the turning of a page or flipping of a switch, all humor left Meko's voice, "Last night one of our workers got murdered!" "What happened, somebody tried to rob the spot?"

"No, not yet. It's what you were talking about before. Lou's peoples."

Meko's little revelation didn't surprise Enkill in the least bit. It was just one of the many troubles he foresaw in their futures.

" The kid's name was Dre," Meko began, " From Carver projects. Good worker, brave-hearted and loyal, had a lot of potential. I was even thinking of moving him up the food chain."

Enkill could tell that Meko was affected by the young kid's demise. In the two short weeks Enkill had been watching Meko, he noticed that Meko seemed to connect with the younger cats like a big brother. He knew that even though Meko put them out there on the front line, he really cared about what happened to them and would always take care of them no matter what. So unlike himself. He even tried to stress to Enkill the importance of treating them like family, giving them the recognition they don't often receive in their own homes, even if they were outside of the team's inner circle.

"How'd it happen?"

"From what I gathered so far. Dre and his cousin Mike were sitting out in front of Dre's projects on 101 St. across from the hospital when they noticed a souped-up black Camry parked a couple of cars down. Three older dudes were sitting inside watching them. First they thought the dudes might have been police. Because these days, they drive anything they confiscate. Since Dre and Mike were clean, they weren't stressing it. They knew they weren't police when one dude, a Spanish diesel cat with a long ponytail, got out of the backseat and starts tryna holla at a couple of passing women.

You know that really hood shit. Then a second cat gets out of the passenger side of the front seat. A slim pretty-boy-looking nigga, Caesar cut wearing some specs. Mike said that when Pretty boy got out, Dre swore the dude looked familiar but couldn't place him. So the two men started talking, and Pretty boy pulled out a pack of cigarettes and looked like he was asking the pony-tailed dude for a light, who made a movement with his hands like he ain't have one. Pretty boy, then walks up on Dre and Mike, asking for a light.

"Dre gives Cat a lighter. After Cat lights his cigarette, he looks at Dre and asks, "Don't I know you?"

Dre responded "No you don't know me." Pretty boy still holding the lighter takes a drag from his cigarette, staring at Dre like he's studying his face then said," I do know you sun, You get money with them up on Lexington, what's that

182

called bro?" he said snapping his finger, " Red Rose, yeah that's it bro!"

"Mike said Dre just looked at him, not saying anything. At this time, the cat with the ponytail walks up with a fake smile, and he's like, "Oh, that's them, I heard of them. I be up there. I think I seen you up there before."

"Dre just looked at the big dude. Pretty boy then offered Dre his hand, introducing himself," They call me Angel. Who you be, young blood?"

"For a second, Dre stared down at the dude's hand, then gave him a weak pound and was like, "Dre." Then Pretty boy got all animated, "Easy bro, easy. It ain't no drama or nothing, you know. It's always respect. I been out here for a while, and basically, I be knowing everybody. A nigga just recognized ya gangsta. Y'all ringing bells. It ain't bout nothing. I probably know ya boss, probably one of my peoples from back in the day. What's his name?"

"Mike said they both knew this Angel cat was fronting, fishing, hoping they'd slip up and give him something. So Dre just told cat straight out, "All that ain't important because if you really knew him like that, you would know what he was doing."

When Pretty boy laughed to his man, "Yo, this little nigga really is gangsta." Mike said he wished they had the gun on them 'cause the big man's whole demeanor changed; he posted up stepping to the side and mean muggin' 'em like he was waiting for something.

Pretty boy then asked Dre, "Little nigga, you think it's a game?" The big man then pulled out the long black gun and pointed the barrel at Dre's chest.

"Mike said Dre ain't flinch or nothing, he stood his ground like, " Fuck that supposed to do, scare me nigga? I knew I recognized you, I seen around the spot before, you be watching niggaz!"

"Pretty boy just smiled, flicking his cigarette away with one hand and smacking Dre with the other. It must have been a reflex because Dre hit him right back. Caught Pretty boy with a swift right staggering him into Big man. They took off running after that. Mike said he went one way and Dre the other way into the projects. While he was running, he heard shots behind him, so he peeked back over his shoulder to find that nobody was chasing him. He then heard more shots and a car then raced off a little later. Mike doubled back through the projects, ringing Dre, hoping to meet up with him. But when my son ain't answer his phone, he knew something was wrong."

Meko's eyes took on a hard, distant gaze like he was reliving the moment.

'Mike said it was ugly. He found Dre stretched out behind one of the buildings face down. They hit him like five times. Three in the body, one in the head."

The two men said nothing for a long moment. They just held each other's stare. This was serious; Enkill knew how Meko felt about the younger dudes. Though Enkill didn't share his sentiments, he understood the streets and the logistics of survival.

Enkill made a promise, "Don't even stress. Them cats is on borrowed time right now. Whatever you want to do, I'm wit it."

Meko responded, "I know that. I got something in the pot right now. We gonna get at 'em in a minute. Niggaz gonna respect this right here!" With vengeful murder in his eyes.

CHAPTER 14

The sky over Scarsdale was a quiet darkness, haunting like a phantom's soul. The chill of the night did little to improve the ghostly air of the affluent neighborhood. The elements or the disturbing stillness were the least of Niccolo's worries as he cut from a side block to the main street. In a complete outfit of mourning black, he paused briefly, pulling his designer pea coat tight around his frame.

He was probing and listening. Listening for the slightest indication that he was being trailed. Niccolo knew his pursuers were close; he had to get out of this country if only he could make it to London. There, he'd make his stand. But for some reason, Niccolo knew in his soul that his passage to the U.K. would be bartered in blood. And very soon. He was just hoping it wasn't his own. For the first time in years, the kingu was mentally disturbed to fear if his ego would permit him to admit it.

From a few streets over, he picked up the drunken ramble from a group of teenagers enjoying a chilly Friday night stroll.

His pointy hard bottoms clicked against the cement as he moved in a steady rhythm, all his vampiric senses alert. Suddenly he froze in front of the closed steel gates of a bakery under a street lamp. Light washed over him in a bright silver tide.

Niccolo stood still, very still. For he'd heard it again. Turning, he looked behind him: nothing. His vision then searched dead ahead for as far as his enhanced abilities allowed. Still nothing. Sending out a mental probe he received nothing out of the ordinary, only more laughing teenagers a couple of blocks behind. But he knew he wasn't alone, the kingu's hand tightened around the hilt of the short silver blade under his coat.

For the past few nights, Niccolo had this feeling. A feeling of being observed. No, he thought to himself, he was being stalked. The thought alone made him furious.

Last night, when he sent out his probe, he heard mocking laughter.

A feminine laugh, he searched for the source in vain. As sudden as it came, it was gone. Niccolo knew it wasn't the werewolves, for they should just be healing, and it often takes them a while to pick up on a trail. Given his head start, Niccolo figured he should at least be a week or two ahead of them, though he was only a few hours from New York because their modes of travel were limited since they didn't possess the ability of flight. Not to mention the distinct scent they carried, one that he was often able to pick up. A talent not possessed by all of his kind, but one that so far allowed him to keep his life even if New York was a close call.

For those reasons, Niccolo knew it was not a werebeast stalking him. It was something that was able to move with a little more stealth. Niccolo started to walk again for another few blocks, and that's when he heard it!

The deliberate loud clicking of heels behind him. Niccolo stopped midstride in a cross intersection of low buildings scanning the street ahead of him, but nothing. Then, to his right and left, nothing. Then he heard a taunting female laughter coming from behind him. Niccolo peered over his collar, expecting to find the street empty as always, so he was genuinely surprised when he saw the tall kingus in the blood-red gown standing on the corner. Her arms folded over her busting cleavage in a rather annoyed manner that could have said she was tired of waiting for whomever she was waiting for. It was time to barter.

Hearing a deep rumbling chuckle, Niccolo quickly looked over to his left and saw, standing in the middle of the street, a large kingu in a violet suit that seemed a size too small he knew at once when he saw the discolored glow of the kingu's eyes.

Ahh shit! Niccolo thought at the sight of the Nosfer general Chango. He looked back towards the female to find her now, only about fifteen steps away. Her chin held high, and thin lips pinched together like whatever she was seeing utterly disgusted her.

"Oh Ezulie, I see you're still a snotty bitch, yeh," Niccolo said contemplatively, the vampiric energy igniting in his gaze.

"You are about to die, yet you waste your last breathes hurling insults when you should be prostrating, begging for a swift death!" Ezulie said authoritatively, her tone radiating the disdain she held the outlaw in.

188

"Ha, me, beg you, Ha HA! I'd rather be bled dry and burnt slow, starting with my feet. I, Niccolo, beg no one, for I am no one's slave. Ezulie, can you say the same? Oh, of course, you can't, for you spend your existence on your knees with Anu's cock in your mouth, competing for favor with this brute and the others. And he hasn't even made you a noble you would love to have such a title, wouldn't you? " Niccolo's gaze narrowed. A sense of satisfaction flared within him when he saw Ezulie's face flush in embarrassment, then twist in anger. His momentary victory was short-lived.

"You are a very foolish man Niccolo," came a deep voice from behind Niccolo. He turned to find Ghedi standing, a hand of inches away. Cursing under his breath, Niccolo took stunned steps backward from the stoic-faced kingu flexing his fingers on the lion's mane handle of his cane. Ghedi, in his fashionable midnight blue three-piece suit, looked more like a dinner guest at some high society function than the merciless warrior vampire he was. A role he relished in the Empire for over two thousand years.

The warrior told Niccolo, "You speak as if you are proud of your stupidity and arrogance when in reality you should be shamed for these deviant traits have caused you to forfeit immortality."

"I forfeit nothing!" Niccolo screamed in the face of Ghedi's accusation, " My blood pumps, and I breathe."

"A burden this night I will relieve you of," Ghedi stated.

"Fuck you! Fuck Anu!" Niccolo spat. No sooner did he utter the obscenities; he felt a burning pain in the back of both of his legs and saw the sky spin above him. Shocked, he looked up from the pavement to see Ezulie fanning his blood from her dagger-like claws into the night, after which her hands retook their original shape.

"Have some respect for your King, degenerate," Ezulie cursed. An orange glow developed in her pupil, which against the brown looked like flames dancing upon dry bark.

"You want me to have respect, hah! For you and the Empire, I have only regret. Regret that I was not successful at purging our kind from the bane that is Anu! Regret that I have not avenged my love and maker, Ishtareena!" ' Niccolo spat furiously, refusing to be humbled, rising to his feet.

Ghedi shook his head slowly, "Now you speak of Ishtareena like she inspired your treachery like you do this for her. Men like you do nothing for others. All of your actions are always self-centered; you use and manipulate others to further your own goals. Men like you are incapable of seeing beyond your delusions of self-importance. Therefore you're incapable of love. And don't ever forget, I knew Ishtareena long before, in a drunken lust, your father mounted your mother. And if I remember correctly, her heart was not yours to claim, for it belonged to another!"

Insults directed at the turbulent emotions in a man fueled by insecurities always hurt the most. Ghedi knew this. He saw the bitter hate in Niccolo's eyes glowing like a burning field on a dark night. With the slight hunching of Niccolo's shoulders, the warrior in Ghedi saw the small kingu was debating an attack.

"You lie! " Niccolo shouted, fangs ripping free, "Just like Anu lied when he accused her of plotting his demise, yeh. Everyone knew he orchestrated that failed to usurp himself and then pushed responsibility on her for denying his advances:" Niccolo was so mad his frame shook. He didn't even feel the blood leaving the gashes in his legs pooling in his shoes.

"I don't concern myself with court gossip. As with all gossip, it is seldom true and sows the seeds of dissension. I've vowed to oppose such dissension within the Empire with my very life if need be. With that, this dialogue is concluded. Your nefarious ways end tonight," said the warrior.

At that moment, it all made sense. Niccolo understood. The prophecy sang its ominous melody in his ears across time. Niccolo broke into a fit of delirious laughter, causing Ghedi and Ezulie to don puzzled expressions.

"Look, the fear of death has driven him mad," Chango said, finding the scene amusing.

"Is that what you think, General?" Niccolo asked, " No, for even in death, I'll win. For one exists now, that wields such a power that one night or day yeh, your whole kingdom will bow before him, or be crushed by his might yeh!-" Niccolo smiled in taunting satisfaction.

"The dark-eyed one you speak of, I've felt his power. An interesting specimen. He has the potential to be great, but not the time left to explore such a road," Ghedi declared.

Niccolo laughed again like a mad cloven-hoofed fiend, feeling the rising tension from the surrounding kingus, sensing Ezulie flinch,

Niccolo reached in his coat, pulling free the short sword in a blinding flash of steel, delivering a wide circular sweep hoping to catch either. Ezulie or Ghedi by surprise. He didn't. His blade sliced nothing but the night. With the little element of surprise gone, seeing his disadvantage, Niccolo preferring to flee, took to the air, willing himself straight upward, a speeding black-clad rocket of flesh against the night.

As far as the powers of a kingu were concerned, Niccolo was a novice compared to Ghedi: the warrior was more than five hundred years his senior. Ghedi ascended speeding like a living comet unsheathing his blade. In two frantic beats of Niccolo's heart, he was upon him.

At the sight of the approaching executioner, Niccolo turned, dipping swinging his blade. The blow was easily blocked.

Ghedi smiled. His perfect fangs shone in the night as he lashed out with such speed Niccolo never saw his arm move. All he felt was the cold steel of Ghedi's sword enter his neck, severing his head from his shoulders. Niccolo's headless body descended, spewing its lifeblood across Scarsdale.

Niccolo's body landed in a twisted heap. Chango retrieved the head, tossing it like the morning's trash upon the corpse. The three kingus stood around the fallen traitor.

Ghedi nodded silently to Ezulie. She knew what was expected of her.

Raising one slender finger and pointing it at the corpse, Ezulie channeled the energy inside her, feeling it fill her in a way that only a handful of her kind could. Ezulie's eyes were burning sockets of orange flame. A small ball of swirling fire the size of a golf ball danced inches over her curved nail, swelling in size until it became roughly the size of a large human head.

She let out a sharp cry, "Like a martial artist's releasing of the chi. The orange ball of flame landed on the dead body was Niccolo, consuming it instantly.

Chango covered his eyes, taking a step back. No matter how many times he saw Ezulie work this talent, it sent the same chill of fear through his cold heart. She commanded one of the Kingu's great mortal enemies: fire. Not even King Anu possessed this ability. For this reason alone, the General made sure never -to spite her in any way. He often wondered what would happen if she went rogue and became an enemy of the Empire. He certainly wouldn't volunteer for the task of bringing her destruction about.

The air reeked of burned kinguic flesh and blood. A smell that no kingu truly enjoyed no matter how wretched the enemy, for it often reminded one of their own mortality. With half of their business on this continent concluded, the three assassins took to the air, heading back to N.Y.C. to complete the other half.

Two men stood in the basement of a rundown apartment building in the slums of the South Bronx. They were watching the third of three dope-fiends nodding against a dingy wall. The large beast, pink-nosed, brindle pit bulls were chained to a boiler barking menacingly at the dirty friends who had just snorted the contents of the small plastic baggie in one of the man's hands. Angel handed the baggie to the older, simply dressed Hispanic man.

The basement reeked of urine and dog. A single yellow bulb hung from bare wiring in the ceiling. Angel stuffed his hands in the front pockets of his blue jeans, looking down around his spec-less high-top Pradas at the dried blood stains and the overturned dog bowls, and was eager to get out of the filthy den. He hated places like this. Dirt made him uncomfortable, but his tonight business was of grave importance, so he bore it. From under the cloak of his tan leather hood, he watched the man study the rose label on the bag rubbing it between two of his fleshy fingers.

The man was Jose Sanchez, or El Gordo as he was often referred to out of his earshot. He was Jose Martinez's, the man the streets called Crazy Lou's older uncle and supplier. The nodding friends had confirmed to him what Angel had already told him, that this was the same product as Snake Eyes - and they'd even somehow mimicked the cut of his slain nephew's stamp.

Jose was a very large man standing close to six feet and over 250 lbs. Even though he was getting up in age, for this June, he would be all of 48, Jose looked like a retired linebacker: a little heavy around the mid-section but powerful. Dressed in simple black jeans, a black sweatshirt, and worn black sneakers, he looked like anything but the notorious drug lord he was. He believed the less flash, the better. Typically a soft-spoken man of few words, but tonight, he stayed true to those traits as he thought of his slain nephew, niece, and grandniece. "Just babies," he muttered.

"That's what I am saying, Pa." said an empathetic frowning Angel. " You know who do this? "

"I am on it. I've been watching their spot tryna get a line on their main-man, I even got peoples out there right now. Last night I ran up on a couple of their workers, putas wasn't tryna talk but," Angel's explanation was cut short by the large man's fanning hands.

Jose stepped in close to Angel pointing a finger while holding the younger man captive with a dead stare, "You find who do this, and you kill. You need help, I get you help."

"I got this, Pa. That's my word. I got this!" Angel swore, hammering a fist to chest. The crazy look in his eyes manifested the sincerity of his intentions.

"When you finish, I take care of you, whatever you need. Familia!" Jose said, resting a heavy hand on Angel's shoulder, knowing that love and revenge were both strong motivators, but when combined with financial gain, there were practically no measures a man like Angel wouldn't take.

Angel reassured Jose again before he left, leaving Jose alone in the dim basement with snarling dogs and the tranced-out fiends. Jose slipped into a trance of his own as he played things over in his head. A practical man, Jose took into consideration the gruesome manner in which his nephew and family were murdered and the fact that the perpetrators opened their operation in practically the same area as the old stamp, knowing word would get back to Lou's crew, and all fingers would be pointed at them and a war would be waged immediately. Not just for turf and revenge but also for respect.

Jose then thought to himself, either this new enemy didn't give a fuck about a war with Snake-Eyes because with the head and heart already gone, it figured the body should be nothing to kill. Or the new enemies were just a pack of crazies: wild loose cannons who could give a fuck if the streets drowned in a sea of blood and bullets. He hated men like that; they were terrible for business. Jose knew, either way, something very serious was taking place. The drug lord watched the snarling dogs straining against their chains. As he approached the two, one-hundred-pound beast, they ceased their growling and sat quietly at attention while Jose unfastened their chains from the boiler. He then made his way methodically up the flight of creaking steps leading out of the basement.

The two salivating beasts eyed their owner as he paused in the doorway. One of the addicts snapped out of her nod, and a dirty black woman in tattered clothing staggered towards the steps scratching her swelling, track-ridden arms, "Where you going?" the junky asked, staring up at Jose. The drug-lord ignored the fiend and clapped his thick hands together, shouting a command to the waiting dogs, and then went through the door, locking it behind him.

The frail woman screamed as she was knocked to the floor. One of the dogs had her by her neck, shaking her. The other junkie, a small Hispanic man with a limp, hobbled for the stairs as he watched the other dog viciously tear into another fiend, a tall black dude everybody called Slim. He saw the beast latch on to one of Slim's long legs and drag the screaming man thrashing wildly about the floor. He knew the leg was broken. After which the beast climbed Slim's chest, Slim put his arms up to guard his neck. That's when he stopped watching; he heard Slim's screams and the dog's wild snarls as he beat his fist franticly against the locked door.

One minute and thirty seconds later, he no longer heard the woman's struggling screams or Slim's. All he heard were his own cries and the soul-chilling wet slapping of hungry jaws as he beat his tired hands against the ungiving door. Behind him, he heard an approaching snarl, and the stairs creak! Forty-five seconds later and two limbs less, the junkie heard nothing at all as his soul glided towards that great hypodermic needle in the sky.

CHAPTER 15

The moon released its silver shower over a brownstone in the Bedstye section of Brooklyn. Inside the brownstone's second-floor apartment, one grieved for another with the emotional passion that only the truly in love was capable of.

Maleeka was affectionately nursing Rejis's wounds like she had been all day. He kept slipping in and out of consciousness. She patted his brow with a damp rag as he lay in a restless sleep on a low couch in the semi-darkness of the living room. The apartment was a rental. Sometimes Maleeka grew tired of hotels and wanted something a little more personal. Now was one of those times. Maleeka pulled the blanket up around his naked frame covering his scarred chest. She was beginning to worry: never had she seen Rejis like this. Sure, they'd both had their share of injuries in the past. Some took a little longer to heal than others. Somehow Maleeka knew this was different. She could feel it in her blood.

It wasn't that the healing process wasn't underway because it was. The gunshot wounds were already closed, it was the sword's inflicted injuries that she paid special attention to. They seem to be resisting the supernaturally fast healing properties of the werewolf's system. The hole in Rejis's head had yet to close. To clean the wound, she had to cut away a portion of his golden locks. The ace bandages she wrapped the crown of his head with were red again and needed changing. He also seemed to be having trouble breathing making her assume his lungs were damaged along with a few other organs. She watched helplessly as his handsome face would contort into agonizing masks while he broke into wheezing fits. He also ran a devilishly hot fever signifying infection. What kind was beyond her? Figuring he should at least have the strength to make a change. Although the moon would have sped up the recovery process rapidly, she positioned him by the window, letting the floating goddess adorn his frame with her silver blessings. But right now, she didn't think it was going to happen. The way Rejis looked, Maleeka estimated it would take a couple of days to even consider a change.

Maleeka sat on the wood-paneled floor, her long legs crossed in an Indian fashion. Her nakedness was covered by a long robe of black satin. In a meditative trance, she pondered the recent elevation of her abilities. Mentally she was always different; her sense of perception bordered along some shady psychic line foreign to all of her kind she'd ever come in contact with; not that she shared this secret with them. It was just something she knew, because she could also detect the ability in others like she had when they tailed Niccolo's dreadlocked spawn. Now he was an interesting one. Maleeka didn't tell Rejis, but something felt subtly wrong about that one. For some reason, his power was like one of the elder blood-drinkers. She would have to be very careful tackling that one, very careful.

Whereas her heightened cerebral faculties made her different mentally, Maleeka now felt different physically. All of her outer wounds were healed. Not even a scar remained. Sure on the inside, the effects of the fight were still present; her limbs ached a little, and she experienced a slight bout of queasiness in her belly that caused her to pray over the toilet earlier. With the adrenaline receding, exhaustion was beginning to set in. Maleeka wanted nothing more than sleep except to see her Rejis up and to smile, hold her, stroke her hair, whisper his dirty nothings that she so loved.

When Maleeka looked over at Rejis's suffering, anger flared brightly in her like a flare gun's rays over a dark sea. How'd it come to this? It was supposed to be a simple, fast job: kill a few renegades, rogue blood-drinkers. No challenging feat. Nothing they hadn't done in the past. They'd thought it would take a week at the most. It had already been over six months of chasing Niccolo cross-country, and the blood-drinker had proven he didn't plan on dying any time soon.

Should have known it was too good to be true, Maleeka cringed at her gullibility. A million and a half dollars for one kingu and his spawns. It should have set off an alarm. Instead, Rejis figured King Anu was just really pissed.

Maleeka had wondered why Anu hadn't sent any of his own, what did they call them? Nosfers, yes. Surely it would have been cheaper. Little did she know King Anu already had, and they'd failed! Again she dabbed Rejis's forehead with the damp cloth from the bowl of water at her side. He was sleeping peacefully now. Maleeka was fantasizing about all the grotesque things she planned to do to Niccolo when she heard a loud knocking at her front door.

Nobody they knew was aware that they were in New York, so Maleeka's defenses went up instantly. Maybe it was one of the neighbors from the first floor or that young fast-talking Caribbean man from upstairs who always seemed to undress her with his eyes. Maleeka planned to make a meal of him before she left. Her steps were softer than a house cat's as she went to the door, sniffing the air. Maleeka picked up a combination of artificial fragrances over the distinct odor of fresh blood.

Standing behind the door, Maleeka picked up a familiar presence: the unmistakable vampiric energy that only radiated from the aged-and. It was not alone. There were three of them. One of them was a female.

The loud raps of a heavy hand on the door came taunting once again.

"Who's there?" Maleeka called out. Irritated anger began to form in her belly like a fetus now that she had a good idea of her unwanted visitor's identities. King Anu knew they were in New York; they'd spoken only a couple of nights ago. The pompous asshole had the nerve to insinuate they were taking too long.

Three long quiet seconds passed before the thick, African-accented voice of a blood drinker she actually detested responded like a winter wind, " Maleeka, open the door... it's Ghedi."

Like a calculator totaling a sum, Maleeka's mind put everything into its proper perspective. First, she thought impossible, then how, but it really wasn't that hard to answer. With him being an Elder, and not just any elder: one of the King's ambassadors, slash enforcer when he wanted to issue a real personal impression. The last she heard, Ghedi was in Rowanda helping a certain Watusi warlord stay in power. So, the question was, why was he here? In her gut, she knew the answer. Given her current predicament, it was one she could do without.

Before she could move to open the door, she heard the clicks of the door's locks turning slowly. The door creaked open. Light from the hallway cut into the apartment's sickly darkness like a golden blade as the three kingus entered.

First came Ghedi. A bald dark-skinned, very thin man whose gaunt face was devoid of hair, except for a thin salt and pepper line that was his eyebrows. His dark brown eyes were set too far apart, along with his wide hooked nose and full pink lips, which gave him an ugly vulture-like appearance. He wore a rather well-made black and white pinstripe suit. Black hard bottoms rapped with his every deliberately slow step. In his boney right hand, he swung a long black cane in low circles with a golden lion's head on its handle and a golden lion's tail on the cane's end. Clearly, the cane was more a fashion accessory than to aide his perfectly balanced stride.

Behind Ghedi came a large powerfully build man that Maleeka's resentment for ran deeper than her detesting of

Ghedi. His name was Chango, a general of the Nosfer. Like Ghedi, he was hairless, his skin so black it looked bluish. One of his eyes were light grey, the other a dark green, both had deep pink lines etched in their irises like a bad case of 'pink-eye At the sight of his discolored eyes roaming hungrily over her frame, Maleeka clutched her gown shut over her breast. He twisted his big black lips into a sour grimace as he stood at Ghedi's side. Gargantuan arms folded over his thick chest, the tight, ill-fitting, double-breasted charcoal suit, threatening to burst at the seams.

To Ghedi's left was a regally tall woman of beauty, slim with caramel skin the glint of molasses. Dangerously cool henna pools served as her eyes. Her hair was brushed back tightly into a single long black braid revealing a face that was a collage of model-quality features of high cheekbones, an angular nose, and thin lips that were painted with a golden glaze. Her defining physical attribute was her breast. She had the kind of perfect breast that many women have paid large sums in search of big round perky cups, and she knew this. So tonight, as she stood in her sleek black business suit, she left the white collared blouse she wore underneath open enough to reveal her flawless cleavage sitting in a nest of black lace. In her six-inch heels, she looked like a twenty something-ish vogue chick when in truth, she was over 1300 years old. A one-time queen of Sudan, and now a vampires who'd made a name for herself in the empire of the kingu. A distinguished name, and not for her beauty which was only exceeded by her intelligence, but for her excessive cruelty, and fatally lustful passions. That name was, Ezulie. Like a silent bronze-faced sentry, at Ghedi's side-donning the sternest of expressions-she probed the apartment.

"Maleeka, it's been too long, over two hundred years. Still, you are a sight to be admired," said Ghedi as the door closed unassisted behind him. Leaving them in the darkness. His pink lips turned up in a greedy smile as his eyes slowly ran over her, unaffected by the lack of light, as was she.

Seeing his admiring gaze, her jaw tightened, "Yes, it has been long. So tell me, why disturb the enjoyable solace that your absence brings? Why now? Ghedi!" Maleeka asked, rolling his name on her tongue like sour fruit. Holding his gaze, the golden feral fire a spark under her lowered lids.

"You were never one for idle conversation. In that aspect, you haven't changed. I've often said, you have the beauty of a Queen, but not the proper training in social etiquette," Ghedi said in his thick English that sounded as if the language gave him trouble. "So let's discuss the nature of my visit, shall we? You and Rejis were hired to perform a certain task. A task that you both were handsomely rewarded for beforehand. A task that has not been accomplished. Am I wrong?" asked Ghedi.

Maleeka's body began to heat, " That depends, darling, on how one looks at it." refusing her a chance to finish her statement, Ghedi asked, " So tell me, how should one look...at it? Is Niccolo dead or not?" There was an irritated impatience in his voice.

"It is true, Ghedi, Niccolo still lives," Maleeka confessed adding. "But he was not all we were contracted to do. Do you forget about the destruction of any spawn? A matter that has become most time-consuming. You see, he's been running around the country, making countless others that we've also had to contend with, given that he's had a head start if you would say. I would say we're making steady progress. When we began this hunt, his numbers were many. Now only a handful remain. Progress, "Maleeka said, slowly pronouncing each syllable. " But for some reason, I don't think you'll agree. Now do you, darling?" she asked, tightening her robe around her waist.

"No, I don't agree, neither does my esteemed King, who feels like you've taken advantage of his generosity. To be frank, he's ferocious, so naturally, his anger is mine. The spawning you speak of is one of the things you were supposed to put an end to. Now that you haven't, our sources have notified us, that it has become a problem entirely of its own. But one you needn't concern yourself with, for if Niccolo was too much for you, then this new one is completely beyond you!" Ghedi told the werewolf.

Sources! Maleeka thought to herself, so they were being watched after all. She told Rejis she felt so, but he just shrugged it off, asking, has the hunt taken its toll on her, for that was his way.

"Where is the great Rejis?" Ghedi asked mockingly, peeking behind Maleeka into the living room at its only two pieces of furniture: a small wooden table and the couch that housed Rejis. "Is that him?" Ghedi pointed to the sleeping figure. "He doesn't look too good. He hasn't moved since we arrived. This place smells of death," Ghedi sniffed the air wrinkling his beak. " It reeks of the poison that travels through his veins!"

Maleeka was unable to hide her surprise, "What poison do you speak of?"

The very one that's ravaging your blond lover's insides as we speak." A small chuckle came from Chango. Ezulie's amusement was more concealed. For a fraction of a second, one corner of her lips wavered upward, ever so slightly.

Taking a step towards the taller kingu, she asked in an octave more emotional than she would have liked, "How do you know this?"

Ghedi, in a slow, deliberate motion, watched his bony fingers glide across the cane's golden mane. Enjoying the frantic strain in the woman's eyes, she fought to control. Savoring his time, when he finally spoke, his voice was a bitter note of condescending arrogance, " Your kind never had much knowledge of magic. You can't even feel it when it's right under your muzzle."

A shoulder-shaking laugh came from Chango. His discolored pupils shone ghastly in the moonlit room.

Maleeka looked at the General, " I'd bet that's the same laugh many a woman has given you after you've removed your pants. Is it not Darling?" Maleeka said, releasing a disturbing sound that passed for a laugh, regaining some emotional balance. Spinning on her heel, she tracked into the apartment over to-Rejis.

Chango looked as if he wanted to rip Maleeka apart. He shook a huge fist, "You bitch!"

Maleeka made a mocking sound that enraged the General further. He moved as if to engage her but was halted by a warning glance from Ghedi that calmed the Nosfer at once.

Magic that does shed a welcomed light on all of this, Maleeka studied the sleeping figure of her maker. Then assessed her current position, "Ghedi, I fear this conversation is not going well. Whatever problems Rejis faces can't be that detrimental because he is healing, not as fast as I would like, but healing nevertheless." She faced the vampire, her eyes feral. The beast was only seconds away. She continued, "Now, as far as Niccolo is concerned, once Rejis is better, he will be a thing of the past. His existence is confined to the halls of memory. And not for any offense he may have committed in your precious court, but for the personal strife that's he's caused me," said the were, her sultry cadence soaked in rancor.

"I don't doubt your intentions, Maleeka, but I do doubt your current ability, you see. My Royal Majesty said you have three more nights to fulfill your contract. We need not mention what happens at the end of the term, for we both know all too well to waste words. So from what I can gather from looking at your Rejis, is that he won't be in assisting condition for at least two weeks to a month. And I've seen this condition before in your kind. I'd bet Niccolo used a blade to administer the poison. Did he not?"

Maleeka said nothing. Her silence said it all.

Ghedi went on, "And I also sense traces of the poison on you, but for whatever reason, it didn't have the same effect. Such is the nature of such things...So now, we have, how do you say? A dilemma. You," he pointed a skeletal finger at the woman whose eyes spoke painful murder. "Only have three nights, and since your Rejis won't be with you. You'd have to accomplish alone that which you failed as a team." Ghedi bought a hand to his pointy chin like he was pondering some complex matter, taking slow gliding steps.

The two kingus followed like haunting shadows.

Ghedi now stood less than an extended arm from Maleeka, ignoring the unnatural heat she was radiating. He looked upon Rejis, " So sad," he said, making a low tongue-smacking sound. "Fate and fortune, the ficklest of harlots," he then switched his attention to Maleeka, raising a hand to stroke her cheek.

"Don't ever do that!" Maleeka smacked Ghedi's hand down, rejecting his false empathy.

"Such fire! Such passion! You are a woman of many talents. I'd hate to see it go to waste. So....I'm going to offer you an opportunity, one I feel you so deserve," Ghedi said, placing a hand on his cold heart. " For I personally don't believe you are responsible for my King's current troubles. I know where the true blame lies," Ghedi lowered his eyes to the immobile man. " And I will be sure that my King is also informed of this. The guilty will be punished," raising his gaze to Maleeka's, "The innocent exonerated, free from association's burdening weight. You, in turn, will join our, how did you say... the precious court has my concubine." His face softened as he rubbed the hand she struck.

When next Ghedi spoke, it was with convincing passion, "You would live like a Queen! With every luxury, your lustful heart could conceive, no more senseless wandering across the world like a savage nomad. Right now, almost every police agency in the civilized world seeks you. How long before one morning, a small army of agents storm where you rest? Drag you out of bed and chain you like a rabid dog. I know you're thinking, you '11 just shift, but then that takes a good ten seconds if you're that physically adept. And what do you think the terrified agents of the law are going to be doing in that time? Huh, I'll tell you. After they get over the initial shock of seeing you become a bitch! They're going to be filling you with so many bullets you'll literally be cut in half! And if there's enough left of you to heal, you'll find yourself in your wretchedly weakened state, strapped to some scientist's operating table five miles below ground while they try to figure out why! And you know the Americans are rumored notorious for such activity. Your options are few. Choose correctly. I've always wanted you, Maleeka," he paused. Only Rejis's sleeping breaths were heard.

Ghedi held out his hand as an invitation. The vampiric glow in his eyes shone like a celestial light, "Be mine!"

The words of Ghedi didn't even hold the slightest appearance of truth to Maleeka. No human could surprise her; she smelled their scent the second one entered her vicinity, even in sleep. It had happened before. These blood drinkers could surprise her on rare occasions like tonight, but not many. And if her body wasn't currently recuperating, she doubted this trio could, especially with her changes.

Three nights, more than enough time to heal, she was sure—enough time to prepare. For Maleeka was no fool, she knew Niccolo had fled the state again, and it would take much longer to locate him this time. So what she intended to prepare for were the treacherous three right now in her midsts. Even if she delivered Niccolo's head, Maleeka knew that would not settle things. Blood would have to be spilled: as always. Assessing the different energy levels they gave off, she determined their destruction would be no easy task, especially not combating them all at once now, if she was able to isolate them, which would be entirely a different story.

A very gory story. One that ended with her jaws closing on Ghedi's face.

"Ghedi leave!" She coldly dismissed her visitors, more than a little peeved that he would even suggest that she could betray Rejis for his lustful sympathy.

"Maleeka, I am afraid I can't extend my offer to you three nights from now. Maybe I'll come back tomorrow, alone, to help better persuade you," Ghedi said in a voice checkered with sexual longing, using his vampiric ability of suggestive visuals, he asked, "When is the last time you've been with one of your countrymen, one of your brothers from civilization's womb? What has it been, 300 or so years? I hear you're furiously loyal to this one," cutting his eyes like a bronze blade down at Rejis. "Maybe you've forgotten what's it's like to be held by one of your own kind. I'll remind you, with the unrivaled gratifying pleasure of the kingu, kindling within you a regretful envy for all the time you've wasted. A fanatically desirous longing for the sensual gratifications to come," Ghedi then sent a flood of graphically perverse carnal images to Maleeka, images that would have instantly aroused and subdued a mere human, and even some of her own kind, but not her.

To Ghedi's surprise, she laughed, a sultry sound of rejection, "Is that your best line? I bet you get all the girls with that one. Kindle within you a feeling," Maleeka said in a ridiculing imitation of his voice. "Rejis is my kind, in case you haven't noticed, darling." she stated and added, "To be honest, you're a little too thin and unpleasing to the eyes for my liking. This conversation is over. Come back in three nights. If Niccolo still lives, which I doubt he will. Then what will be, will be. Now leave!" The feral savagery that paced like a golden beast within her pupils emphasized the finality of their conversation.

"I meant you no harm or offense, just making a point no matter how crude you may find it. In three nights," Ghedi said, making an apologetic short bow, then turning as if to leave, his free hand moved in a flash.

The kingu's solid fist took Maleeka in the temple, spinning her to the floor. Ghedi's other hand twisted the lion's mane on the cane's handle. With a flick of his wrist, the ambassador produced a long straight blade.

The sword shone like silver death in the moonlight as he held it above his head and grabbed Rejis up by his hair. The werewolf mouthed an incomprehensible sound while his eyes fluttered like lazy wings.

Ghedi brought the blade down in a lightning chop across the helpless were's neck and heaved in the air his blood-dripping prize: the head of the werewolf Rejis.

Rejis turned to Maleeka, his eyes a bright devious inferno of fire; red, orange, and blues.

Maleeka screamed, "Aaaaahhhh!"

At once, she was on her feet. The explosive mixture of outrage, despair, and disbelief produced a consuming need to kill. Her eyes computed to her brain what had just happened. No! But a part of her knew she must accept if she was to survive.

Ghedi's sword flashed again, slicing the disoriented woman high in the shoulder. Another strike of blinking speed bought the sword down through the tender flesh of her breast, forcing her backward, pulling a short scream from Maleeka's emotionally gagged throat. The kingu accelerated forward, bringing the sword up from the floor in a reverse arc.

Maleeka saw the blade sweeping up from the floor and read its fatal intentions. With no time to perform a change, she did all she could do. She stepped backward, hoping to lessen the damage and not a fraction of a second too soon.

The point of the blade entered Maleeka's skin under her navel, traveling upwards as she threw herself backward; She felt the cold blade run over her sternum, continuing its murderous climb. Scratching over the hard bone of her ribcage. Its bloody tip exited under her collarbone, missing her jugular by a micro inch, reentering through her chin, ascending, splitting her lips and the cartilage of her nose's tip, exiting. Maleeka felt breaking glass behind her and a sudden rushing winter breeze. She was falling.

Maleeka fell two stories. Her body connecting with the chilly pavement made a loud thud! There was pain.

" Oh shit! Son, you seen that? She alive?"

Maleeka picked up her bloody face and saw that she'd landed right in the path of a group of passing young men. The shocked expressions on their faces meant nothing to her.

" Ma, you alright? Shit, somebody call an ambulance!" said a tall, dark-skinned man.

Maleeka pulled herself into a sitting position, ignoring the aiding stranger's concern and what was beginning to be a crowd of pointing onlookers. She stared up at the window from which she'd fallen like some debased angel to the earth, the golden halo glow stolen from her eyes. Suddenly there was a deafening explosion, and a large orange fireball shot out the broken window like a dragon's breath.

She watched, and in a matter of seconds, the entire second floor was ravaged by flames. Her eyes watered, and

213

salty tears trickled down her bloody face. A deep feeling of loss and dispirit rage fell over Maleeka that she expressed in a gut-wrenching scream, animalistic in sound but so filled with human loss it silenced the chattering of the strangers gathered.

Maleeka shook uncontrollably. She sobs a banshee's pain. As tears flowed, she beat her fist against the pavement. Black smoke floated overhead. A pair of strong arms cradled her, stroking her hair and back, trying to offer comfort. In a gesture of surrendering acceptance, Maleeka buried her battered face in the man's parka coat. It's thick down, muffling her cries.

Somebody from the crowd said in a sympathetic voice, " Yo, she must have lost her babies inside there:"

No, not her babies. Her baby, her Rejis.

CHAPTER 16

In East Harlem, the clock was five ticks from midnight as a mild winter wind blew across the dim basketball court of Wagner Housing Projects. The raving motors of speeding vehicles could be heard from the F.D.R. Drive and the Triborough bridge behind the housing complex.

Seated on a bench facing the empty ball court, Indio took a long pull from the blunt. Holding the smoke in his large chest, he carefully flicked the ashes, ensuring he didn't burn a hole in his new purple and black bubble goose coat. He exhaled after a few seconds releasing a ghostly grey cloud that traveled over the deserted court and dissolved in the night. With his free hand, Indio reached down by his black field boots, retrieving a long slender bottle from a brown shopping bag. He placed the bottle to his lips and took a delightful swig of the cool, fruity alcoholic nectar. Alize was Indio's drink of choice. He wasn't a heavy drinker. He just liked a little buzz every now and then.

Indio had met her earlier tonight while he was sitting in his whip, a black tinted Chrysler- parked on the corner of 124 St. and Third Ave. He was doing a little surveillance on that Red Rose spot just like Angel instructed him to and watching who came and went, trying to get a glimpse of a lieutenant or somebody who looked like they were calling shots. He'd been sitting there cramped for the past three hours, his legs had fallen asleep, and so far, all he saw were the pitchers. They moved real smooth, and he didn't even notice when they switched shifts. The previous ones just disappeared, and new ones took their place. The only reason Indio noticed the new men were because of the long lines of addicts forming around them.

Indio cursed to himself. He had only zoned off for a few minutes. That's when he looked out the window and saw Mami. A milk-skinned young Hispanic female in a pair of tight blue jeans squeezed over a perfect heart-shaped rear, sporting beige Nine West boots and a matching leather jacket. From the puff in the front of her jacket, he could tell she also had an impressive rack. The woman's black hair was pulled back in a bundle of curls. He felt he had no choice but to try his luck with such a sexy creature.

She told him her name was Nancy, and she was heading downtown to visit her sister. When Indio asked if he could see her later tonight, she said okay; when she finished with her sister and gave him her number. Later, when Indio went to pick her up, she asked him if he smoked weed. When he said yes, she said she didn't want to do anything fancy, just smoke and cool out. Thinking this was definitely his kind of chick, he stopped by a spot he knew and the liquor store. When he suggested they go to his place, she said she hated smoking indoors, it made her paranoid, but they could go to his house afterward with a suggestive little grin that raised Indio's temperature by a couple of degrees.

This was the second blunt Indio passed to Nancy. She took it with her candy apple nails, took a slow pull, and released it out her small nostrils. When she saw that Indio was watching, she giggled all silly. Just like she'd been doing for the past hour. A little horny voice in Indio's head said, "that's it, Mami, smoke it up, cause in a little while I gonna work it all out of you."

Indio took a long swig from the bottle. After he bought it down from his lips, she passed him back the blunt, removing her thin coffee rimmed tinted glasses, cleaning them in a small carrying case she pulled from her jacket before replacing them. Seeing her glassy light hazel eyes with the sun-fire rays for the first time tonight, Indio thought, dam, this bitch is bad! Nancy then held out her hand for the bottle, "Let me get some pi. Normally I don't, it makes me crazy, but I feel like being crazy tonight," Nancy smiled, taking the bottle in her small hands, drinking deeply with big gulps. Indio watched her, noting the large diamond wedding ring she wore.

The way Indio saw it was, whoever her husband was, wasn't handling his business, but he would gladly handle it for him. She was probably mad at the fellow and had just finished complaining to her sister. Now she was hanging out with him for a little get back. Indio smiled to himself. Whatever it was, he didn't give a fuck. All he wanted was a piece of that ass. Her issues were her issues. When he was done with her, he would send her back home to her lame duck of a husband who was probably worrying himself sick, calling all her friends in search of his wife at this very moment.

She handed him back the bottle patting her chest lightly with a silly smile.

"Easy ma, easy," he smiled, placing the practically empty bottle on the ground. Then took the two remaining puffs on the roach and tossed it. Feeling like now was a good time as any, " What's really good, ma?" Indio asked, running a hand up Nancy's thigh.

"Whatever, you tell me," she responded, moving in closer to him, so their bodies touched. Indio then leaned into her. Nancy came forward halfway to meet him.

Their lips touched, interlocking in a deep kiss. Indio's hand wandered inside of her jacket, squeezing her soft mounds, cupping them. Pulling her nipples roughly between his fingers as Nancy moaned in agreement kissing him harder. One of her hands worked loose his belt buckle, unfastening his jeans, pulling down the zipper, journeying into his pants until she found what she sought.

Massaging his hardening cock in one of her hands, Nancy nibbled on Indio's earlobe, darting her hot wet tongue in and out of his ear canal, toying with his ponytail.

Indio, "Ahhh!" he loved it. His ear was sensitive.

She then licked down the long curve of his thick neck, stopping under his chin, sucking, pulling, and biting lightly.

Nancy pulled Indio's fully erect penis from his jeans out into the night. The hard blood warm organ throbbed in her hand. She ran a finger over the tip smearing its juice over the head. Placing the finger between her lips, it disappeared in her mouth, " Ummm, good!" She told him, smacking her lips.

Her whole seductive shade thing was driving Indio crazy. He saw his own lust in her tints. He could take it no more. Grabbing the back of Nancy's neck with one of his large hands, he pushed her face down into his lap.

Nancy complied, inching away a little to get a better position. She went to work at once. Her mouth closed over his penis, taking it halfway down. Wet lips and tongue slowly slid back up his shaft. Each time she went down, she took more in until she was completely engulfing him greedily, which in itself was an accomplishment. Nancy made loud slurping noises, dripping saliva down into his bushy crotch, making the big man cry out, " Damn! That's it Mami ohhh!"

Indio's eyes were closed. The effects of the intoxicants and her mouth had him in another world. He swore this was the best blowjob he'd ever received. Most girls barely got it halfway down because he was kind of large, but not her. She took in every inch and didn't even gag. He didn't even have to keep hold of the back of her head. For the last sixty seconds, Indio kept feeling as if he would cum at any second. He was fighting a losing battle with himself not to be vocal, but it felt so dam good.

"He looks like he's really enjoying himself, doesn't he?"

"Yes, Sirrrr."

At first, when Indio heard the two distinctively different male voices, he thought he was tripping: the weed and drink were getting the best of him. It had happened before. But when he opened his eyes and saw the two black men in suits standing over him, Indio's mind traveled from knocking on the pleasurable gates of ecstasy to the cautious pit of alarm. Attempting to remove Nancy from him, Indio suddenly felt sharp teeth enter the flesh of his swollen organ. The alarm became fear.

" If you have any future plans of ever reproducing, if I were you, I would stay still, very, very still." the dreadlocked man laughed, his dark eyes ablaze with fine silver rays that caused Indio to swallow hard. Indio chastised himself for leaving his gun in the car; he thought he wouldn't need it being on familiar ground.

"Yo bro, what you want?" The panic within Indio was audible in his voice.

"I think you know the answer to that homeboy," stated the taller slenderer of the men, pulling out a long platinum chain from inside his shirt. On its end hung a red-jeweled rose that sparkled ominously in the night.

Indio wanted to scream. He immediately knew what was happening to him. He had to survive, he told himself, looking closely at the chain's owner. The man looked familiar, but he couldn't place him. Trying to buy time, hoping maybe the housing police would roll through," I know you?" Indio asked. No sooner than he did, Nancy applied a little pressure. Indio winced as blood began running down his rapidly deflating prick.

"Yeah, you saw me before. We were in Attica together, A-block. I never liked you. Anyhow, in case you can't remember, I'm Meko, and this over here is my man Enkill. From this point on, son, you ask no questions, only answer them. If you cooperate, I might let you live! You hear me?"

"Yeah, bro," Indio said, rapidly bobbing his head up and down like it was attached to a yo-yo string, holding up his hands in a defeated gesture. "Okay, I'll tell you whatever you want to know. Just get her off me!"

"'What a bitch ass nigga," Meko snickered and then thought, what other option does the man really have?

"Yo faggot, one of you niggaz bodied my little man Dre the other night. You pulled the trigger?"

"No man, nah bro, I swear it wasn't me!" Indio shook his head franticly in denial.

"I know you was there. If it wasn't you, then who was it?" "It was Angel, yo!"

"Word, Angel, huh," Meko stared hard at the scared man. His ice grill intensified by the inhuman glow of his pupils. "Angel, huh...why you been watching my spot?"

"Yo Angel told me to. He said ya'll might have murdered Lou."

Meko's right fist connected with Indio's nose– crushing the bridge. The big man saw white flashes as his head snapped back. Blood spewed from his broken nose, and Indio bought both hands to his face, kicking over the bottle by his foot. Meko grabbed his ponytail jerking the man's head back, spitting in his face, " Fuck! You trying to play me, son?"

"Nah, nah," Indio sounded like he would burst into tears any second.

"Angel this, Angel that, Angel killed my man, Angel made me do it, fuck is you, Angel's do boy? Huh, Do you hold his dick when he pisses?" Meko stormed, smacking the man.

A frightened Indio didn't know how to respond. The glow in the men's eyes drained all the strength from his limbs.

"Where the fuck is Angel? Where can I find this man?" Meko questioned.

Before Indio could respond, Enkill cut in, "Let me kill this nigga. Fuck that move, son!" Holding the short silver ax above his head, trying to push past Meko, who placed a restraining hand on his chest and said, " Chill sun, he gonna tell us, right," Meko said, looking down at Indio, who at the sight of the ax made the connection to Lou's gruesome murder and broke down into tears.

"He live uptown!"

"Ease up, Nancy," Meko ordered the kingus, and she released her hold on his bloody member. Meko then continued the interrogation, "Where uptown?"

"Yo in the Bronx, at 151 St. around the corner from the Grand Concourse. The biggest building on the block, 489, he lives in apartment 3-j with his girl". Indio stuttered, unable to rip his eyes from the ax, his mind flashing back to the headlines of a couple of weeks ago.

"He got a number?"

"555-6269"

Nancy whipped out a phone, punching in the number. After a few rings, a female picked up, "Hello."

"May I speak to Angel?" Nancy inquired with the class of a project whore.

"He's not here. Who's this?" the woman answered.

"His girl!"

"If you was his girl, you would be here answering this phone bitch!". With that, the woman hung up. Nancy looked over at Indio thinking how pitiful he looked as she put the phone back in her jacket.

"See, I told you, bro. I don't even fuck with that nigga like that, yo." Indio's words were a nervous ramble, with persuasive perspiration and tears mixed over his bloody face.

"I bet you don't," said Meko with a disgusted expression on his face, "You just catch bodies with him, run errands, go to his house, chill, and eat his food. You probably be screaming on his chick. I hate niggaz like you...Nancy!"

Nancy's eyes ignited behind her specs with gleaming gold at the sound of her name. Her jaws morphed into a fanged death's cave that she closed down on Indio's entire genitalia, balls and all. With one savage twist of her neck, she ripped them free. Blood splattered Meko's pants. Indio screamed, strangled, and tortured as he crumbled from the bench. His cries cut through the still of the project night like gunfire.

Greedily Nancy chewed the male organ; her neck grew serpent-like as she swallowed it.

A castrated Indio screaming like a mad eunuch curled up on the pavement, gripping his ruined groin. Nancy's movements were lethal as she stood and effortlessly flipped the large man on his back.

Her claws found the screaming man's neck. With one violent jerk and a wet pop, the gangster's head dislodged from his shoulders. The kingus then stood holding the offering to Enkill, "For you."

Enkill glanced incredulously at Meko, then back at the kingus. "What the fuck I'm a do with that?"

The kingus laughed a crazy sound and tossed the head out onto the court that rolled out into the ghostly darkness of the vacant court.

Enkill then asked Meko, "You made her?"

"Nope."

"Then who?"

"Charise."

Enkill landed with the swiftness of a raven in a cloud of mist on the lair's balcony. He paused ever so briefly as his probe located not one but two unfamiliar kingu signatures within. A wave of his mental hand opened the balcony door and closed it behind him. Swiftly he announced his presence with an authoritative probe and made his way to the source of the unknown signatures.

In one corner of the room stood a 150-gallon L-shaped fish tank on an ash grey rotating base filled with piranhas.

The small, carnivorous tropical fish darted around mindlessly through the tank's colorful corals. Framed on the wall - a few feet away - was an emotionally moving portrait of the Black Madonna: cinnamon-toned Isis sitting on her throne with her baby son Horus suckling from her breast. Further down was her husband/brother Osiris, and then came Thoth.

The furniture was a variety of cutting-edge curves and sleek designs done in grey leather and smoked glass. Across in a corner under a window was a circular marble table for two. The table was supported by one leg in its center shaped like a wine glass's stem that grew out of the marbled floor like some oddment stone weed. Its smooth surface was polished onyx except for the two-tone grey and ivory chessboard built into the center. The pieces ranged from six to eight inches in height. Each was a brilliantly handcrafted human figurine of the most sparkling crystal. The detail was exceptional, a row of fierce-faced warrior pawns, a proud lance-wielding knight on a stallion. The stern dominating glint in the Queen's eyes as she plotted a strategy to bring about the rival King's demise, to the ascetic look of the bishop like the world no longer held any wonders and the flesh was a temporary prison he waited patiently to be released from.

A studio-quality sound system played a progressive rock tune on one wall that screamed jarringly. Facing a giant wall-mounted flat screen was a curving davenport, the grey of a sky threatening to storm, on which sat like a storm-goddess, Natasha.

A grape-like cluster of dimmed, golden bulbs lit the room like a fading sun. Natasha sat regally cutting a fourteen. The long split down the side of her skin-tight black leather, dominatrix-inspired dress allowed a milky-toned leg to be seen. Down by one of her extra high heels sat a young man in black. A leather vest hugged his sleekly built pale white torso. Colorful tattoos of warring devils and angels fought down both his arms. Tight leather pants hugged his lower body. A slow trickle of blood dripped from a slash on one of his wrists to the floor. He sat on his hind quarters like a dog, head high, grey eyes haughty, scanning the room's new arrivals like he possessed the most dignified of positions. From his spiked collared neck ran a thin chain that Natasha held in one hand as she dangled a wine glass in the other with a thick crimson liquid that Enkill sensed at once as blood.

"Hey lady, how have you been?" Enkill asked, taking in the jade radiance that jumped from under Natasha's mascara when she smiled, warming him as he pecked her lips, tasting the blood.

"I am fine. What about you, stranger? I haven't seen you in over a week."

"Been a little busy, you know, but I see you've been keeping yourself occupied," he said, ignoring the dog-man looking at the two new kingus she sat between.

"This is Fatimah," Natasha said, introducing the pretty coffee and cream complexioned Middle- Eastern young woman. Her hair fell in long wild black waves over her collar framing her small makeup-less face perfectly, like the portrait of some ancient huntress. On Fatimah's petite curves, she wore a raven-wide collared blouse, fitting black jeans with a worn, ripped look, and high-heeled black boots that reached up to the slashed denim under her knees.

Fatimah got up in a manner so fluid and smooth that Enkill found it reminiscent of Natasha as she embraced him. Small hands with long ebony polished nails glided across his back. She spoke with a melody as if singing a song, "Oh Enkill, finally we meet. The man subject of so much."

Enkill saw gentleness in the newly made killer's smile and a fire in her eyes as he squeezed her perfumed frame. Tasting her lips lightly like one would a dear old friend. Sometimes upon first meeting a person, their genuineness just reaches out and touches you.

To Enkill, this was one of those times, " I've been the subject of much?"

"You are the nucleus of us all. You will always be the subject of much," she stated.

Enkill looked closely at the kingus, who couldn't be a mortal day over twenty-five, but spoke in a sage-like manner that revealed a maturity beyond her years. All he could do was nod reflectively in acceptance of the truth.

Natasha then introduced the rather tall Asian man sitting at her side, "And this is Chen."

227

Chen got up and offered a slender, hard hand with the tattoo

of a giant black spider above his knuckles, How's everything? It's good to meet you." Chen's voice was unnaturally deep but somehow fit the. slim man with long black hair twisted back in a single braid. Under his thin eyebrows were dark slants that wore the promise of great menace. His mouth was a tight pink line. Whereas Fatimah's fleshy lips wore a mix of a loutish half smile, Chen's was tight-jawed and stern. He looked like a man suppressing a violent urge that he was only seconds away from acting upon.

"Same here. I'm just tryna keep us ahead of the game right now," Enkill answered, wondering how Natasha met the serious-faced man. Not that he minded the man's demeanor, on the contrary. Enkill would prefer to surround himself with no-nonsense individuals. As of now, he viewed Chen as a welcomed plus to the team, "How's everything with you? How's the change treating you?"

"No need to say life's changed drastically, so what I will say is that the change has been for the better." said Chen, casting a brief look at Natasha. And Enkill saw a faint smile soften the man's features, briefly. Seeing Chen standing there like that in his loose white oxford and blue jeans, Enkill understood the relationship, or at least he thought he had an idea.

"I'm sure in some way or another we all feel the same way," Enkill said, then asked, " Yo, I take it. Natasha filled you two in on what's happening at this stage?"

The two kingus assured him she had.

"Of course I did," Natasha said, giving him a look that said, how could she not?

Enkill left Meko with the trio, walking over to a lazy boy that Charise sat poised in like a Queen with Nancy standing over her like a royal guard.

"Hey beautiful, what's up?"

"Nothing much," Charise shrugged carelessly in a silver turtleneck, a couple of her braids shifting in the movement.

"I've met your new friend. You choose well," said Enkill.

"Now, if only I did so in all matters," Charise retorted.

Enkill heard the twinge of aggravation in her voice as she brushed invisible lint from her black jeans. He knew now was not the time or place to address such a matter, so he filed it away for later.

"Where's Ty and Marisola at?" Enkill asked no one in particular, turning away from Charise.

"They're uptown at the spot," Meko spoke up.

"Alright, I want somebody to tell me something. What the fuck's going on in here, and don't say nothing because I feel it," and feel it, Enkill did as he took a folded arm stance by a short triple platform glass table. The whole vibe of the room felt funny, like something needed to be said.

Natasha took a sip from her glass and spoke," Well, for starters, I've been having this eerie feeling of being watched.

And it's not physical. It's mental, like someone's listening to my thoughts. Then when I probe out to catch it, it withdraws. Gone, without the slightest trace." She said so conversationally. "How long has this been happening?"

"About a week and a half. At first, I thought nothing of it, like it was the result of my heightening perceptibility, until about a couple of nights ago, it got intense. I was walking down in the Village, and it was like I could hear a voice in my head.

The only thing I could compare it to is when I used to be in one place, and he another, and Niccolo would call upon me."

Enkill listened thoughtfully to Natasha's words, for he knew exactly what she spoke of. He himself had shared the same experience, but he was more physical: much more physical.

One night last week, as he wandered mid-town, Enkill had the distinct feeling of being trailed. Like strange energy was just a few steps behind, only with his eyes he found nothing. Still, he knew it wasn't just in his mind, even when a probe turned up nothing.

Enkill ascended up to the roof of one of the area's skyscrapers and waited. The markings on his arms were an inferno as he pasted himself to a wall of shadows, gripping the hilt of his ax cloaked in his own dark mist.

The energy presence got stronger until it felt as if it was surrounding him. This time when Enkill probed, he got a handle, like his mind touching another's. That's when it retreated, and Enkill gave chase. At a racing speed, he followed the fleeing energy signature for a good twenty minutes across the N.Y.C. skyline, finally losing it in the shadow of Lady Liberty over Ellis Island, but not before he caught a glimpse of its source. The tall, dark figure of a male in a cloud of grey vapors with eyes of copper flames watching him before it dematerialized over the dark waters of the Hudson River.

So now, Enkill knew the source of this energy wasn't just some mental phantom but possessed a physical body, and Enkill also knew it was a kingu.

What troubled Enkill now was how to touch the topic. He had told none of his experience with the watcher. The reason being to admit to such a problem might imply that though they may all feel so -he might not be that much above them as far as being a kingu goes if he too faces the same threats, fears, and insecurities. Or it would just reinforce what he said about the need to always be prepared and go nowhere unarmed.

"What did the voice sound like to you?" asked Enkill.

"It sounded female... like condescending laughter," Natasha said in between sips.

So that means theirs more than one of them, he told himself and said, "Um, you know what's really ill? I had a similar experience. The only difference is mine was with a male that I actually saw."

"Yo, you can't tell me that!" Meko blurted out in surprised concern.

"I know, I was tryna put everything in its proper place first. I was going to drop it on you earlier, but the conversation kind of went a different way. So I figured I would approach it later, when we're all together," Enkill delivered a half-truth as he paced in small circles, which wasn't all bad because he did plan to tell them.

"So, how did you see him? Did he speak to you? What happened?" Natasha quizzed, stroking the head of the dog man at her feet.

Enkill then ran down the details of his experience to the assembled group while they took in every word like devoted parishioners listening to a Sunday sermon.

"That's something to think about, but why did he run?" Meko wondered out loud.

"Perhaps he's toying with Enkill or attempting to feel him out," the room's attention was now focused on Chen as he continued in his deep bass, "Maybe their trying to see where our strengths and weaknesses lie before they attack." Chen's logistics rang an uncomfortable bell of truth with all present.

"I was thinking something similar, but one thing bothers me. First, has anybody else had any type of experience?" Enkill asked, searching the room. No one spoke, so he went on, "How did they just come upon Natasha and me? This city's big. How did they locate us, and how many of them are we up against?"

"That's a good question right there. One I won't mind having answered," Meko traced his hand over his chin.

"Hold up. How do we know they're even against us?" Charise asked. "They could just want to know who we are."

"Did you forget everything Niccolo told us about our standing in the kingu community?" Enkill snapped. "Speaking of, I wish we could somehow get a line on him," giving Charise a look.

Charise rolled her eyes, "Well, you're not going to the mid-town spot. That is a waste of time because you know it's burned down. And I think he's dead anyway because a couple of nights ago, I spoke to a friend who was a thrall of his if you will. And she was asking me about him all teary-eyed, talking some sorry shit about how she used to be able to feel him in her head, now she can't. She said he told her she would always be able to feel him. No distance would be too great unless one of the two of them were dead."

"What! Why you ain't tell me this earlier?" Enkill asked, the darkness in his eyes swimming. Charise was really beginning to get to him.

"It slipped my mind, and it ain't like you've been around to tell you if I had remembered!" Charise said with a little too much attitude and neck movement for Enkill's liking as he transferred his wordless gaze from her to Meko, then back.

Chen sensing the rising tension, spoke up, telling Charise, "Listen, whatever personal feeling you may have against anyone in this room, don't let it jeopardize us all."

"You're a new jack. You don't know shit about me!" Charise broke, "And I ain't got no personal feelings against nobody!" She came to her feet. In Charise's eyes was an emotion that heightened her voice, "And since when we started trusting everything Niccolo said anyway?"

Enkill spoke slowly, "Listen, Charise, I am not going to play this bullshit with you. You know what the fuck is going on. Plus, we learned from a different source tonight what's happening among our kind, and you know what? It kind of checks out with everything kingu wise that Niccolo put us on to."

"And what source is this?" Charise took a step towards Enkill, posing with both hands on her hips.

Meko cut in. Filling the group in on their meeting earlier tonight, as he spoke, he placed his body between Charise and Enkill, who were trading visual poison.

Enkill then said, "Yo, until we get everything under complete control, like determining how great of a threat these watchers pose when traveling outside, choose a partner. Daylight hours when you sleep, it's inside of here," before Enkill could finish, Charise interjected.

"Why we gotta sleep here? You don't sleep here!"

"One, you're not me. Two, I don't sleep every day."

"Whatever, fuck this. I am out, and 'I'm not sleeping here!" Charise stormed for the double doors, heels clicking loudly with Nancy following. Charise grabbed the doorknob, turning and pulling to find that it wouldn't budge like an invisible hand was holding it in place.

"Am I gonna have to rip this motherfucker off? Or somebody's gonna stop fucking playing with me!" Charise turned around to face Enkill across the room, brushing Nancy aside, "You think it's a joke, don't you?" Her arched brows joined together, sinking into a sharp point. Her ears lengthened, then flattened to her skull. Charise's eyes became glowing slants, and lips pulled back into a fanged snarl. Long curved claws completed her split-second transformation to a demonic beauty.

Enkill just laughed, a deep, powerful sound like the revving of a sports car's engine, which infuriated Charise further. She let out a loud deafening screech that made Natasha's human-dog cover his ears, and roll on the floor in agony, bloodshot eyes bulging as if they would pop from their sockets. The empty wine glass in Natasha's hand exploded, a long crack appeared in the fish tank, and several others in the windows.

All the standing kingus took a step backward except Enkill. He stood deathly still except for the slow raising of one arm, open palm until it was shoulder level.

Slowly Enkill closed his hand as if squeezing an invisible object. The ear-shattering sound that Charise was emitting ceased. Shocked, she grabbed at her neck with both hands. Gagging. Her serpent tongue slashed wildly as she struggled against the incorporeal force that held her.

Enkill lifted his arm higher, slightly twisting his wrist. Charise's body came off the ground. He was angled strangely like one hanged, bloody saliva spewing from her tongue. Feeling her breath going, Charise suddenly went still. Her neck then morphed, extending enough that her heels once again touched the floor. In her eyes blazed triumph and defiance.

Enkill smiled. The dark mist poured from his sockets.

Suddenly Charise was hoisted seven feet up in the air. Blood began to leak from various small tears in the flesh of her neck, and Enkill hadn't moved a limb.

"You see, it's not done by hand. That's just for show. It's done inside the mind: the true source of all strength," he said, placing both hands at his sides.

Suspended in mid-air, Charise struggled, blood running down her turtleneck. Without warning, she was driven down violently to the hard marble floor face first with a smashing thud. Nancy attempted to come to her maker's aide, only to be lifted with death-defiance speed off her feet, smashed into the ceiling, then down into the marble beside Charise. Nancy tried to rise and fell backward. Clearly disoriented, a small wound was opened on the side of her face, and one must have been somewhere on her head because a slim trickle of blood leaked down her forehead. With fearful eyes, she looked up at the dark-eyed vampire.

"This is your first and only lesson Nancy, don't ever involve yourself unless you're told to," Enkill warned before turning his attention to Charise. "You see, Charise, this is what I've been doing while you've been muff diving with your new little girlfriend right there. I've been trying to get my shit together, to make sure our shit's together. So we'll have a fucking fighting chance. Look at you! Talking about you go where the fuck you feel like, you can't even defend yourself, and I ain't even put a hand on your, sorry ass!"

Enkill's words cut into Charise like the hacking cleaver of a butcher. They hurt. Charise reared up on her hands, morphing her neck back to normal proportions. A nasty gash ran down from her brow to cheek, somehow missing her eye. A few of her teeth felt loose. Whipping the line of scarlet saliva that hung from her lips, Charise looked into the faces of her teammates and saw mixed expressions of shock and pity. Except for Natasha, her eyes held a smug satisfaction. Charise knew the green-eyed bitch was enjoying her humiliation. How could she allow this to happen, like this?

When her gaze fell on Enkill, Charise felt stupid, angry, and shamed all at once. He was looking down at her like she was the lowest thing on the face of the earth. She wanted to apologize and run into his arms. All she really wanted was his attentive affection. Charise was mad about being checked, for she had a proud and fiery nature. But it wouldn't have hurt so bad if it had been in private, just the two of them. She would have lowered her wings to the man she desired to please above all others. Just not in front of everybody. Charise thought of how everyone would view her now. Damn, she fucked up!

When Enkill and Meko walked toward Charise, her heart leaped. She whipped the blood from her eyes that was caking her lashes in anticipation. He looked calmer. Maybe he was coming to cradle and comfort her. Tell her how sorry he was, and beg her forgiveness. She would grant it. But when Enkill passed her, leaving the living room with not so much as a look of recognition, like she was invisible. Charise's heart sank, a layer of its compassionate warmth stripped away, never to be replaced. Still, she wanted to chase behind him, screaming, "why?" For her, physical wounds were superficial. Already they were healing. It was the mental ones that were going to leave scars. But Charise didn't move a limb, save for the burying of her face in her arms as bloody emotional tears seeped down her face. Charise did the only thing she felt she could at that moment. Even though she begged herself not to, she cried. A gut-wrenching wailing sound that originated somewhere in her soul.

CHAPTER 17

Under the dining room's golden chandeliered light, Enkill and Meko sat a few seats away from each other at a long rectangular table of thick black glass.

"Yo son, you don't think you was a little rough on homegirl?"

"No," Enkill stated, "Strong soldiers need strong leaders. So you can't always just talk and not act. Your words become empty, and people stop listening. I did what had to be done. What will stop everybody else from following suit if I let her show out? Then what do we have?"

"I understand and agree with your logic, but Charise, don't strike me as a soldier like that. You can't make her into what she's not, especially if it's not what she wants."

"Then what do you think she wants?"

"Just a little affection and a hard erection."

The two men laughed, but in the joke, Enkill saw its truth in the joke: "I know, man, imma get at her later."

"You do that. Now on some next shit, that was kind of ill back there. I see you really puttin' it together on this vampire shit. I am really feeling that" Meko leaned on his elbows, casting his friend a look.

"Yo, you just got to explore yourself. I know you got some shit inside of you. You just got to take the time and bring it out, "Enkill told Meko encouragingly.

"I know, I just be busy and all with everything, you know," Meko knew Enkill was right, but he was so swamped with everything that sometimes he felt the night didn't have enough hours. He was so busy with Red Rose that he couldn't even enjoy the fruits of his labor like he wanted to. Every time he looked up, it was sunrise.

"All I know is you better get your weight up," Enkill smirked, waving his hands dramatically. The unoccupied chairs at the table floated to the ceiling.

"My shit is up, don't try none of that Jedi shit with me."

"Hey, I wanna ask you something," Enkill said, replacing the chairs. "Back at Raphael's earlier, did you feel anything strange about them? Could you tell they weren't normal humans?"

"No," Meko answered.

So that meant if the lagaoo were enemies, then they would have had one up on you, Enkill said inwardly and let the topic pass.

For about half an hour or so, Enkill and Meko discussed how they could expand their current operations until Ty and Michelle joined them.

Greetings were exchanged as Ty took a seat, and Michelle hugged Enkill warmly and said, "I heard what happened. You want me to have a talk with her?"

"If I say no, you still are anyway.

"No, I am not," she winked.

He laughed, "Whatever," kissing her forehead. "Tell me something, Ma. What's up with you? Is everything okay? Ain't nobody tryna bite on you, right?"

"I am okay," she assured him. "Nothing I can't handle," Michelle said, shooting a look at Ty, who looked away at the chandelier whistling.

"I am a little tired. Imma go take a little nap. But first I am a go holla at my girl and see how she's holding up."

"You do that," Enkill kissed her cheek,' "And tell her I want to speak to her before she shuts it down for the day."

"Okay."

The three men watched the woman as she left the room, entranced by how her tight denim skirt squeezed over her swaying hips as she walked. The click of heels on the marble was hypnotic.

"Damn, that bitch is bad!" Ty said, breaking the spell by pulling down the hood of his black sweatshirt.

"Why don't you get at her?" Meko asked him.

Ty sucked his teeth, clicking a finger against the table, "Kid, she a little funny style ya heard, she on some Enkill shit."

"Isn't everybody these days," Meko said, looking to Enkill. The smile his dark-eyed maker wore was snug and cocky.

"Yo, I heard how y'all handled ole boy tonight. That's what's up," said Ty. "Nancy also told me ya'll also got a line on Angel."

"Yeah, we'll be paying him a visit one of these nights very soon," Meko promised.

"So, how'd the meeting go?"

At the sound of Ty's question, Enkill realized that nobody told Ty anything since he had missed the festivities earlier. So with a split-second touch, Enkill relayed all that had transpired. When he had finished, Ty asked, astounded, "Yo, they some kind of were-beast? Say word. Yo, what's the chance of that?"

"That's all right," Enkill said, "But you know what's even sicker, if we wasn't what we are, we wouldn't know what they were. Imagine how many such creatures you might have come in contact with in the past and had not known. Remember, Meko was introduced to dude by a second human party, who had no knowledge whatsoever of what Raphael was either."

"So what do you make of them, though?" Ty's eyes narrowed suspiciously, "Remember what Niccolo said about the were-beast?

"With everything taken into consideration, business associates. If the future holds more, we'll see," Meko said, standing and flexing. He then reached in the inside of his jacket hanging on the back of the chair, pulling out a zip-lock bag of marijuana and a photo leaf. The weed he crushed on the table as he proceeded to roll.

"So what ya'll make of all that shit going on in Europe?" Ty asked.

"It adds up halfway with what Niccolo told me, but still, we need more info," said Enkill.

Ty shook his head in agreement pulling from his sweat hood his own photo, mimicking the process Meko was engaged in, "They told me about the whole watcher thing too. Marisola is gonna be my partner. I'm feeling how she gets down," said Ty.

"That's cool with me," Enkill said, wishing everybody responded as smoothly to things as Ty did. After a few seconds, "Yo, that shit get you high?" Enkill asked. His countenance was of disbelief as he watched Ty stuff the leaf with a rather large amount of the green bud, then roll and seal it with his saliva.

"Not like it used to, just a short buzz, you know," Ty said, placing the blunt in his mouth and lighting it with a fancy lighter fashioned like a naked woman. Ty inhaled deeply, deeper than any mere human could, steaming away a fifth of the blunt. When he exhaled, it was like a steam engine or some great dragon as a huge grey cloud poured from his nostrils and mouth.

"Wanna hit some of this shit?" Ty asked in a raspy voice, taking another pull and handing the blunt towards Enkill, who declined with a wave of a finger, not seeing the purpose.

"Man hit that shit and stop fronting," Meko said as he suavely puffed away on his own drug-filled cigar. He then told Ty, "Yo Ty, you think Michelle is bad, wait until you meet that lion chick Quillana in person. The visual you just caught is nothing compared to being in the same room as her, feeling her vibe."

"Say word, I'm coming with y'all next time y'all go check, ha," Ty told them.

243

"You know Imma get up in that right," Enkill said with a confident bounce of his brows.

"Not before me," Meko said, challenging his partner's boast.

"Fuck that, let's get a train going. An orgy or something, I know she got some friends, "Ty stated humorously, tipping ashes into an ashtray. The three men broke into a burst of conspiratorial laughter.

Enkill heard and felt them approaching. Something was wrong. The doors to the dining room flew open. Michelle entered with Nancy, "I can't find Charise anywhere, and it's like an hour before sunrise. She's gone!" Michelle's tone was one of nervous concern.

"Shit, man! Some people just need to experience everything on their own, I guess. Let's just hope she stays in one piece," Enkill rose from the table, his mood soured. As he walked past the two ladies, Nancy touched his arm and followed him a few steps into the hall.

"Enkill, I am sorry, I was out of line," Nancy didn't have a chance to finish. Enkill halted her apology catching her gaze, "Don't worry about it. Sometimes we all get carried away, myself included," he smiled sympathetically, running a finger down the small healing wound on her cheek. He understood her position perfectly and respected her loyalty to her friend. After all, Charise did make her.

Enkill strolled into the living room, gazed upon the sleeping dog-man cuddled up on the couch, and headed back out into the lightless hall, then one flight up a curving

244

staircase with an ivory banister. Emerging from the stairs put him in the middle of a luxurious hall of off-white tiles with over-lapping golden rings. Enkill's room was the second of two to the right. As he passed the first, its door opened.

"You look so stressed. Come talk to me."

"It's that apparent?" he said.

Natasha stepped back from the doorway, allowing Enkill to enter. As she closed the door behind him, the faint traces of a little mischievous smile could be detected.

Security-wise, many renovations had been made in the penthouse for its new occupants. Specialists worked around the clock for seven days straight before everything was satisfactory, and still, more work had to be done.

Like all the others, Natasha's bedroom was windowless and steel reinforced from the walls to the door, designed to withstand a twenty-man battering ram assault. It also had a manual bolt lock and a special computerized timer set to sunrise and sunset hours controlled by a password that one punched into the console on the wall by the door. Only a room's occupant knew a room's personal code, except Enkill, who knew every room's password. Each room had a spacious walk-in closet and a shower and bath attached. That's where the similarities ended.

Natasha sat on her room's most dominant piece of furniture: a king-sized bed resting on a solid red Oakwood frame. Each of the four bedposts almost reached the ceiling and were carved into snaking necks with the heads of the horned horse like a beast. Around each of the beast's neck was a collar of black wood, and each collar was attached to a beam connected to the post. On the beams hung a rich scarlet curtain of silk, creating a partial canopy effect. Directly above the bed was a mirror that was its exact width and length.

The curtains were parted.

With the allure of a sea nymph, Natasha sat within the bed's ocean of red, wrapped in a short towel that barely reached her thighs. Her hair was wet. It hung in slick waves over her face. She had just come out of the shower, "Give me that, please," Natasha asked, pointing to the floor. Enkill reached down to a thick carpet that a dropped coin would have disappeared in and picked up a small jar of some kind of crème and gave it to her. He stepped back as she started applying generous amounts to one leg extending it up and out in front of her. The towel parting. The dark slick hairs of her crotch could be seen as she massaged the crème into her skin.

Standing in front of a dresser fashioned after the bed frame, an entranced Enkill watched the kingus silently in the light of six tall ebony candles situated around the room in small blood tone bowls, which fragranced the air with the wild scent of a rose garden.

Damn, she's fine, even with no make-up, Enkill thought as he observed Natasha's performance of her ritual. Dancing shadows floated over her nakedness as the jade even-kingus discarded the towel, rubbing the crème over her entire body.

Natasha's hands and limbs moved in erotically slow and graceful movements, a phantasmal beauty in a dance of seduction.

With her grooming done, Natasha floated up into the bed. Twisting with a sensual slowness through the air, muscles flowing beneath her shining skin. Softly she landed on her back, gazing up at the mirror above, one knee up and waving, just enough to give a peak at the moist lips of her glistening treasure box. Her back arched off the bed as her glowing vision found Enkill's. Natasha's voice was the whisper of a soft wind, "Come."

And come Enkill did. Removing his shirt and the carrying straps from the base of his back with a thought. The ax hit the carpet with a muffled thud. As he stepped out of his shoes, his slacks and boxers followed. He was already hard.

"I thought you wanted to talk."

"I do, but later. Come," Natasha winked, the emerald glow of her vision burning bright. The tips of her fangs pinched into her bottom lips. He climbed on top of her between her open legs. Grabbing his erection, she guided it inside her warm wetness. Feeling his length full of her, Natasha wrapped both arms around his back, releasing a husky moan nibbling his neck, pricking the skin.

"You feel so fucking good!" He grunted.

"Of course I do," was Natasha's response kissing him. The two kingus tongues danced a passionate tango as he worked his hips in short thrusts into her, sending small tantalizing currents through her, which Natasha absorbed and returned, her walls squeezing him like a fist.

"Oh shit!" he cried out in delightful surprise.

"You like that, don't you?" she said.

When they'd finished, there was no talk about Natasha's newfound ability or anything else for that matter, the kingus was on the verge of sleep, and sunrise was only minutes away. Enkill secured her room and slipped into his own. After a quick shower, he changed into some blue jeans, a black sweater, a parka, and ski boots. He then put on a pair of dark-tinted specs. Grabbing up his ax, he secured the penthouse and left via the front door. It was also steel reinforced with a timer that only allowed it to be opened during sunlight hours by himself or Michelle.

Enkill hit the roof and immediately took to the skyline, moving swiftly towards downtown's Westside. It was an early Saturday morning. Being a weekend, the city was not really awake yet. Only a few early risers moved beneath him. He was high over Central Park, around 86 Street, when Enkill noticed how strange he felt.

A hot tingling sensation spread across his skin, starting with his face. Enkill looked up into the golden abyss that was the sun, and for the first time since his transformation, he experienced pain.

It was like standing too close to a raging fire, and a gust of wind blows its heat in your direction, singeing eyebrows and lashes and drying your iris. Snatching away your breath, forcing you to cower, but this was worst.

Screaming, Enkill almost fell out of the sky. His glasses spiraled down to the earth beneath him as he covered his face in his parka's hood, righted himself, and pushed on the twelve or so blocks to his secret pad. A large three-bedroom apartment in an old fashion gothic-looking building on the corner of 72nd and Central Park West called The Dakota. He chose the building for its rather interesting history.

Enkill flew stealth-like through a half-open window, crashing on his living room floor in a smoking bundle of glass.

Mrs. Perez jumped up from the comforts of her new rocking chair as fast as her old limbs would allow. She put both hands to her mouth so she wouldn't scream as she stared uncertainly at the smoking figure on the floor, her heart thumping.

When the figure moaned and rolled over to its back, she saw the partially burned face with swollen eyes of onyx crying tears of blood, cracked swollen lips pulled back in a grimace of anguish, fangs jutting from its gums, like a mother witnessing her child being hit by a speeding car, Mrs. Perez's heart dipped, "Oh my God, Enkill!" His pain was her own.

CHAPTER 18

In the fabulously furnished living room of a presidential suite, just one of its owner's countless properties scattered throughout the globe, on a couch of midnight blue sat its owner, Ghedi.

Naked from the waist up, the kingu's chest was smeared with the fresh blood of his victims. The blood-drained body of an auburn-haired teenage girl lay on his lap and her friend's body at his feet. A young model, thin black girl, her blonde weave was caked with blood and pushed to one side, revealing the baseball size hole in her cranium through which her brain had been removed.

Ghedi was fed and in jovial spirits. He smiled a smile of wicked humor at Ezulie sitting across from him on a loveseat, looking like royalty in a black Versace evening gown. Her hands of expensive stoned rings and scarlet polish folded tightly in her lap with a posture so perfect that she rendered the loveseat's back obsolete. Tonight Ezulie's long hair was held up in a fancy bun with countless gold pins with sparkling diamond heads, and it looked as if she wore a crown. Her voice was emotionless as a stone, "What do you find so amusing? Is there a reason you're giving me a smile you should reserve for your prostitutes?" She asked, pointing distastefully at the two bodies.

"Relax, Ezulie, for I was gazing upon you and noticed you looked fashionably exceptional this night."

"As I do every night."

"You are really too modest."

"I know it's one of my stronger traits," she retorted.

Ghedi clapped his thin, blood-sticky hands together and laughed.

A sensual glow danced in his pupils, "Has anybody ever told you, Ezulie, you're a splendid company?"

"Not in those words, but last night a man did tell me how he would love to see me again. But somehow, I think he changed his mind after I castrated him and broke both of his legs and arms, and left his bloodless and defiled body naked on the hood of his car, in front of the home he shared with his wife, with the word adulterer, written in red lipstick across his chest!" Her blood-toned lips cracked into an impish smile.

"Now I feel deeply honored."

"Why?" She asked.

"Because you see that smile there," pointing a finger slick with blood, "I thought would be reserved for one such as Charise. Speaking of whom, when you include her on the night's menu, I do hope I'll be invited; she looks like such a delicious piece," Ghedi said, licking his lips amusingly. Red tongue lapping at his fingers.

"What makes you think she's going on any menu?"

Ghedi ceased fondling the corpse's hair and just stared off at the ceiling pondering her words. He didn't like them. "Just given her current status of an outlaw, you know, spawn of Niccolo's spawn."

"And you know that status can very well change if she pledges allegiance to King Anu."

"What makes you think she will?" Ghedi asked. "You've already said she's very fond of the one called, Enkill.

"Fond, yes. Enthralled no. You see, she was more likely to take his word as law: finality when she'd just heard of others of her kind. But to meet others like herself on her own, as she met me," Ezulie's orbs glowed under raised brows, "She no longer views us all as enemies."

"Even if she pledges, what makes you think King Anu will accept her?" Ghedi asked, leaning, resting both elbows on the body, watching Ezulie closely, examining her conviction. If the truth is told, Ghedi held Ezulie in high esteem; she was both wise and cunning. Her option he respected, but she did have her ways. At times she liked to patronize him for her own self-amusement. He was trying to make sure this wasn't one of those times.

"Why won't he? She has served his purpose by leading us to their lair, allowing us to fulfill our mission," Ezulie stated like it was the most obvious thing in the world.

"She may have aided our cause, but don't forget Ezulie, it was not intentional. You trailed her back to her lair; she didn't bring you. And how do you think she's going to react once she finds out you are responsible for the destruction of her boyfriend and dear friends," Ghedi reclined back into the seat. "She may act as if she doesn't care now, but we both know how strange and unpredictable situations can become when matters of the heart are involved."

"It is the truth you speak," Ezulie agreed. "But we also know the nature of the kingu: Self-preservation. When she realizes their hopeless plight, Anu's resistance will be pointless!" She stood, gliding smoothly over the footrest towards Ghedi with open arms asking, "Do you really think she would choose death over immortality, especially once she fully understands immortality and the many fruits its tree can bare?"

He chuckled, "And she'll come to fully understand this with your help?"

Ezulie didn't like to be laughed at. She didn't find anything about herself amusing. "Of course," the kingus said. "When I'm finished grooming her, she'll be encouraging the others to pledge their undying loyalty to the empire."

"You overestimate her intelligence," Ghedi shook his head.

"You underestimate it!" She shot back with a tangerine flare in her orbs.

"Ezulie," calling her name earnestly, "Don't forget, they are not like us. They're from different places and ages. Look at the society that birthed them! And even if your Charise did manage to convince the others to pledge, Anu will never accept Enkill. His orders on him were specific, as they have been for the last eight-teen centuries for any who showed what the King deemed as The Mark of Abu. You remember how he handled the last to bare the mark!" Before his words could conjure the images of fire and torture associated with them, Ghedi went on, "You're all too aware of his sunlight wanderings. So you know exactly what he's capable of, even if he doesn't. He's simply too powerful to be allowed to live. I felt the strength of his essence. It's prodigiously impossible. I suspect magic, but of what source, I can't tell. And even if he's tamed for a century or two, a long time before that, he'll come into a full understanding of his power." Ghedi stood, dumping the body. Stepping over the other and around a hovering Ezulie.

When the warrior spoke again, his voice was heightened not in anger, but a passionate emotion, a testament to his unwavering loyalty to the Empire, "Who's to say he won't develop royal aspirations? It's no secret The King is not loved among a great portion of the kingu. But they fear him, so they pay the Gza and obey. He is feared because he is the most powerful." He turned, facing Ezulie, clutching a bony fist. The muscles in his sleek torso tensed, "Those that don't agree for now hold their tongues for fear of losing their heads!"

"From what I've been hearing, those you speak of haven't been holding their tongue of late."

Ghedi's voice calmed to a thoughtful poise, "Yes, you're correct, and after we finish here, that is the next problem we'll address. For now, they whisper, speaking in hushed tones among those of similar mind," a few silent seconds passed as Ghedi made his way over to a ceiling to floor window veiled by a thick curtain of navy. His fingers marched along a long table of thick cranberry oak. Pushing aside the heavy curtains, Ghedi gazed out over the bright city night, down at the immense view of Central Park. Stripped trees stood like skeletons propped on a dark stage in a ghoulish play.

"Ezulie, those like you and me; the Nosfers like Chango, we will crush them! That's why they whisper. Because they are not yet strong enough to fight, they secretly conspire and grow in numbers. Still, they are a small band with no real power to stand behind. No power to lead them. What if they infected this Enkill, poisoning his mind with their disease of insurgence? What then?" He proposed without turning from the window.

Ezulie watched his slender muscled back. She did not need to see his face to know his expression was one of the utmost seriousness. She knew like herself the warrior Ghedi was; fearlessly loyal to the court, but to her, he was overlooking something.

"You say they have none powerful enough already. There are some who would argue that point with you, but I am not one of them. Just know, putting aside the spawns addition, that there are many Elders Ghedi. In another half, a millennium or so, me and you will be considered Elders. And how many exist now that fit that criteria, Ghedi? There are many Ghedi!" She said his name with tenderness as she floated up beside him. As her heels touched the carpet, she rested a hand on his shoulder, "Especially in the region the news of the unrest is coming from. Also, there are many who were once powerful figures in our empire, who are also flocking to the region, Perusu and Nosfer alike."

"Excellent, that way, we'll destroy them all in one place, at one time."

There was no give in Ghedi's voice. Cold and unwavering like sharpened steel across a warm jugular. But that was the way of men like Ghedi. Warriors. They believed the solution to every problem lay at the end of their blade. To Ezulie, this problem seemed a tad more complex. "Don't forget Ghedi, though Anu is King. There have always been those of our kind who've lived outside his rule. In far-off regions, even right here in the states. Small bands who've claimed their independence."

"That's because they don't remember the wars: kingu killing kingu; packs of were-beast preying murderously upon solitary and small groups of us without fear of consequence. They don't remember the times of lawlessness, before Anu, before our Great King!" his voice rising. She massaged his shoulders soothingly.

"No, they don't," she said, "For many of them were not yet conceived in their mother's wombs. And if they've heard of the times, they either don't care or believe. And if they've survived the times, then they've forgotten them. Just like Anu has forgotten them !"

"What do you mean, Anu, forgotten them?" He asked.

"You see, for centuries, he's considered the few rogue elders and renegade kingus of no significance. Weak, few with no channel to directly challenge him. In this time, he's allowed them respite to conspire and grow, feed, all the while maturing in power. So coincidentally, what was once not worth mentioning even in idle conversation, now requires his direct attention."

Her words cut like sharp ice into Ghedi. "You paint a very grim picture," he finally responded, his tone reflective.

"The picture is grim indeed. Much blood will be shed by all participants involved," solemnly Ezulie prophesied, then asked, "Where's Chango?"

"Right now, as we speak, he's the brush, painting the picture we speak of."

"Ezulie nodded, letting her sights venture towards the stars as she rested her chin on Ghedi's shoulders. He let the side of his face touch hers. The two vampires shared an intimate moment of silent understanding—the reaffirmation of a bond formed by centuries of blood, death, and mutual respect.

It was getting late, and Angel was tired and hungry. It was already midnight, and he hadn't eaten in hours. He was in East Harlem, walking down 127 St. and Park Ave. The streets on this side of the tracks were dark and dingy in the gloom shade of the Metro North's railroad overpass. The neighborhood was rundown; it seemed to have been missed by the previous mayor's rejuvenation of the Harlem project.

Two men accompanied Angel. One was Jose, a corn-braid-wearing older Hispanic man who walked with a menacing stride like he was always looking for trouble. The second man was Diente, a large bald-headed young Dominican with a really nasty temper and terrible eyesight. He could barely see half a block in front of him if it wasn't for the gold-rimmed designer Versace specs he always sported.

The trio had just finished partaking in the pleasures of the G-spot: a whorehouse that specialized in pretty teenage Mexican imports, located a block off of 5th Avenue. Having shot their loads for the night like most men, it was time to either sleep or eat. Choosing the latter, they were heading up to the Bronx to check out this little diner they frequented.

"Fuck, you park so far away for?" Angel asked, digging inside his white leather jacket to fetch a light for his cigarette.

"Yo, what do you expect, bro? Do you see any parking up there? We circled the block twenty times," Diente replied, sounding slightly irritated.

"Yeah, whatever nigga. I am starving. Nothing like some good pussy to work up an appetite," said Angel exhaling a cloud of nicotine.

"Yeah, you know that I could tear some shit up right now," Diente agreed as a chilly breeze blew, causing him to button up his leather pea-coat.

"Fuck you hungry for? You were only in there like two minutes," Angel said, jeering the youngster, winking out the corner of his eye at Jose.

"What nigga! I was breaking that bitch back like this!" Diente started demonstrating loudly as he continued, "From the back, deep strokes. You heard it. Yo Jose, the other bitch told me she and Angel was in there playing cards," he laughed, throwing a heavy arm over Angel's shoulder.

"Damn, bro, get yo big ass up off me," Angel amiably ducking under Diente's arm. Angel liked messing with Diente. He had a great deal of respect for the younger man. For he'd been putting in brutally messy jobs with the crew since he was sixteen. That was over five years ago. Angel also teased him because he was one of the few people who could do so without the big Dominican going off the deep end. It was Diente's undiscriminating use of a gun that made Angel bring him along this night. Later on, he planned to go look into something. See if they could strike a little payback for Lou and Indio. At the thought of his fallen brethren, a current of anger flared through him.

"Yo bro, you see that?" Jose whispered in a serious tone that immediately raised the other men's guards.

"See what?" Asked Angel as he strained to see up the block ahead of them. He saw nothing. As they stepped off the curb into the street, passing under the train's overpass, Angel dumped his cigarette and reached into his waist, finding comforting security in the cold steel of a nine-millimeter glock.

"The Moreno and chamaco?" asked Diente, referring to the couple walking a little ways behind them.

"Yeah," Jose answered.

"Yo, I seen them when we came out the spot," Diente said, unzipping his coat. Feeling inside, taking the safety off the two large handguns he always carried: his twin chrome 45s. Diente left his coat open for easy access.

"Might be a dude and his chick just taking a walk. Let's cross the street," Angel suggested stepping out into the traffic-less street, looking both ways as if scanning for traffic he knew wasn't there. When Angel's line of vision roamed over the couple, who were now about a little less than a half a block behind, he got a strange feeling, like they were watching him. Angel could have sworn he saw the short black man's eyes glow momentarily like a firefly. But he knew that was impossible. He credited it to the street-lights reflection catching off something on the man's face. Maybe he wore glasses. Nevertheless, he felt uncomfortable as he told his comrades, "Be on point." The trio reached the other side of the street and cut down a side block lined on both sides with brownstones in need of repair and decrepit-looking tenement buildings with inexpensive vehicles parked out front.

Marisola and Ty-born walked, his arm around her waist as they followed the three men.

"Yo shorty hear me when they get to the middle of the block," Ty said.

"I think they're leery of us," she replied.

"It doesn't matter none," he replied back, flicking his tongue over one of his fangs.

Another set of eyes watched the two kingus follow the men. A set of eyes that had been in the shadows watching them since they'd left the lair.

Angel and the two men were walking in silence until something made Jose look behind them.

"Shit, bro!" Jose swore loudly as he pulled a long chrome Desert Eagle nine millimeters from inside his black bubble coat, causing both Angel and Diente to spin around, drawing their own weapons.

The couple was now only like fifteen steps directly behind them. As the words left Jose's mouth, the Hispanic female reached into her rather large purse producing a short black sub-machine gun. Simultaneously the man lifted the long, black handgun he was holding down by his leg and started firing.

BIIR-RAT-TATT-TAT!   The sound of gunfire lit up the block, disturbing the silence of the ghetto night. A barrage of rhino from the sub-machine gun tore into Jose's chest, puncturing his lungs in two places. But that was the least of his problems. One of the bullets entered his heart, shredding it like tissue. Death came instantly. The force of the shots carried Jose's bullet-ridden body into Diente, who stumbled to the ground firing his weapon at their attackers. He watched as he hit the female with three shots high in her chest. To his surprise, she didn't even stagger or lose a step. She just kept firing, coming forward. Diente dived between two parked cars, losing his glasses, and returned fire wildly.

Diente cursed himself for letting his glasses fall. How was he supposed to shoot if he couldn't see? Crawling around to the front of the car, he crouched low, his back against the front wheel facing the street, trying to regain himself as exploding shells echoed in his ears. When Diente felt the car shake, he looked up behind him to see the woman standing directly over him on the car's hood. She was smiling. The unexpected glow in her hazel eyes caused him to pause, one second too long. Diente watched in dumbfounded awe as a bullet from her gun entered in between his eyes and exited out the back of his head, taking his mushy brains and pieces of skull with it.

From a building's doorway, Angel beheld in horrified amazement the murder of his comrades. Sticking his head out the doorway, he fired in a wild rage at the woman in the car, hitting her in the back with an onslaught of bullets.

Angel was seduced by satisfaction as the woman jerked from the impact of the bullets, but his bowels nearly busted when instead of falling, she turned to face him. Her red lips twisted in a fanged frown, an unnatural glow in her eyes. Angel felt a bullet hit him hard, slamming him back into the door. It was open. He fell into the building lobby. From the lobby's floor, he looked behind him to see the short chubby Moreno blowing imaginary smoke off his pistol's barrel, laughing, mocking him, right as the lobby's door swung shut.

The lobby was dark but seeable. It stunk like urine and garbage. Graffiti marked up the chipped green paint of the walls. Fear motivated Angel as he jumped to his feet, shoulder burning where he was shot. At least he still had his gun. Darting through the lobby up a flight of stairs, Angel heard the lobby's front door open and knew his pursuers followed. He kept running as fast as he possibly could, taking flight after flight until he reached the roof.

For some reason, Angel's mind flashed back to the newspaper headlines concerning Lou and his family's murder: "Monsters Invading City." Nobody took it literally; it was just the brutal mutilation of the victims and the little girl's death that gave the suspects their label. But after what he had just witnessed, Angel wasn't so sure. His bullets seemed to have no effect on them. Angel knew he hit the female with enough lead to bring down anybody.

Maybe she had on a vest, he rationalized. But what about the eyes? The glow that chilled his insides he couldn't explain. Nor could Angel explain the teeth. Both she and the Moreno had teeth like dogs. After the fifth flight of stairs, Angel pushed open the roof door. Glaring around into the darkness, he searched for a place to make an ambush or a last stand.

The night's air was cool but not cold. The temperature could have been subzero. Still, to Angel, it would have made no matter. The adrenaline that raged within him was warming. He tried not to think about the blood leaking from his wound, causing his shirt to stick, and the numbness invading his shoulder. Blood seeped down his arm to his fingers as he reached into his ankle holster, and retrieved a chrome .38 Special, then fumbled in his jacket for another another-clip reloading his nine.

Kneeling down a little ways from the roof's low ledge behind a large grey metallic box, Angel pointed both weapons at the roof's entrance. Scanning the roof's perimeter, he looked for an escape route. The roof's surface

263

was bare except for the metal shed supporting the entrance, the box he knelt behind, and the row of discarded garbage bags along one side of the ledge. Angel saw that this particular building was surrounded on both sides by brownstones, so if he had to jump, it was going to be a long way down to another roof, something he didn't look- forward to. He reached in his jacket, searching for his phone. It was gone. He must have dropped it when he fell downstairs. For the first time in Angel's life, he wondered, where were the fucking police?

Marisola and Ty followed Angel into the building stopping in the lobby. Marisola had been shot more than five times; never in her life had she suffered such an ordeal. She wasn't mortally wounded or even physically hurt. Her vampiric organs were already working to repair themselves. Something being a newborn, she didn't quite understand yet, therefore: a little uncertainty gawked at her mind as she saw her life's blood seeping from her. Seeing Marisola tracing her fingers questioningly over the bullet holes that had reddened the front of her once black jacket, Ty asked, "Ma, you okay?"

The bottoms of Marisola's fangs curved down into her lips as she snarled, "I will be when that nigga is dead. Imma eat his ass! Come on!" Marisola took off up the stairs, following the scent of Angel's blood with Ty behind her. Reaching the bottom of the fifth flight, the two kingus watched as Angel went through the roof's door.

"Nowhere to go now, kid," Ty growled. "When we come through the door, go straight and up. Imma go right and low."

Marisola snarled her comprehension.

A flight and a half below them, the shadow listened with inhuman hearing to their movements. Being careful only to move when they moved, not wanting to alert them of its presence just yet.

Ty and Marisola slammed through the door, moving with vampiric speed. Angel fired sporadically, hitting nothing but the door and the night. A single shot whizzed past his face taking off the tip of his nose. He cried out, involuntarily closing his eyes.

His cries were met with laughter.

Opening his eyes, Angel cursed as he saw the female on one side of him, about ten steps away standing as still as a statue. Staring at him with hard hazel eyes of flame, her mouth fixed in a fanged grin. A small wind blew, picking up her long loose hair and wrapping a few strands around her face. To Angel, she was a vision of demonic beauty.

On his other side, moving towards him, walking or floating, which Angel couldn't decipher, was the Moreno. Angel was sure he was dead. Suddenly the roof's door smashed open flying his way. The door flew over him, grazing the top of his head, knocking him dizzied to the surface sending the .38 flying from his hand.

Marisola was stunned when the huge black form burst on the roof, moving with a blinding speed in a graceful yet hunched-over motion. It grabbed Ty by one of his legs spinning him over its head as if he were weightless. Then flung Ty so hard into the roof's ledge, Marisola heard stone and bone break alike as the two collided.

Seeing the danger, Marisola screamed, letting off a beam of shots at what she knew was a man of sorts. She fired but couldn't seem to hit the large man. It dodged the rounds hopping forward until it stood before her. Its hands moved with the quickness of a lightning flash, smacking her face, shattering her jaw, snatching the gun with its other hand, and tossing it off the roof. Before Marisola could fall completely, it yanked her up by her hair and wrapped a hairy, dark taloned mitt around her neck, squeezing, lifting all five-foot-three of vampire that was Marisola up to its eye level.

Marisola stared into an enormous face that was a cross between an ape and a man with two discolored eyes. One glowed a pale grey with pink veins, the other a green so dark it looked black, letting Marisola know it was all kingu.

"I am Chango," Gruff voiced. The Nosfer General introduced himself with a crooked smile showcasing a set of large razor-sharp pearl tone teeth. Marisola looked into that mouth and saw both top and bottom fangs that were twice as thick and long as her own.

The watchers, she told herself.

Marisola swiped at Chango's face with long mutated nails. Chango sensing the move, jerked his head back. As her hand passed his face, he closed his mouth on it. He was chomping down, breaking bones, grinding, and chewing flesh. Marisola screamed as she brought the short blade hidden in the small of her back viciously across Chango's grey eye. He released her hand, crying out, and flung her across the roof. The kingus landed hard with a series of tumbles, dropping her blade.

Seeing Marisola's distress, Ty shook off the knocking in his head and pulled the thick short sword hanging over his shoulder inside his jacket. Charging up behind Chango, Ty drove the blade savagely into the Nosfer's lower back, "Yeah Motherfucker!"

Ty's momentary elation transformed into blood-chilling surprise when the huge kingu turned and grabbed him with an elongated double-jointed arm by his bald head and drove him to the ground with such force Ty's head smashed through the roof's tar surface, splintering the wood loudly underneath.

Chango then picked Ty up with both hands by his head, putting long thumbs, which were nothing but sharpened bone, deep into Ty's eyes: bursting both eyeballs like grapes. Ty wailed, scratching wildly at the kingu's grip, blood streaming from his eye sockets.

Chango hooted fiercely, digging his other claws into Ty's head, palms against his jaws, and then the nosfer began to squeeze, pushing both hands towards each other with strength that was even great for their kind. He squeezed until the bone of Ty's vampiric skull gave in from the pressure, cracking. Collapsing.

Brain matter and blood ran from Ty's nose and ears.

Blood, broken bone, and brain oozed in Chango's hands. He continued to push in his vice-like motion until his bloody hands practically touched.

Ty no longer screamed.

He made no sound at all as his body spasmed, and Chango shook his hands violently from side to side. Ty's blood danced into the night's air. His neck was breaking, skin tearing as the body was jerked about attached to his crushed head by a few veins and arteries that were rapidly giving way under his dense body weight.

From the spot she'd fallen, Marisola witnessed an unbelieving horror: Ty's headless body flying across the roof. His life-blood spilled in a thick red arc across her as Ty's body landed a few feet away with a lifeless thud!

Chango grinned at Marisola. His good eye glowed as he opened his blood-glistening hands, showing her the mushy flattened remains of her partner's head.

That was too much for her to bare.

In the short time, Marisola had known Ty, she'd come to honestly like him. Even appreciate his, at times, irritating sense of humor. Above all, he was one of her own.

Revenge cloaked Marisola's mind as she got up and shot forward as if fired from a cannon at Chango. Snarling jaw hanging, lopsided tongue, slashing like a rattler's tail. The eerie maddening sound issuing from the pit of her soul came out like a screeching wail through her broken jaw. Mangled hand at her side, other a raised hand of curved talons like a deadly scythe.

Chango waited for her advance. Countless centuries of experience had taught him patience.

Marisola flew upward, then descended, raking her taloned hand at Chango's neck in a movement so fast a mortal eye would have missed. But not a battle-hardened Nosfer General. Chango, with swift ease, dodged the decapitation attempt and struck out with a fist powerful enough to shatter a hundred-pound cement block like glass, hitting the kingus in the left side of her chest.

The blow on contact smashed Marisola's ribcage sending bone fragments into her vampiric heart resulting in paralysis. The impact sent her flying off the roof into an adjacent building's wall across the street. Her temporarily paralyzed body, unable to brace itself, then fell five stories hitting the cemented sidewalk with a loud splat!

Chango then approached Angel, who was cowering in the shadows and grabbed him by one shoulder, yanking him to his feet. It was the same spot where he'd been shot earlier. Angel winced in pain. When Angel looked into the bestial face of the nosfer, his knees gave out in fear. Chango held the terrified man up easily as one would a tantrum-throwing child.

Angel watched in rational disbelief as the beast's ape-like face shifted to a more human appearance, and its overall body mass shrunk in a matter of seconds. Only then did

Angel realize it was actually a black man in a black suit that hung off his frame in blood-splattered rags.

Still, even in the man's transformation, he didn't release his hold on Angel, who stared into the man's strange eyes. One of which was red with blood dripping a trail of bloody tears down one side of his face.

Pulling Angel close, Chango spoke in his thick English, "My enemy's enemy is my friend."

Angel was so speechless the gun dropped from his hand. Chango then threw Angel over his shoulder, and he took to the night's sky. Beneath them, police sirens flashed and screeched.

ACKNOWLEDGMENTS

Brandi Hester -Harrell , Publisher
Mahogany Pen Publishing

Tiffany "GLAMM" Malloy

Ashley Simpson

Twisted Films Production Team – Special Thanks to my
entire production family, from cast to Nico.

Thank you sincerely…

In a world of monsters, fear the angels.
Soul of the Kingu

ABOUT THE AUTHOR

 Lorenzo is a creative and entrepreneur, native to the concrete jungles of New York City. After discovering the wonders of literature, his passion for words would birth the literary experiment and the journey to Atlanta that would become Reckless Indulgence.

www.ingramcontent.com/pod-product-compliance
Lightning Source LLC
Chambersburg PA
CBHW030247030726
47493CB00023B/873